Little Peg

BY THE SAME AUTHOR

The Fifth Station

Little Peg

KEVIN McILVOY

Atheneum
NEW YORK 1990
COLLIER MACMILLAN CANADA TORONTO
MAXWELL MACMILLAN INTERNATIONAL
NEW YORK OXFORD SINGAPORE SYDNEY

My grateful acknowledgment to: Margee McIlvoy, Leslie Argo, Beverly Bogle, Barthy Byrd, Kathy Davis, Paula Moore, Maja-Lisa Moran, Darlin Neal, Eileen Patterson, Rita Popp, Cynthia Rose, Libby Scheidegger, and Barbara Waters.

Atheneum
Macmillan Publishing Company
866 Third Avenue, New York, NY 10022

Collier Macmillan Canada, Inc.
1200 Eglinton Avenue East, Suite 200
Don Mills, Ontario M3C 3N1

Library of Congress Cataloging-in-Publication Data
McIlvoy, Kevin.
Little Peg / Kevin McIlvoy.
p. cm.
ISBN 0-689-12107-5
I. Title.
PS3563.C369L58 1990
813'.54—dc20

Sections of this work have appeared in different form in *The Missouri Review* ("Second Hands"), *Crazyhorse* ("August Twelve"), *Turnstile* ("In Your Hands"), and *Witness* ("Duty").

10 9 8 7 6 5 4 3 2 1

Printed in the United States of America

For Ann Rohovec: a promise kept.

For the wives, daughters, sisters, mothers, and grandmothers of Vietnam veterans, who offered no less than their lives.

There never was a war that was not inward: I must fight till I have conquered in myself what causes war.

Marianne Moore, "In Distrust of Merits"

PART ONE

Straw

I am in my own mind.
I am locked in the wrong house.

Anne Sexton,
"For the Year of the Insane"

1 · *In His Hands*

(FALL 1988)

I quietly ask myself, "Who is it?" before entering even my own home. At the door of my classroom I follow the same ritual. Francis, my roommate and friend, comes to the classroom with me. Her birth name is spelled with an *e*, but she writes it with an *i*. The idea, she says, is to remind herself what a difference that one vowel makes.

Nontraditional English One, Section B is a 6 P.M. Monday and Friday class, lasting ten weeks. In the second week of the fall semester seven of my eighteen students have dropped the course. Most of the students in Introduction to Making Fiction lack the money (or, in a few cases, the guts) to go to the college or even the community college, but they believe my course will help them test the waters.

"I'll lecture about something if you'll shut up," I say to the chattering group.

I have no idea what I will lecture about. Maybe Freytag's Pyramid. I ask, "First, who will read from her journal?"

"Were we supposed to bring our journals, Mrs. O?"

"You're always supposed to bring your journal, Norm."

Francis is doing something strange again. She has taken a small bottle from her purse and seems to be cooling her fingertips on the glass, touching without looking. Francis, I think, you are *so* fine. They've never seen anything like you. A real storybook character.

Many of the students are watching, but no one sits up straight at the long table. Eleven variations on slouching. But usually it means something when Mitchey Shultz nudges her journal before her on the table. "Caught you, Mitchey. Go ahead, read us something."

"It isn't much," she says.

"Go ahead."

Mitchey opens the pocket-size journal and has one quick read-through of the entry before she decides she will share it. Her grin must be viral: everyone is grinning.

"It's entitled 'Tea.' "

" 'Tea.' Great title. Good. 'Tea.' Go ahead." It takes this much effort with Mitchey, who always volunteers but has to be encouraged.

She reads: " *'Tea.'*

"The boys like it when she serves them tea. The boys like the way the kettle hisses then whistles, and the boys like the way the air changes when the tea is plunged in the hot water."

She is reconsidering the next part. She reads it. *"The boys like having it poured and they like seeing the unstained cup placed before them on a saucer. The water darkens, the air sweetens, and the boys like to have her lift the tea bag out of the cup then squeeze it with her fingers and take it away but come back, and they like her to say, 'Drink.' "*

The writing is a complete surprise. I say, "What can I say?"

Andria Charley says, "Was that the assignment?"

Norm Navares mouths the words "Oh, baby." Norm sits next to Mitchey because he has believed all along she had this in her.

"Key-rist!" says Burns, whose moustache is still only faint braille. I imagine reading his moustache. It says, "Are you kidding me?" Burns, a Nontraditional repeater, always writes it like it is. All of his short stories have been about characters with names like Candy and Spit. His last story, two triple-spaced pages long, was entitled "But Who Gives a Fuck?" and in it everyone met a violent end.

Peter Thompsenson, who sits at the corner of the table farthest from me, is trembling like a hummingbird. He thinks he knows what Mitchey means about tea: he feels covered wingtip to nose-tip by all the golden pollen in her voice.

"Who else will read a journal entry?" I ask. "Peter?"

"Huh?"

"Would you like to read?" I suspect he has never refused a teacher's request. If I asked him to erase the board with his short, unwashed hair, he would do it.

"I—"

"A little one, Peter?"

He pulls his journal from his rear pocket. "I did one on prose rhythm. Like Mitchey." The pages are smeary because he obsessively reworks and revises. "This doesn't—it doesn't have no—any—title."

"Fine. That's fine. Okay?"

"But I could call it 'His Fist,' I think."

"His Fist." I wish I hadn't called on him. It was cruel.

"Go ahead?"

"Go ahead, Peter."

He shakes his head yes, a gesture he offers himself to help him go ahead. He reads: *"You couldn't open it a chink because it was so strong and everything, was like a chunk of concrete, could break something if it wanted, smelled kind of like wet concrete, was cold with holes like the holes concrete's got, when it hit something concrete it might get chipped but didn't get crushed or anything, or even open up even a little."*

Most of the class members are watching Francis, who sits next to Peter. She is following every word, looking at him with absolute adoration. Burns and Norm worshipfully gaze across the table at Mitchey.

The Invisible, the students who are not absent but are also not really present, are self-erasing. Susan Orstal. Dennis Tiber. Erminia Maestas. Tim Hutto. One minute they sit before me.

The next minute, if a question seems too imminent, they fade. Minorest characters.

I ask, "So. What did you think of 'His Fist'? Norm? Burns?"

Norm says, "Good." Burns slowly turns his total attention on Peter, who is also a Nontraditional repeater. "Peter," he says, "I always like what you do." Then he looks at Francis and asks her, "What *did* he do?"

Peter starts to explain but I say, "I'm going to lecture now about round, really round, and obscenely round characters and then I've got another assignment to throw out and I'm going to throw it way out there and we can all go fetch it and bring it back to the kennel here on Friday."

Andria Charley wants to know if her story is still due for discussion on Friday. She has gotten her long ash-brown hair shredded by angry birds or paid a lot of money to have somebody make her look hard-bitten, but her wavering voice betrays her.

"We're all looking forward to it, Andria."

"Yeah," says Burns, halfway out of his chair.

"I was just asking," says Andria

"No other questions?" I look them over. Lewis Blake, one of several older students in the class, is missing again. "Anybody know where Lewis is?"

"Happy hour," says Burns.

"Do you think so?"

"Class over?" he asks.

"Not yet. Don't forget to read the Updike, Oates, Kurtz, Butz, Bortsch, and Bottley pieces in *The Many American Amber Grains*."

Peter Thompsenson is rattled. "What?"

"I'm joking, Peter. The Oates in your textbook, okay?"

"Okay."

"And look, everybody, I want you to think about round characters and not another thing in the world, so that's why we're quitting early again. But I have an assignment. Write this down.

"You have to draw your own scheme or map for how a short story works. Make it a map. Make it practical but brilliant. Provide details of description; include topographic details; and be ready to defend it."

Peter asks, "How long?"

"How long? Eleven inches. As much paper as it takes, I guess, Peter. Okay, Peter?" He nods yes. "Bring it with you, everybody. Class dismissed."

After class, Francis and I drop by Rickee Wells's office to say hello, but she is hiding out, probably working on a new poem. (She says "poom.") Rickee is a Real English Professor Poet in The Department of English on the main campus. She is also a fledgling real estate tycoon. Her motto: An apartment should not mean, but be.

"You in there?" I ask through the door.

"Can't talk. Sorry, Peg."

"Hi there," says Francis.

"Hi, Francis."

I understand that for Rickee, The Muse is real as rain. In another book I might be a Real English Professor, like her. I would have already lived many lives in many houses of straw and stick and stone. Like Rickee, I would have split myself in two completely different halves, poet and professional woman, and then joined the two in unlikely lovely, holy self-matrimony. Rickee and I would be best friends. In another time, we might yet be. "See you, Rickee. Good luck on the poem."

"Sorry. Hey, wait." Through the hollow wooden door, Rickee's words sound like stones spilled out of pottery. "Want to hear it?"

"The poem?" asks Francis.

"Great," I say.

"Certain?"

"Sure." Francis and I lean against the door. We can hear

Rickee rattle some papers, scrape a chair across the tiles of her office.

"It's called 'Ivu.' Ivu's the Eskimo word for 'the suddenly leaping shore ice.' Ready?"

"Wait." Francis puts her weight on both legs.

"Francis," I whisper, "you are *so* fine."

"Ready?"

"Yep," says Francis.

"We have / more words for Ice / than Love. / Crumbling ice like / unsteady, wrinkled palms / ice like skin on / boiling milk / ice like waking eyelid / unbroken / unbreaking names. / We have more words for Ice / than Awe."

"Hey!" Francis is confounded.

"Rickee, I like it."

"Certain, Peg?"

"One of your best."

"It's rough."

Francis looks at the door. "Ice. What an idea for a poem."

"Thanks," says Rickee. "I must get back to it. Thanks for listening."

"Sure."

"So. So long there, Rickee."

As we walk out of the building, Francis asks, "Was that a first part? It sounded like part of a something poetic. Why did she call it 'Ivol'?"

" 'Ivu.' I don't know, Francis. I guess it's an awesome word. Don't you think?"

"But if you don't know what it means . . ."

"Francis, did you see what the thugs have done to our building?" At the entrance to Hugh Milton Hall someone has blacked out the lower-case *h* in Hugh.

"But," says Francis. "Wait a minute."

"I guess she'll have to put in a footnote or something explaining about what 'ivu' means, won't she?"

"Well, I guess!"

* * *

Francis and I talk about the poem on the bus back to Everview, where I can use Paula Analyst's Kaypro word processor and Francis can finish a letter to my daughter Molly. It will be written as if by me and will be signed by me.

After a snack in the dining room, we follow our once-a-week routine of tuning in to "The Brazilian Hour" on our local FM. Our moderator Sergio answers the listener letters. He pronounces his name "Sear Zhee Oh."

"We ligke to rezeeve letters zhou zend," he whispers. "And now thee tremenda Martine Davila.

"We hobe zhou enzhoy thizya one."

Sergio never talks aloud. He whispers. What zhou cannot hear tastes delicious there between the luscious, moist layers of his voice. I know. Sergio has been a constant, accepting friend. I can count my faithful friends on one hand: my daughter Molly, my friend Francis, my university friend Rickee, and my truant student Lewis Blake maybe, and Sergio. Barely a handful.

My ex-husband and I are estranged. In 1971, when we had been married barely eighteen months, James came back from Vietnam okay. He deplaned uninjured, handsome in his uniform, and closed his arms around me and our daughter so hard I had to say, "The baby, honey. Careful." Then he fit into a good job as a snack machine vendor for White's Snack Foods here in Las Almas. He might have put too much energy and time in his work, but he'd say, "I'm still adjusting some, Little Peg," and that's what he would do: adjust himself.

I have been at the Everview Residential Treatment Center for almost as long as I have been married. In the early seventies it was called Everview Halfway House, and it had no wrought-iron gates and archways, and the large adobe building was not divided into two "wings." It had no concrete identifying sign with sun/mountain/stream logo. It had no permanent staff. We called it Halfass House. It was purchased by the Everview Corporation, "a health care organization," which conglomerated it. In 1975 they built a two-story one-hundred-room psychiatric care center right behind our small building here in Las Almas. Vistaview. We call it Neverview. Sometimes we call one The Little House and the other The Big House. Our building looks like the guard station to a maximum security prison. Since all that happened, our treatment center hasn't exactly become more structured or efficient or even effective, though the driveway has been widened into a parking lot and the building facade has been pasteled and decaled and awned and hedged to look more institutional. The plan is not to keep anyone for more than eighteen weeks here, but no matter what is happening in Neverview, exceptions to the rule are still the rule at Everview.

I have taught English in the Nontraditional Program at New Mexico State University, Las Almas Branch for over ten years. My specialty is Creative Writing, which I teach only part-time. I am allowed halfway into the normal world while I live halfway out of it.

It's a good thing I'm a solid person. I am six foot one and a half inches tall. Slightly over one hundred and ninety-five pounds. I was large even when I was very young but I have always been called "Little Peg" by my oldest brother Anthony and my father; once, that was an affectionate irony, now it is an ironic affectation. My mother and my younger brother Ben never called me Little.

God made me from a large block of mottled white stone and he rushed the job, didn't chisel or chip much away. So, I have few well-defined features except for two almost unindented dimples at the corners of my mouth.

Sergio would not mind my weak ankles. Sergio would kiss my thighs and the little bit of fleshiness behind my knees and, when he got to my ankles. Oh. He would be moving toward them with excruciating leisure and patience (whispering, "Zo zoft iz zo zo zo . . . zoft"). When he got to my ankles, he would kiss the veins and taste the Amorale perfume I would rub into them if I had some; then he would brush the thin line of his moustache on the places ("Close zhyur eyes, dearez") where I had pumiced my heel calluses and trimmed my toenails neat as neatly spaced and lovely teeth.

Beauty is up your eye, in my reserved opinion. My shoulders and back are broad. My breasts are thirty-eight years old; I'd like to forget them but if I don't tell everything now, God help me later. They're big enough, I guess, but low on my chest; they form a ledge just above the rounded ledge that is my waist.

I do good things these days with my hair. The history of my perms is the history of my mental health. Right now I'm in a perm named "True" that keeps it swept back from my face in slight ripples of dark auburn wave flowing thickly down my back: a look that's uncontrolled but controllable and that says, *I'm natural.*

I will be a beautiful old woman. I will chain-smoke, wear belted cotton dresses, and be thin as a mint: an advertisement for aging. Who will care?

Francis and I both watch the radio when it is on in our room. If we try to read or to look at each other, we find we have to turn the volume up. I can see two of Francis in the shiny dials.

When Sergio offers a commercial break, Francis asks, "You have Andria Charley's story for discussion at the end of the week, don't you?"

"Guess so," I say.

"Well?"

"It has some holes in it," I tell her. It has more holes than it has spaces between holes. I'll have to ask her to stop reading so much Virginia Woolf and watching PBS. We might have to talk about the contrivance in it. What do you think, Sergio? Zo mush do underztand, no? Form or Content, Sergio? Do you sometimes listen to the tremenda Martine Davila and argue: Form over Content? Content over Form?

Sergio, I can hear the jungle around you. Is that possible?

I know what Paula Analyst would say. She says the world is too exact for us to bear. Paula Analyst is an analyst in need of help. But she is my analyst, and so I listen to what she offers.

Your chair, she says, *is the locus of certain coordinates. What are the coordinates? We need to know if we're going to be able to cope, Peg. Think of your chair as an exact place. An exact place is no place. A perfect place to begin. Do you understand?*

"No," I say.

Good, she says. *Begin.* Her resting expression is a Rasputin smile.

"You're a kook," I say.

That makes her laugh. *Begin.*

"I went home for my wedding anniversary."

Yes.

"April ninth, 1970."

Why?

"Where else to go—my husband James was in Vietnam."

Where?

"No where. Vietnam. Da Nang. He said a hill near Da Nang."

Good. Go on, Peg. Information.

"Hill 38. It was my first wedding anniversary. How many days were left for James to come back? I don't remember."

How many days, Peg?

"My mother was fifty-five. My father was fifty-seven. He had fought in France. James and I had been married two months and—we both knew how many days, too—two months and twelve days—when he left for basic. Molly was conceived in Japan. A leave that September. Let's stop."

All right. Stop.

"Wait. Wait."

We can stop.

"I drove my brother Ben to the airport when he left too. We sang, 'He's Got the Whole Wide World' the whole way to El Paso."

Are you exaggerating?

"Yes."

Don't.

"*Some* of the way to El Paso. You know how the song goes?"

Sing.

"Come on."

Sing.

" 'He's got the whole wide WORLD in His hands. He's got the WHOLE wide WORLD in His hands. He's got the WHOLE wide WORLD in HIS hands. He's got the WHOLE world in His HANDS!' "

Oh, yes.

"On the swings in the backyard we used to sing it through all the verses we knew. 'He's got the little bitty babies in His . . . He's got my mother and my father . . . He's got my sister and my brother . . .' We made up verses. 'He's got the liver and the tuna in His hands.' "

How old were you on the swings?

"Nine or ten. Eight or nine."

Carefully, Peg.

"Eight. Can you believe that? I'm sure. Eight."

Slow down, Peg.

" 'He's got the turnips and the lentil beans in His hands! He's got the spinach and the powdered milk in His hands! He's got the oatmeal with raisins in His hands! He's got the WHOLE world in His HANDS!' "

Then?

"Did you know what? Did you know all over Vietnam are old, old white stone grave markers that say, 'Liet Si'? Ben wrote me. Said it made Arlington Cemetery look like a tiny family plot."

Where were we?

"It means 'Hero.' "

Where were we?

"I was twenty-one years old. My brother was nineteen when he left for Vietnam three months and two days after James. My brother's full name is on the memorial. Twenty-two characters etched into the memorial. A six-hour plane flight from here. Nightmares sometimes that his name is worn away by wind or rain, by God's big clumsy fingers. Benjamin Edwin O'Crerieh. Worn away."

Long enough. We can stop.

"I'm done."

Where are we? How did we get here?

Tomorrow I'll visit James and Molly Ann.

Are you following your medication schedule? Exactly? You're sure?

Here in our room, Francis and I are in a storybook state of being. Denouement. It is sunrise. Or sunset. The clouds—three of them—cast one perfect cruciform shadow over the unopened curtains.

Francis says, "Want some coffee?"

She is menopausal. That really is how she has been diagnosed. I have sneaked a look at her staff file report. The file says: Menopausal. Depressive. Self-destructive. Diet. Exercise. Positive reinforcement. And below that is a calendar conforming to five columns headed with these titles: Condition/Short-trm/Lng-trm/Self Report/Staff Comments.

Francis and I have coffee. It makes me laugh when I think about the clouds, the curtains, the coffee, how neatly we descend the last steps of Freytag's Pyramid, which is the topic of my Friday lecture.

We listen to the end of "The Brazilian Hour." The program is always about one hour long. Isn't that strange? But many hours seem to have passed.

"We hobe zhou hab enzhoy," Sergio, at last, whispers. "Keeb enzhoying."

Hab a nize day, Sergio, my friend, my dear moderator.

2 · *Self Report*

Writing a letter to my daughter Molly, Francis got stuck on Churchill.

"Did Churchill have six pairs of spectacles?" she asked. "Was it five?"

Her ring finger tapped the *s* and her index finger tapped the *f* on her Cadet RemRand Portable, but she didn't strike either key. A single consonant, a single vowel could be immeasurably important. "Winston," she finally said, "we shall have to take a stab, shan't we?" and she typed, "6 pair of spectacles."

She had been awake since 4 A.M. hammering out the first draft. Writing these letters to my daughter Molly was not something I asked her to do; Francis did it, she said, "just because." At first, I would ask, "Shouldn't I write these letters, don't you think, Francis?"

"Well, Peg," Francis had said, "of course."

The conversation always abruptly ended there because Francis said nothing more. And I realized that if it made any sense to be writing these letters (which it didn't, since I saw Molly every week), then, of course, I should be writing them, but I never did; and my own letters would probably not ever be half as fine as Francis's.

Now, when the alarm went off at seven and I wished her a good morning, Francis was eager to read the letter to me.

I asked if I could take a shower first, but Francis said, "All right," clicking her fingertips on home row, which meant it wasn't all right.

"The shower can wait, I guess."

Francis said, "Here goes," and rolled the paper up on the platen.

"*My Dearest Molly.*" She stopped. "Should I keep the 'My'?"

"Let's keep it."

Francis had crooked lower teeth like me but her smile never showed them. Her crooked index fingers clicked on *f* and *j*. A storybook character.

> *My Dearest Molly,*
>
> *I'm thinking about you again. I'm always thinking about you. How are you?*
>
> *On the tv yesterday I heard some more about Imelda and Ferdinand Marcos and I thought that was interesting. What do you think?*

"Imelda and Ferdinand?" I asked.

"She's studying them. I bet she's got them in Current Events class. I want her to know we're—you're up on current events."

"Okay. Why not?"

> *What do you think? I was wondering if they'll put a picture of Imelda's closetful of shoes in the history bks.*
>
> *In my history bks I can remember seeing a photo of Churchill's 6 pair of spectacles and the 6 cases they came in. It made me wonder.*

"Wonder with an *o*?" Francis asked. "Or an *a*?"

"Let's make it *a*, Francis. Was it six?" I asked; I thought I remembered ten or twelve, a tableful of spectacles.

Six. And you know how I know that I know that? This is interesting to me. This makes you stop and consider. I can actually picture the multiple-choice question I had to answer in school: a) Six, b) Two, c) Four in the cases, Two out of the cases, d) None of the above.

> *Well, what else?*
>
> *I have a new job in the Neverview building. My friend Francis and I clean and buff the floors in the whole building on Thurs. nights. On Sun. and Wed. nights we vacuum. Then, the last day of the month we wax, and we each get $30 a wk.*
>
> *Have you bought a new pair of shoes lately? I'll bet shoe sales go down for a while.*
>
> *I know we're seeing each other today so I didn't need to write a letter. But I wanted to be able to give you something because*
>
> *I love you so much.*

I looked at Francis's hands resting on the typewriter keys, her thumbs over the tab, her wrists resting but alert. "It's a beautiful letter."

"Here," said Francis.

I signed it "*Me*" and folded it. When I came back from my shower, Francis was gone for her daily trip into town to walk. I had gone with her only once. Francis went everywhere, up every main street in Las Almas. She walked too close to the curb. She looked inside the cars as they passed and always waved a little fingers-only wave to the ones with children in them. And she didn't really walk; her stride was so urgent, she almost ran. It ached me to think how the people in town must figure Francis to be one of the "walkers," the street-roaming crazies.

Self Report, continued.

It is a Sunday morning in September. The Everview bus lady has given several of us a morning ride on a small bluff road just beyond the northern edge of Las Almas. On this high edge, I can see most of the Mesilla Valley. It is softened by the dew, as if some artist wanting to romanticize it stippled it with the smallest dots of pale rose paint. I recite to myself about the dew because when I love things I can't help naming and renaming them: Dew. Dewiferous. Dewifluent. Dewifluous. Dewigenous.

On my bicycle I used to get ahead of my brother Ben and fishtail the dust into his face if he couldn't keep up. Or to be sure he stopped when I stopped, I would sideswipe his bike with mine. I was only two years older than him, so by the time I was ten he had caught on to me.

We had a particular place we bicycled to, where the Rio Grande ran just under El Hado mesa on the southwest end of the valley. It was a part of Black Mesa, but it was more bare and more shadowed by steepness. We had bicycled through Mr. Stahmann's pecan orchards that said KEEP OUT (and, scrawled underneath, PELIGRO!). As we figured it, that was fair warning to anyone who might come to our secret place, a closed curtain of rushes fourteen or fifteen feet high.

One March at the windy time in the valley, the late afternoon was like evening because of the smoke-black dust blasting from El Hado's face. The rushes clacked against each other and their straw heads tangled and untangled in a hissing sound. Between the rushes and the river we sat down and pulled Baby from the grocery bag. A twenty-inch life-size rubber newborn, Baby came with her own snap-on plastic diaper and pink cotton jumper. I don't know what Baby Lifesize cost in 1960, but you can buy her today for $19.99. I have seen many of her.

We sat Baby up. "Mmmmm," she said, awake and unsurprised when I forced her head off.

Ben showed me how it was her head that made the sound. He rocked Baby's head, making it sigh again, closing and opening its eyes. Ben had instinctively learned a gesture of my father's in which he would quietly, only slightly, shake his head no at some notion known only to him. You'd see Ben or my father look down at a bowl of Malt-O-Meal and do it, or at someone in church.

I asked, "Don't you want to float her?"

"Huh?" he said. "Yeah. Course." He brought out his stuff: black electrical tape, a toy compass, a box of matches, a few yards of fishing line filament with a hook at the end. I had a little finger-size flashlight and a map of New Mexico taken from the dash of our parents' car. I also had blank paper and two sharpened pencils. We laid it all out, lined it up: a survival kit for "the people in peril," the Mexicans downriver. The idea was the same every time, though we made it more and more elaborate according to new things we learned about Mexicans from our parents. It had to be secret help because they might be a Mexican family, and so there were probably eighteen or nineteen of them and they were probably running from the law. The best thing was that the people in peril were *aliens*. If you were floating things downriver to *aliens* anything you floated down would be wondrous. We knew at least that much.

"Ready?" Ben asked. Even though he was already eight, he had just learned to tell time. He looked at his wrist. "Three fifty-six," he said.

"Mmmmm," I said to Baby's torso. The torso said it back.

"Okay, Ben." I stuffed the fishing line and hook inside the matchbox and handed it to him.

He dropped it into her and looked inside. "Okay," he said.

I put the flashlight and pencils together, rolling the blank paper around them. I rolled the map around that, but then decided I had the order wrong, so I rolled the pencils in the map and the map inside the blank paper.

"Okay," Ben said, diagonally wedging the package into her rib cage. "But it'll rattle around inside."

"Yep," I said.

He looked at me, his eyes opening wider. The expressiveness of his face was dependent on his eyes and mouth since neither his frowns nor grins ever creased his smooth, impassive forehead.

"It has to rattle," I said. "Or they won't know anything's inside."

He had gotten a pencil mark above his nose, so I wiped it off with a damp finger. "Messahanus," I said in imitation of my mother.

"Jeez, Peg."

He wiped my spit from his forehead. His hair did not have as much black in it as mine, but it was the same auburn shade. All the features of his face were so much like mine that I might have been only his moult, a person still inside the skin he had shed.

The compass also rattled in Baby's head as we screwed it back on and punched her limbs in place. We took off her jumper to tape up the seams of her neck, arms, and legs. We covered her tilt-open eyes, her pursed mouth, and perfect, open ears. We looked her over for a last leakage check. "Functional," I said. "Functional," he said. It was a word we had heard our father use. She had a diaper but, needless to say, no genitals or anus. We decided the holes at the roots of her lifelike hair might leak, so Ben taped her head.

He said, "Here you go," to her—or to me—and asked, "Ready?"

I answered, "Set sail." I might have felt nostalgia for Baby if she hadn't floated so beautifully. I might have felt some horror at the sight of her bandaged up like that, but I held hands with Ben and felt awfully good that we sealed her up tight. Downriver, the people in peril, without light or heat or compass, would retrieve her and find inside her everything they needed.

I must be talking out loud without knowing it. Dewopathy. Dewimancy. The bus driver says, "Huh?"

"Dewimancy," I say. "It means 'divination by dew.'"

"Going to rain?" she asks. I like her.

"No chance."

As we take the University exit off Highway 25 and descend into Las Almas, I am happy. It is amazing to me how easily happiness can come back.

* * *

On the door of my husband's house, very high up, but eye level for me, was a brass plate which said MR. JAMES AIGLEY. It made my knuckles hurt to knock, but it was a matter of ritual and principle.

"Hey," he said when he opened the door, "it's Little Peg." He said it both to himself and to me, which was his way.

I said hello and told him I was happy and fairly okay mentally so it was safe to let me in.

"Oh, hey, come on in," he said. "Molly's at church but you sit down and let me take care of you." His newly trimmed hair was parted high; his sideburns were short, narrow, neat, and the skin of his face a little agitated where he had circled his electric shaver too much around his mouth and over his chin.

He had breakfast, coffee, orange juice, the morning paper, anything I wanted, he had it. I sat on his stiff, short-backed sofa. His carpeting was clean. His window curtains were Lustre Glaze Chintz (we had picked it out together) which feels so good to gather in your hands or in a curtain sash.

James and my arrangement has been unconventional. We might be "separated." Who can tell? In '73 I gave him no choice but to take me to court concerning Molly, and as a result, I was declared unfit. He has legal custody but allows me to visit whenever I like. (My scheduled times are Sundays, Mondays, and Tuesdays.) Would you think we would be divorced by now? Would you think our relationship would be hostile? Nope. For fifteen years, for week-long periods, I have lived with James and Molly while I have moved from Everview to various apartments and then back in with them before eventually returning to Everview. People strange enough to agree to such a life should be called "estranged." That will do fine to describe James and me.

I asked when Molly would be back.

"A minute. Relax and let me get you something." He was pouring cream into my coffee, remembering just how I liked it, giving it to me whether I wanted it or not, like always. His hands were steady around the cup, and I touched his fingers with mine as I took it from him.

Though I know what I need, I don't always know how much. Memory has to fill in the gaps.

James trimmed his nails by neatly chewing them off. His fingers and the backs of his hands were nearly hairless and were always raw from overscrubbing. After lovemaking, I used to hold his hands near my face and talk to them.

Now it made him uncomfortable to have me looking at them. "You're early, Little Peg."

"Sorry. I'm in a great mood, James." He sat on the identical sofa across from my sofa. He rested his hands on his knees and leaned forward as though he wanted to look more directly at me, but then he avoided eye contact.

I remember I would touch his hands with my nose and lips; smell and even almost taste the weedy mustiness of me on his fingers; then whisper into his palms, "How do you know how to touch me like that? Did I teach you? How?"

"So. Things are better?" he asked.

"All the time, James. Leveling out." I told him it was nice of him to ask but could I drink my coffee and us not talk, because it threw me off to talk to him when I was really happy and I'd rather save conversation for Molly.

It was hurtful of me. I never meant to be hurtful but if I would recall something pleasant, some one good moment with him, I got mean. If I visited and remembered how we were, the tense anticipation, mostly the nothingness, I could be friendly because I could pity us both enough to want to reconcile things a little.

James was always pleasant and kind to me on my Sunday visits. It convinced me he remembered only the nothingness.

We sat quietly. He poured himself some juice. He said he had fresh eggs, cheese, salsa, tortillas, lots of stuff he could serve up quick, he'd be glad to, just ask, okay, Little Peg? If I wanted to lift the scab of another ancient, unhealing ugliness, I would have told him to stop calling me Little Peg, call me Peg or shut up with your lots-of-anything-I-want because you're ruining my happy mood.

He had left the living room to load the dishwasher when Molly came in. She was excited to see me, but as we hugged each other I told her, "I'm okay and feeling happy, Molly, and I think we can have a good time this time." Because of the way some of our visits had gone, I always thought I should either warn her about me or put aside doubts.

"Oh, Mom, we have a good time every time and you—you—" She's not like me about that. She can start a lie but has a bad time finishing.

James called from the kitchen, "Do I get a hug?"

He didn't get one.

While she was changing out of her clothes in another room, I joined James in the kitchen. I asked, "Hey, Molly, how was Mass?"

"Father Sylvester gets off on baptisms, doesn't he?" she called out. "Took it to the limit, Mom. He thinks a lot about conception and all that. His sermon was about seeds and mustard seeds and fertile earth. It was kind of embarrassing."

"He's very young," I said.

"I mean, you could tell what *he* was thinking."

"If she isn't getting anything out of it," James muttered to me, "why make her go?"

"I don't make her go."

"You still ask."

"James," I said, "you haven't turned the dishwasher on."

I didn't know why I asked her to go to Sunday Mass except that in a Mass I had always gotten some good, straight contact with God and His apostles, disciples, popes, bishops, nuns, ushers, organists, the faithful who weren't afraid of the nutsiness in eating His body and drinking His blood right in front of Him and each other. Symbolism or no symbolism, even if you discounted both heaven and hell, sins and states of grace, immaculate and maculate conception, Mass was still a powerful jolt.

When Molly came back out she asked James if he wanted to go with us; this was a joke among the three of us, and we played it out every time I visited. "Yes, I'd love to go," he said.

"Too bad," she said. "You can't." It was not funny, it never was funny, but we couldn't help ourselves: we played it out, we all three laughed.

Molly has bought us a dozen doughnuts and two extra-large coffees at the Wagon Wheel.

We've been talking about boys. I've been trying to say wise things about how if a woman wants knights she better expect armor and if she wants priests she better expect commandments, and for both she better shave her underarms.

We've slogged down four doughnuts when talk turns to birth control. And the question about what to expect men to be. "Toads," I tell her.

She says, "Daddy misses you, you know. He talks about missing you."

I can't wipe all the sticky icing from my fingers. "Your father's an okay man. Mr. Adequate."

"Hey, Mom."

"Okay, I take it back." Inside I'm not taking it back, I'm pushing it forward.

"What's up?"

"I'm happy, Molly. I'm really in a good mood today. We could have more doughnuts."

"Nah. All that sugar. So. What's up?"

"See? You say 'So' all the time like I do. But you're so pretty and you say 'Hey' and 'Nah' like James says. And look how you hold your doughnut and mouth and coffee cup all real close together. Like him. So. It makes me—I don't know—ruins things, I guess."

Nassar, the manager of the Wagon Wheel, walks by and says hello. He has a discount agreement with Everview. All the Everview residents have a little card we show him. Francis has scratched out her name on hers, and written *Bug.*

After Nassar has walked past, Molly says, "We worry about you."

"God. You're so mature, Molly. Look how mature and sensible you are. Like James: he's so awfully mature. 'We worry about you.' God! Does that sound to you like it does to me? Like *we* can adjust, *we'll* adjust fine. But what about you, Mom? What about our Little Peg?"

"We—"

"I'm happy. If you could've seen the dew I saw this morning, Molly. You should have seen. So. Tell me something about you that will upset me. How about it? If you'd talk to me like an adult—your mother—I'd like that. Tell me something horrible."

"Mom."

"You know: horrible. Eat me up with motherly horror. Well? It would sure make me happier than 'We worry about you.' "

Molly has to work at a grin. When I describe her to friends I'm usually wishing I could show them a picture instead; when I'm showing her picture, I'm usually saying, "She's prettier when you see her." She has my good complexion over all of James's features: a narrow, handsome face, a tigress's chin and jawline so resolved and regal it almost does not permit smiling. She has my auburn hair, except unpermed and fuller than mine and richer in crow-black shiny touches. At her birth, the doctor injured her left eyebrow. Maybe only I still notice the slight shadowed flatness at that one plane of her face.

"So?" I ask.

"Nothing big."

"That's okay."

"People at school sometimes want to know about my mom. You know—you."

We've talked about this before, but never settled anything about it. For many of the sixteen years I've been in and out of Everview we've talked about it. I realize that people probably still ask. "Do you tell them about how I teach in the Nontraditional Program?"

"I did." She can see she's got me confused. "I used to."

She drags her napkin across her mouth. I notice how carefully she's cared for her nails, which makes me want to get back to the subject of boys. But one thing at a time, I tell myself, because Molly *used* to tell people I taught and doesn't anymore. "Why?"

"Mom, you have to know how it is."

"I don't? I don't. You're right, I guess."

"Okay."

"So. I'm all ears."

She moves her coffee cup away from her on the table, which is faked up to look like a wagon wheel. "Weird," she says.

"Weird coffee?"

"Ha. Ha. Very funny. I'm not joking, Mom." She glances around her, circling her glance back to me. The Wagon Wheel has people in it and lots of talk but no one is listening to us or each other or probably themselves. If they had seen the dew I saw, it would be different. She says, "I tell them you're a patient at Everview."

"What?" I say. At first I want to explain that we aren't "patients" at Everview, that it's not an asylum. I already know that won't matter. "No, Molly, you're right, I guess. Lies lead you nowhere, right? It's okay, that's okay." I take hold of her wrists. "Do they make fun of you—me? Molly, I'm sorry. People can be animals, Molly. But animals can be people again too, see what I mean? They won't make fun long because it dies—you'll see—it dies down."

She turns her wrists in so she can take my hands into hers. "They don't make fun, Mom. They think it's weirdly weird or something. I tell everybody."

"It makes you more popular?"

"Weird," she says.

After all, it's what I wanted. A horrible piece of unleavened truth I could lodge in my throat. I offer a sarcastic thank you.

I have many things I need to say to her about why I am at

Everview. I cannot tell her the complicated truth, so I always tell her something else that should have been something more. When she has bluntly asked me, "What happened to you?" I have answered as dishonestly as men answer who are asked, "What did you do in the war, Daddy?" I have said, "I saw *Valley of the Dolls* and *Return to the Valley of the Dolls* on the same day in April of '71."

She drives us home in James's beat-up but clean, sparkling clean, Nova. They offer me lunch.

"You're very kind," I say. What a stiff, cold thing to say. I can't help myself. "No. Thank you. No. But how nice of you to offer."

"I love you," my daughter says.

"Me, too," says my ex-husband, who can always make it sound as if he means it in front of our daughter. An okay guy, but a jerk.

I hug her, and I feel in her unbreaking embrace that she would hold me forever if that could protect me. "Here," I say, "I wrote you this," and hand her the letter I didn't write.

In class on Friday I lecture about The Five Mysteries of Fictional Life. I have careful notes written on crisp salmon-colored notecards from Paula Analyst. On the other side of the cards are detailed instructions about my various medications.

"One. The Character, or in some cases, the Unreal Character, slowly becomes Real a) to herself or himself or to itself, b) to other characters, c) to the reader, and, finally, d) to the professor of literature.

"Two. The Character's life gets complicated and inexorably full of Man vs. Man vs. Woman vs. Man vs. Nature vs. Society vs. Herself or Himself Conflicts. All or none can overlap; some are minor, most Major, some are planned or misplanned or unplanned by the characters. Some are God's doing.

"Pay attention, Norm. This is good for you.

"Three. Character Relationships unseal, seal, the seal breaks, skirmishes follow, isolated battles, war happens, then truce, then peace, children are birthed, a visitor arrives, one leaves, failures come or personal triumphs, symbols are shaved, beveled, grooved, until they fit in throughout and everywhere (crosses, guns, clocks, columns, clouds, orchids, caves, and unopened books are out; cakes, cake candles, burning or not, table settings, microwaves, purses, chair legs/arms, remote controls, and sheathed/unsheathed knives are in; trinities of any kind always have been and are still welcome)—and this is where foreshadowing and backlighting and shifts in point of view and flashbacks and flash-forwards and authorial restraint and intrusion and expansive and compressed narration and canned and convincing dialogue and the size and shape of your diction figure importantly.

"Let's stop a minute here. About where are we on the Pyramid, Burns?"

"We're peaking, Mrs. O. We're about to peak."

"You were paying attention. You really were paying attention, I guess, Burns.

"Four. Every Character, minor or Major, anaerobic and archetypal, has a climax, a good one, or disappointing, or disappointing but enlightening, or if the earth does not move it has an epiphany, or if no epiphany then a moment of clarity, but if not clarity a cleansing whiteness or mystifying darkness that is absolute; characters make love, make lust, reach out or up or down or slash out or sleep in each other's arms.

"Five. After climax all or some of the Major and minor Characters change or develop, leave or stay, choose or choose not to choose, bust up or come together; in many cases, they die, in some they are seriously injured, in some psychically healed, in E. M. Forster's day it usually happened over cigarettes/foreign beer/chocolates, but now it happens over coffee/cocaine/wine/fresh fruit/whole-grain homemade bread, in a promising or threatening or ambiguous climate, at a postclimactic time of morning or evening (though hacks always have it happen at sunrise or sunset), in a quiet or disquieting moment, or sometimes nothing happens after climax at all except a few single-syllable dribbles of dialogue or flaccid narration.

"This whole thing," I say, "is neat and easy and so thoroughly departmental and is called Freytag's Pyramid after Gustav Freytag, who never wrote a story or poem or play in his life but after whose example we pledge our allegiance."

I have another notecard. I have many other notecards, and if I taught in the regular university instead of in the Nontraditional Program, I could use them all. I ask, "Any questions?" The Invisible have all raised their arms, and then erased them. I am hoping someone will ask who E. M. Forster is, or rather, was. I put him in almost every lecture. No one ever asks.

I tell the class I must wait to pass out copies of "One Set, Proofs," which is supposedly Andria Charley's story. It is not.

I think I'd better explain.

At the beginning of the ten-week session I announced that students could write their short stories about anything they wanted as long as each story directly or indirectly made me, their teacher, the major character. The character could be me now, or me earlier in my life, or the story could speculate about my future. Any unusual variations—my friends, my family, my associates as major characters—would have to be approved in the first two weeks of the semester. In researching their stories, they have been allowed to ask me personal questions and I have permitted myself the right to be absolutely truthful to them—or to lie.

I further stipulated that if what they wrote was not good enough to go into my own book-in-progress, they would have a second chance, and, after that, not a chance in hell of passing the course. Seven of the students dropped. The remaining students are from that large part of the population who, in any national survey, answer that nuclear disaster is certain and unpreventable. None of them have told my supervisor.

I thought I should explain this. Still, I don't want it to be a worry. The students' work *is* fiction, right, since they don't really know me, the real whole me? And anyway, in every case—every single case—I have actually thrown out their stories, replacing them with my own versions of my life that I will stubbornly defend as true.

Though I have placed her name in the upper right-hand corner, this is not Andria's short story.

Andria Charley
2322 Houston Ave.
Las Almas, N.M. 88001

One Set, Proofs
(Peg, 1959)

#1

She was the girl standing behind the giant pumpkin on the seed packets. Only her head and neck showed, and her hands around the thick, twisting stem.

The Burpee photographer had called in June and told her mother about her winning the contest. "My name," he said, "is Ed Fraley! And your little girl—is one lucky girl—because she has been chosen—from hundreds of contestants—to be next year's Burpee Big Max Pumpkin girl! What do you think of that? You're wordless, huh? I'd be wordless too. Your husband home, Mrs. O'Crerieh? No? Well, look, I can phone back. No? Well, we got details to take care of if the answer is yes. Yes? I'm so happy for you, really happy and glad. Well, I got to shoot her right away—get her on my schedule. What do you think? Okay? Okay! Okay. Next Monday? July fifth it is."

Her mother said, "What about—"

"She should have several outfits ready. No bruises or cuts or like that on her face? You'd be surprised. Several outfits—homemade that *looks* homemade is best. Is her hair still straight?" he asked.

"She has a cute perm," her mother answered.

"Okay," he said.

"It's new, Mr. Froley, and it's darling."

"Okay. All right, I suppose."

"We didn't guess she would win."

"She's a beauty. A tall one, huh? You should be real proud, Mrs.—I'm sorry—I don't know your first name."

"Marcella."

"And your husband?"

"John."

"You say hi for me, will you? John's a working man?"

"Yes, he—"

"Say hi for me. Tell him to call me with any questions. Ed Fraley. F-R-A-L-E-Y. Ed. Here's the number."

#2

She and her mother had fussed over her hair, whether it should have a ribbon to pull it back from her face and forehead. Her mother won, and they used a narrow white strip of satin.

They had gotten up hours before Mr. O'Crerieh in order to clean the house. They had taken her younger brother Ben to the baby-sitter for the day. Before he left for work, her father had said, "No acting foolish, Little Peg. Take a nice picture." He and Mr. Fraley had made the arrangements about the money, he told his wife, and it was a fair shake, she shouldn't worry herself over it. "It's a long drive from Denver to Las Almas," he reminded them, "so make the man some breakfast."

They kissed him through the open car window. "If we get a letter," he said, "call me at work, honey." He always drove home for lunch if a letter came from her older brother Anthony, only seventeen but a freshman at UT-Austin.

No sooner had Mr. O'Crerieh gone than the Burpee pickup pulled into their driveway. The man who came out did not look anything like the way Mr. Ed Fraley sounded. But at the door he introduced himself as Ed and, because of something about how his upper and lower teeth were an unmatched set, they took his word for it.

He said, "Hello—why, look at you, you beauty. Mrs. O'Crerieh, hello. I thought you must've lived on a farm so I circled town. Nice town. Found some good shooting locations out there, so no time wasted. Want you to see my pumpkins—

want to see them, girl?" He said it all in one inhalation and one smooth exhalation.

Mr. Fraley's arms were almost hairless, but were tawny and hard like her brother Anthony's arms. His neck was unwrinkled, smooth as his words; his face was friendly and human. Her mother had told her once that you could find some trace of animal in almost any man's face, that she should look around and see. Except for her father and brothers, it was true: men looked like their dogs and pets and like other people's pets; some looked less tame than others. Mr. Fraley's face had nice, definite human bones at his cheeks and jaws. A good shaved human chin. The thin hair on his head was slicked back, ending low on his neck; slightly damp, it was the color of cream-and-sugar coffee.

"Wait'll you see my pumpkins. You're like your picture. You're going to do perfect. Over here—come on." He unlatched the cover over the bed of his pickup and lifted it away.

The giant pumpkins were covered with green tarps marked

BIG MAX
Beware Temp

and as Mr. Fraley uncovered them he explained, "They're wax so I have to be careful of heat and bumps in the road and problems like that."

Her mother stepped nearer to them. They were too large to see entirely.

"Go ahead," he said.

She tapped the top of them with her fingernails. "They're not hollow."

"Stuffed full of shredded paper. Keeps their shape up." He said, "What about you, girl?" He put his hand on her head and pressed his fingers in. "What do you think?"

"Why do you have two, Mr. Fraley?"

He laughed. "This's a smart one." He scratched her scalp, then took his fingers away. "I'm going to show you why there's two when we start shooting."

But first they made Mr. Fraley's breakfast.

"He eats like a bird," her mother said afterward in the kitchen.

"I heard you," he said. "I like to shoot without much on my stomach, ma'am—plus, I don't like to miss morning light. Best shooting light was a couple hours ago—we got to hurry out. You two ready?"

"We have to change our clothes," said her mother.

"Yeah, she needs that, you're right." He said, "Don't mean to be rude—hurry, though—hurry her up. Bring two or three outfits with—combs, brushes."

In her mother's room she carefully pulled the dress over her hair. She rolled her new white socks down a little bit more until her ankles matched to her mother's satisfaction. "Stand straight when he photographs you," she said. "Look." Her mother pushed her chest out, shoulders back, and raised her head enough to unwrinkle her neck. "You do that." She did it well.

They climbed up into Mr. Fraley's truck cab, her in the middle.

"You aren't sitting on your dress?"

"No, ma'am."

"Mr. Fraley wants you to look nice, hon."

He was happy to be driving, she could see. He sped up and leaned into the turns from Branson onto Espina, University onto Main, and finally onto old Highway 28.

Magnetized to the dash was a small plastic St. Christopher statue with the Christ child on his right shoulder; on his left shoulder St. Christopher had a dry little ball of chewing gum.

She nudged her mother and nodded at it, but she didn't get nudged back.

#3

He had already chosen a particular spot in Mr. Stahmann's pecan orchards, the oldest, grandest orchards in the Mesilla Valley. He pulled over and pointed. "See, you got a good big circle of light there all shut in by the shade. Nothing like it." He pulled the truck onto the shoulder and then slowly, almost rocking the wheel in his hand, he entered the grove.

She heard her mother mutter, "Mr. Stahmann won't like you doing this, mister."

"He the owner?"

"Yes."

"Got an attitude?"

"I don't—attitude? I don't know, Mr. Fraley."

Mr. Fraley stopped. "Let's shoot," he said. He walked around the truck, helped her mother out, then her. "This light's mine," he said and put his hands out before him in order to let some of the sunlight pool into and overbrim them. "I own this all day."

His camera was already attached to the tripod when he slid it from inside the truck and set it up. As he unlatched the hinged truckbed cover and lifted it away, he said, "Mrs. O'Crerieh, I can use you." And he helped her up where she could grab two of the four rope handles on the canvas under the first pumpkin. He took the other two handles, and they cradled it to the ground, positioned it in the light.

"Now," he told them, "you're going to see why there's two."

They cradled the second pumpkin to the ground. Her mother stared hard at it. "Of course," she said, in that same tone of voice that she might ask a timid question.

The second pumpkin was much more perfectly manufactured than the first. Each pale orange wrinkle and each deep almost red crease had in it the tension of something still growing.

"See what I mean?" Mr. Fraley asked.

"No," she said.

And her mother said, "Yes. Okay, this is a female."

"Lady Max. You can't tell, girl?" His laughter was unkind. If her father did not like a meal or the color of her mother's fingernail polish or the way the table was set, his laughter was that same way.

"Mr. Fraley," said her mother, "can we go on with everything, please?"

"No disrespect meant." He shook his head and turned from them. He took a bottle of something from the truckbed and lightly sprayed the surface of the pumpkin, polishing it with a soft rag out of his pocket. Then he asked, "The little one ready?"

"She's ready."

He produced a box, which he opened up at one end. "This," he said, "is a light meter. Shows the shine your skin gives off." He demonstrated how the needle swept slightly left or right according to whether the meter was pointed at her hand or her dress.

"Look here," he said, and they did the meter readings on both pumpkins. When he took a measure of her face, he was pleased; he grinned, and snapped the box shut.

"Did you see?" she asked her mother, who nodded yes. But she wanted her mother to actually see her reading, how the needle rested on one place, which was exactly the amount of light that was her.

#4

For the next two hours, he posed the pumpkins and her, occasionally rubbing a damp, oily cloth over her face followed by a deep-pink scented powder. Teaching her how to squint without wrinkling up her whole face, showing her what to do with her chin in order to relax her mouth, he coached and coaxed her.

"Here, Mom, put this on her real light," and he handed her mother a pumpkiny lipstick.

"Hon," her mother said after she dabbed it on, "do this with your lips."

"I know."

"Like you've seen me do it. Like this. Press and pull in. Pucker." She turned to Mr. Fraley for his approval of the results.

"Great, great." He let her mother come again to the camera and look through the lens at the composition, her daughter squarely in the center. "Okay, Miss Beauty, I want some

Sweetness—your Daddy's Big Little Beauty Winner Look. Okay—almost—lift the chin—can you put those arms wider over Prince Pumpkin?—got it—got it."

In two hours he had used four rolls of film. After she changed outfits again in the cab of his truck, she had a question that wouldn't wait. "Did you know my brother Anthony is an Orrow TC in college? Have you been that already?"

"Nope. Let's have Smartness—practice a little bit—like you got your hand raised at school—put your hand up if you want. Don't lose that! Put that hand down, but don't lose that now—could be—hold it—don't move—yeah, yeah. That could be the one."

Her mother asked, "Is something wrong with you?"

"What?" He was changing the lens of his camera, one fist around the camera body, one fist locking the new lens in place.

"Is something wrong?" her mother asked.

He ignored her. "Let's get you like this. Neither hand on the pumpkin—but like you just slapped the top of the pumpkin—don't slap it!—could be saying, 'I won!'—your mouth is too closed, open your mouth—little more—big, open-mouth smile now—no—no. No. Help her out, Mom? Good. It's there. Almost. Hold it!" He took the picture. "Your big brother smart?"

"He is. You should see how smart."

"A smart college boy," he muttered. He came from behind the camera in order to rearrange her shoulders and head. "Light's awful. Let's come back around three and shoot some more with Lady Max. We can leave it all—take the camera, though—get a tarp over the two."

They drove half a mile to the Stahmann Gift Shop, where Mr. Fraley bought them candied pecans and RCs. "So," he said, "your dad works in a brick factory." He pushed back the thin hair on his head, and gripped the nape of his neck as if he was gathering in a heavy rope. She didn't have to look to know her mother did not like him.

"What's he do?"

"He's a foreman," she said.

With his mouth full of pecans, Mr. Fraley asked her mother, "What's he do?"

Mr. Fraley, the girl wanted to say, *don't talk with your mouth full.*

Her mother spoke to her instead of to Mr. Fraley. "He's responsible for the men. The men on his shift."

He finished chewing. "Makin' those bricks." He grinned as he swallowed.

When they returned to the grove, he pulled a handwritten note to himself from his back pocket. "We're going to need some breathlessness. More sweetness. Some affection again."

It was a lot to ask. But her mother helped show her, and Mr. Fraley helped move her body the right ways. And lots of them she could do all by herself. She was surprised how many poses she already knew.

#5

Closer to five in the evening she gave off less light.

He said, "You're going to be a tall one, anybody can see that. I got to manage that." He brought out a padded stool, which she was to kneel on behind Lady Max. That made it all look like a pumpkin with a head on top of it. Her mother told Mr. Fraley she hoped those weren't what he picked because you couldn't sell seeds to people with plain silliness.

They had not been getting along well. His face finally showed his anger. He said if she knew what he knew about what people want to see she'd be making a living taking photographs, wouldn't she? "No. You almost don't see women photographers around. Because you take a good guy photographer—he knows how—if he's good—to sit and light and pose them and get a set of proofs that show what folks want to see."

He took his handkerchief out of his pocket. He said, "Look up here, sweetheart," and he wiped her face dry again, rubbing her lips clean also. "We're done."

"Yes, we certainly are," said her mother. They strode ahead

of him out of the grove. Her mother silently helped Mr. Fraley cradle the pumpkins into the truckbed.

When the pumpkins and the camera were loaded and the truckbed cover was latched into place, they drove out of the circle of light, smaller now because of shadows fencing it in more closely. At their home, her mother found a letter from Anthony in the mailbox. She turned the letter over, touched her thumb along the seal. "What do you think, hon? What do you think he'll say?"

She knew. He would say very little, what he needed to say, the things that would make her father happy. Anthony was good, the way he always worried over her father. Then at the bottom he would say, "Hello there to Little Peg and Ben and you too, Mom."

Her mother went inside to make the telephone call.

Mr. Fraley leaned on the porch rails. She wanted to ask him about how the meter readings worked if there wasn't any light. Did you give off light without your clothes on? What kind of people gave off the most light? Which ones didn't give off any?

"I wish," he said, "your mom and me could've got on better. You're a kind of people I know how to work with. You're perfect to shoot—I mean, I could shoot some family shots—make you all look good—a perfect family portrait—a ten by twelve or like that."

When her mother came back out, he was in the truck. "Mrs. O'Crerieh, I thank you. Burpee thanks you. Got to go—make some proofs—" He offered a handshake through the open car window, but her mother probably did not notice. He said, "You got a little princess here—a big little princess. A good one, I mean it. Check and proofs'll come on the same day. I'll call from our office in Denver. That's July 26. Look the proofs over—I make the choice—but I want to hear what you and Mr. O'Crerieh got to say."

"Let's go inside," her mother said to her. They didn't say goodbye to Mr. Fraley except for a polite wave behind the screen door. She watched her mother and waved like her.

They called the baby-sitter to ask if she would bring Ben home. "You make me proud," her mother said when they went into the kitchen. "I'm proud as I can be of you." They brought out the plates and silverware and glasses. She wouldn't let it go: "You're a parent's dream. Our pride and joy." After the table was set, they stood together and looked it over. The setup seemed to arrange itself around the unopened letter her mother had put at the center of the table. It would be wrong to ask that the letter be moved.

She crossed her arms over herself as her mother did and started to ask how she liked the table arrangement. But her mother asked, "Are you proud of me too, like I'm proud of you?"

The End

3 · *Extrapyramidal Tmetic Carnival Options*

This chapter has a Brazilian beat, many cc's of the Prolixin Brazilian beat. It creeps in by prescription. I can't help it. I let it creep in.

Sergio says, "We wheel hab Carnibal. Zhu ligke thadt? Juice vor today? Good."

Do you listen to "The Brazilian Hour"?

You can taste his words. When he says "good" it sounds like "food."

You should listen.

Last night, Paula Analyst and I had to go looking for Francis because she didn't show up at dinner. On the way around town, I told Paula lies about Francis and me and our neighborhood, our grandmas, boyfriends, our periods. The fact is, Francis and I never met each other before Everview. You know how a spider will leave one unsticky thread in her web so she can avoid her own traps? I didn't weave a single, tangled strand of truth. One particularly ornate lie I told was about how Francis and I double-dated and how we took smokes to the drive-in and pushed the cigs back in our teeth whenever The Tongue was coming, or spilled hot ashes on The Boob Claw. I told Paula that Francis and I had our own "python" jokes about those boys' ever-alert penises. When Paula laughed at all that I assumed she believed me, so I believed me too. Completely.

It could be the psychotropics I have taken. I have had extrapyramidal drug reactions but they're over, so I'm good as tuna. Lately, Prolixin, gentle swan of the psychotropics, once a week. Right in the butt.

You're not okay. And she's not okay, Paula said after we got back to Everview in order to wait for word about Francis.

I had asked her: "Am I okay?" I had asked her: "Is she okay?"

Eventually, Francis called Everview from the Sears in the new mall. She apologized for frightening us. When Paula and I got there, Francis marched us to a friendly life-size Cheryl Tiegs. "Does this make you sick?" she asked.

Cheryl was waving hello. Nothing in her whole cardboard physique could make the wave a goodbye also. Cheryl was prancing on her own cardboard words: Summer! My New Sears Summer Look! And Yours! Affectionately, Cheryl!

Francis asked if we could go somewhere for chocolate milk. Paula said they had it at Everview. She parked in front and gave me permission to use her Kaypro, which was already in my room. We thanked her.

Paula was upset with us. She pushed her sharp lower teeth out a little, which is okay for a northern pike or muskellunge but makes a human look dangerous. Unreal. She said, *You're acting crazy, you two.*

I squinted to fix her in a narrow space where I could be sure she was real; I mean, not someone I only imagined.

Drinking our milk with our medication, Francis and I talked about it. Andria's story had upset Francis. She thought I shouldn't have done what I did.

"I just retyped it," I said, which was a lie I only needed to repeat in order to believe. "I just retyped it." (So, how do I know it's a lie if I believe it? I just retyped it.)

"But I—"

"Okay," I said, "I guess I was angry at James and everybody."

"And then," Francis said, "you know. You put in your older brother and that mean man."

The dining room table we sat at was vast. Probably twenty chairs were tucked under it. PROPERTY OF EVERVIEW was stenciled onto the center of the Formica about every fifteen inches.

"Anyway," said Francis, "it *was* a sweet story, wasn't it? And you made it—you know—you made it mean."

"That's right," I said, "I made it mean."

She wanted me to promise I'd never do that again.

"You sure?" I asked.

I solemnly promised never to promise that.

Maybe my medication kicked in. "Francis," I said, "I want one or two things just the way I want them."

She said, "I can see that."

I knocked the table with a knuckle. "I hate this," I said. "Property of Everview."

She looked down the length of the table. "Key-rist!" she said, the same way Burns said it in class.

"Quit it, Francis. Look, they've put it all over. Property of Everview. Like one of us is going to tuck the tables under our arms and walk out with them."

Francis said, "That might not be the reason." Her lips moved as she silently read the words on the table. "They might be—what if they're—naming things for us? We might need that."

She smelled as though she had been sampling scents in the mall. "You stink," I said.

"Me?" She lifted her left wrist to her nose. "I smell like Cheryl Tiegs," she said.

"Oh, quit it."

"You quit it, Peg. I think naming things is good. If you want to remember, you name." Her palms raised from the table, and pressed down on it again. I remembered what she had told me about her miscarriages. She had lost three children in nine years. Daughters. And she had named the last two.

At the center of the table, we touched each other's hands with the tips of our fingers. We looked at each other and then poured blank gazes into the empty glasses. Should I have been ashamed to admit that it thrilled me to touch that way? Why would people want to make us ashamed of that? When does that kind of pus first come into people's souls? I wrote Peter Thompsenson's story the way I did because I wanted to understand.

Peter Thompsenson
P.O. Box 239
Las Almas, N.M. 88005

John Glenn, American Hero
(Peg, 1961)

In one summer, three good things happened that couldn't be explained and that must have been connected. Mr. and Mrs. Demas's house three houses over and across the street burned up. The Rios' three-trunk pecan tree next door died in one night. So did all the pecans in their shells. Peg got breasts.

Her mother showed her how to wear the thing. It had an eye hook at the back. It had a pink butterfly bow at the front. She didn't grow them all at once. But one day in the middle of the summer her mother said that she was still a little girl, when did those come? And drove with her to the Woolworth's department store where they bought the thing.

There were new rules. Peg should put the thing on every morning. She should not let Ben see the top of her as she did before. She should not let Ben see her put the thing on or take it off. Ben should not play with the thing.

That made her angry at first. She held it up to look at it. She had seen her mother's things, and it looked like them, like a horse's harness. Her mother said that she was blossoming, she didn't want to show everybody her blossoms, did she? That made her angry too. She hid them, thought of all the sunlight she was hiding them from. In the bathroom, she took the thing off and looked hard. Each one was eleven years old. They had blossomed at the same time. It *was* kind of amazing for it to happen. Later, her mother explained that God gave them to her and He knew what He was doing. It was a mystery of life, like a woman's cycle. They would talk about that when the time came.

Peg didn't want to be a smart aleck and tell her that there

were women's cycles and men's. Men's had a crossbar. Women's didn't. When the time came, she would tell her mother she already knew.

It was Saturday. Peg and Ben's parents always took a nap on Saturday afternoons when the special rule was that all children stay out of the house. Though it would be big trouble for them if they got caught, Peg and Ben went to the carport and pretended to drive the car to anywhere they wanted.

Ben was only nine but he drove because they were pretending and, even pretending, the man always drove. He was calm as a clam behind the wheel. "Dear," he said, "would you hand me my sunglasses?"

She took them from the dashboard. "Here you are, honey."

"That's better."

She asked if they were taking the highway upstate. He said that he heard it was a nice drive. They could go through Michigan, Maryland, try to find Texas. Ben was a silly pretender. She wanted to know if they could stop in Oregon to look at a burned-up old house she had heard about and a mysterious dead tree along the highway.

"Dear," he said, "would you clean my sunglasses?"

Since he had to concentrate on his driving, she pulled the sunglasses from his face. Her parents had discouraged her from pretending so much. She was older and that was "unhealthy," her mother said. Peg breathed onto the lenses and polished them with one of the tails of her blouse. Then she put them back on him, tucked her blouse back in.

"Where is this burned-up house?"

"You take the turn here."

"Uh-oh."

"Missed it." Peg could expertly mimic her mother's miffed voice, and she liked doing it. She asked him to pull over to the shoulder, where she could read the map she had taken from the dashboard.

They rolled the windows down because that time of year was hot in whatever state you were in. Peg looked at Maryland and

Texas on the map. She traced her finger over the rivers, all the rivers, the shields that were the road signs, the arrowheads that were Indian country, the blue stars that were the major cities, and showed him where the Alamo was in Texas.

"I *can* read, dear," Ben said, pretending to start up the engine again. She pointed to a tiny encircled green pyramid on a stick and told him he would have to turn around to get to the dead tree. As they were pulling back onto the highway, they heard giggling through Peg's car window.

"You better not," Peg said, touching his hand on the wheel as he pretended to turn the car in that direction.

Ben stopped, turned the engine off. "What is it?" he asked.

"It's them."

The bedroom window was open completely. It was a roll-out window that opened almost directly into the open car window. They could hear their parents making sounds people might make rowing a boat on a river, rowing and laughing and rowing faster.

They heard her father say very quietly, "Thank you," which made her mother giggle again. Then he said, "You've got the giggles, huh?"

Her mother said, "JohnyesyesyesJohn," lower and louder. "Yes! There. Mmmm."

It was quiet for a minute or two. "I heard someone today," said her mother, "I can't put her out of my mind."

Peg scooted nearer the voices. Ben scooted next to her.

"Well," her father said, "what?"

"Not much." She laughed strangely. "I feel so good. Wait. No. Yes. Do you feel this good, John?" It sounded as if she breathed in deeply. "I think it's funny."

"Hmm-mm."

"I went to a different parlor for my hair. Do you like it?"

"Fine. Wonderful. Fine."

"It cost more. The woman who did it was telling all of us in the shop about how famous she is. She cut John Glenn's hair before he went up in space."

"No barber?"

"She swears. He wrote a letter, she says. He signed a picture for her. When she has her own shop she's going to frame it."

"John Glenn. You believe her?"

"She says he wrote her about how he didn't like having his hair just cut so nice and then stuck under that helmet. All his radio stuff was in the helmet, she says, so it was important to keep it on."

"I bet she's right about that."

"But he cheated. He broke radio contact and took it off and let his hair go free. He needed the freedom, he said, the Friendship Seven was tight, and his hair felt good lifting up off his head. That's what she said he said."

"That's the craziest—"

"She said his eye roamed over the whole earth, looking for Las Almas, New Mexico." They both were laughing now. Peg and Ben tried not to laugh, but couldn't help themselves.

"She says he said to himself, 'Thank God for Jen Thompsenson!' and 'What a good cut!' "

"It takes all kinds. I—"

"John. Did you hear something?"

Peg and Ben slumped down in the car. They heard her mother at the window ask, "The kids?"

"Probably nothing."

They stayed low. Her mother said, "Okay," and her father chuckled oddly as though he was chuckling with his mouth closed. He asked, "Didn't John Glenn have a crew cut?"

Ben touched Peg's left breast.

"Ben?"

His hand rested lightly, respectfully, on her as if he was helping her pledge allegiance to the flag. "Could I see?" he whispered.

"What?"

"The thing. Where you grew. Could I?"

The idea of saying no to him was new. She said no to him, of course, about pushing nails into water bugs and drowning moths, but she never had to say no to him about important things. And now. He only wanted to see. But her mother had told her the rule as if telling her about an eleventh commandment. Ben shalt not see the thing nor Peg under the thing. "No, Ben," she said, lifting his hand away.

"She'd be mad, huh?"

"Real mad."

"Hers grew a lot," he said. "I saw hers."

"But she didn't know you saw them, did she?"

"No." Still crouched low, he moved away from her.

If she wanted to, she could let him see the thing, touch where she grew, and her mother would never know. "I'm sorry, Ben."

He said it was okay. He scooted over to sit behind the steering wheel, where he could concentrate on the outside rearview mirror. He put his sunglasses on and pretended to idle the car, waiting to pull onto the highway. "Do we have coffee?" he asked.

She pretended to pour some from a thermos. She blew on the coffee to cool it before Ben took the cup and drank. "You're mad, I guess."

Through the bedroom window, directly into the open car window, her mother's voice boomed, "Ben! Peg! You get out of that automobile this minute!"

Inside the house, she asked them, "What did you think you were doing? Do you know a car is dangerous? It's a dangerous thing. I've told you that a hundred times if I've told you once. Have I told you that? Answer me." Her eyes were messy with tears. "You're my—dearest—little—if an accident happened, I —Peg—Ben, what do you have to say for yourself? How will you two turn out is what worries me. It really worries me."

"Answer your mother," her father said.

Peg was thinking that she had little Jujubes inside each breast. They might grow like her mother's. If they grew, they would be harder to hide in the thing. She would have to get things like her mother had. With wires. She had shown Peg the thickness of the rubbery things. The wire was like fence wire. She looked at Ben and tried to read his thoughts. *We didn't hurt ourselves.*

Her mother said, "Wait and see what your father does," and "You scare me half to death with your wildness."

We found out about some stuff. We heard some stuff. Ben said, "We didn't hurt nobody."

"Get to your rooms right now! And I don't want you—either one of you—in the other one's room, you understand?"

Peg didn't let me see.

She talked about "hell to pay" and said to their father, "Get up, John. I'm at the end of my rope with—"

He said, "Honey. They're kids." Peg knew her father might spank her and Ben.

In her room she could hear her mother's whimpering, which was only a little softer than the happy kind of whimpering they had heard through the car window. Her mother said, "I know. I know they're only children."

"Honey," he said, "come here now."

"No, John."

Peg whispered down the hall, "Ben?"

He whispered back, "Yeah?"

"I'm sorry." Peg wished they could see each other.

She took off the blouse and then the thing. She lay on her stomach. Ben must be thinking that somehow her breasts were the cause of it all. He must be wondering about it as she was. She thought she knew his thoughts well enough to think them herself. *We went to everywhere and never took her chest out of the thing.*

His voice came down the hall again. "They're not too mad."

From the bedroom downstairs, her mother hoarsely said, "We are *too* mad. Don't you ever do anything like that again."

"Come on, darling," her father said.

"They—"

"Come here." The springs of her father's bed made a half-sprung sound. Then they made a sprung sound that unsprung her mother's laughter again.

The End

I am watching Francis sleep. I can hear her heart, which sounds like mine. A samba.

Francis is so much like me I could have made her up. When I'm her age I'll look like her. Her silver hair is sloppy-boy-short and is thinning but lustrous. Her nose was probably cute once for the fleshy tip of it, but now it looks susceptible, like something that could or already has caused her pain.

Francis's eyes are always changing; they make me think of those fossils in resin, the ones with insects' bones arrested in flight. On her staff file report is a question about Francis's eyes. *Retinitis pigmentosa*? it asks, *Ck. dosage Thorazine.*

I could have made her up. I ask you to help me. If I made Francis up, who made up Imelda and Ferdinand and George Herbert Kaddafi Gorbachev and Gustav Freytag and Mother Betty Theresa Crocker and, politely, Ted Koppel and, I'm serious now, who cut the cardboard for Cheryl Tiegs and Ronald Milhous Richard Reagan? And what about Sergio? And how to explain the jungle I hear behind him and the Peg I hear there in the jungle at 92.2 FM?

I wake up but I don't have to open my eyes because they're open already. "Francis," I say, "help me."

"Huh, Peg? Where?"

"Help me. Write this. Write this down. I want to write to Molly."

She rearranges her nightgown. "Are you okay?"

"I'm not okay."

She pulls a cowboy shirt from a hanger and puts it over her nightgown. Buttoning, she sits at her typewriter, poises her fingertips over home row. "I'm ready to start," she says.

"Good." My arms are freezing. I pull some bedclothes from my bed and wrap myself into them.

Dear Molly,

You should know some things. You should know some things. How the war happened. When the war happened. The names we gave it. Where the war lived. Where it lives now. I know.

You were born with your fists closed. I opened them. You closed them. It made me laugh and laugh. And when you do that now, hold your fists up and say anything, say, "You there, Mom?" or, I don't know, say anything, your fists closed around something that was inside your mother when you were inside her. Then I know I don't know how the war happened or when the war happened and I shouldn't have said I know, should I? Your tiny fingers, perfect, lovely empty hands is what I know.

Sarah was what we wanted to call you. He said in his letters it should be an old name. He had been in Vietnam 316 days. Who knew this country was so old? Who knew? he wrote. And when he got the news that I named you Molly Ann he wrote back: Molly! It's the name of a fish, those little fish in a bowl. Ann!

Then, this happened. He started signing his letters "James." The first letter he did that, change from Jim to James, I read it over because he should not have been able to do that. It should not happen, I said to myself. All his words stupidly not his words. Not, "If I could touch you, Little Peg. Miss you. Write me, please! Love me. I love you!" Not exclamation marks but the period, like the head of a nail driven into paper. Not the word "love" in the branches of every sentence, but bare branches. I wrote him, "My love, my heart." I wrote, "This should not happen!" I tore it up.

I rocked you in my arms, Molly. I spoke and whispered and sang you to sleep with what he always called me, what I always hated: "Little Peg. Little Peg. Little Peg." Your fists tightened like in your sleep, until your father came home and your mother was gone there and had not come had never come back. It is called Vietnam. I am writing you from this place. It is not a dream. I ask you to help me. Is it a dream? A very old country. The grave markers like white dots on dominoes. So many. No dream. Everywhere. No dream, the ones in stone, the ones face down or splintered. No dream. A little beautiful country, and a marker for my brother Ben. And mine, my marker, uncarved. Not a dream.

Francis asks, "No more?"

"No more."

She leaves the letter in the typewriter. She lies down on her side, facing me, her eyes open, indefinite as a newborn's. "I didn't make paragraphs, Peg. I forgot to indent."

"So?"

I have my two fists under my pillow and with my head rested over them I can hear two muffled oceans at opposite ends of the world. If not for Francis, I could not hold myself from being drawn under and drowning.

"Francis," I say, "you smell like goodness."

She must be asleep. It must be in her sleep that she asks, "Do you want to know their names?"

"What names?"

"I gave them names," she says, and that is all.

The next morning is a strange underwater swim because I am off my proper dosage again.

I unsnap my beat-up attaché case. The class respects that unsnapping sound and they give me their attention. Taking attendance, I welcome Lewis Blake back. I'm always more on guard when he's there. He's a Nam vet and has said in front of all my class that he thinks I'm full of shit but that he's in love with me. So far, I can disarm him in class but I might have to teach him a lesson someday.

"You all have copies of Andria's story, 'One Set, Proofs.' Today we'll also discuss Peter Thompsenson's story, 'John Glenn, American Hero.' " Peter starts to correct me about the title of his story, but he stops himself.

Except for the half dozen who are The Invisible, everyone looks ready. Who could help loving them for how ready they are? Always excited about their own work, the most hardened of them are unnerved by their concern for Peter. And Peter's throat is so keen, so severable that I can imagine his shirt and collar being lifted out of the way as he frowns at the shallow basket, my attaché case, in which his head will be carried away. If it would not upset the university Nontraditional Program I would impale weak stories on pikes outside my office.

"Well," I announce, "I've brought the first fifty pages of my book, *Little Peg*, so put everything away." I pass a stack of Part Ones to my left and Part Twos to my right. "Parts One and Two. It has Peter and Andria's stories inside. You've got twenty minutes. While you're reading I'm going to lecture. It's okay if you don't take notes."

Lewis Blake is staring. Right through the voile of my dress, I suspect. "What is this shit?" he says. "What about Peter and Andria?"

If this were grade school I'd make him close his eyes and put his head on his desk. "We'll get to Peter's story. Do the reading, Lewis."

"It's okay," Peter says. He is actually relieved.

Lewis nods ominously at him, says, "Sooner or later, Petey."

I announce that I'm going to lecture about how the short story writer should never have as much fun as the novelist.

"Ask yourself some questions. Is the novelist having fun? Too much? How many successful excesses are excessive? Lots of tmesis in the novel? Too much tmesis?"

Mitchey wants to know what tmesis is.

"You should be reading," I tell her. "Tmesis refers to the parts of a book that don't belong but are allowed to stay."

She gawks at me with that Mitchey-mouthed frost lipstick look. I'm annoyed when students too studiously consider what I'm saying in lecture. She asks, "Why aren't we allowed to put any tmesis in our stories?"

"You're short story writers, Mitchey. It's not allowed. Do your reading." She's a more beautiful and confident developing young woman every day. It's harder to like her.

I resume. "Here's a good question. In the novel are three or more foreign languages used? Greek? Occasional Franco-American Chef Boy-ar-dee?

"Are ideas predominant? Characters? Are characters full of—ideas? Ideas perambulating characters?"

I look out over the class and am pleased to be completely ignored. I'm at my best with the lecture as filibuster. "Which of these ideas are short story ideas? Which are novel ideas?

"1) How like the combustion engine is the human soul!

"2) What stereotypes must be reinforced? What myths must be revised?

"3) 'Expansion. That is the idea the novelist must cling to. Not completion.' (E. M. Forster said it.)

"4) Will males have transplanted wombs fifteen hundred years from now? Will we call them wombs?"

The list is over forty items long. I ask, "What does now plus next plus next equal?" My sentences pour, streak, stroke, snake, snarl, gnarl, gnaw. "Are belt buckle museums wrong?" My metaphors hold fast, loose, bleed, spread, sprawl, stain, each as unrevisable as guilt, as unassignable as blame. "If I break pattern *in a pattern called a war—Christ! What are patterns for?*

"That's plagiarized. I don't remember who wrote it. One of the Lowells, I think. I'm upsetting myself here. Slow down. I guess I should slow down. Am I upsetting you?"

Apparently, I am not upsetting them. The words that come to mind when I look at my class: hooded incandescence. Blake is not reading my novel, but is turning pages throughout my body. Puts his fingertip on the corner and pushes page after page. I ask him, "Will you burn out mine eyes, these eyes that never did nor never shall so much as frown on thee?"

Mitchey, Future English Major, asks who said that, was that Byron or somebody?

Shakespeare. But I'm keeping her and all of them in the dark where they shine so much brighter than in the light of my own already overgenerous illumination.

Oh yes, I give off light. I'm beginning to remember how much exuberant light I used to reflect.

"Have you finished reading?" No one has, but no one admits

it, not even Peter. Lewis Blake has turned another page of me, has pressed my spine on the desk before him and has spread me open. He is moving his lips over me, reading roughly, quickly. Someday I will test him for vocabulary and comprehension.

Mitchey has slid her hand onto Norm's forearm. Norm gives me a look that asks me not to call on him, not now.

The class hasn't finished reading, but The Invisible have stopped and are staring at me.

Andria mutters, "This isn't my story."

"New and improved," says Burns.

"But it has my name on it."

I'm prepared for her objections. "Think of it this way," I tell her. "It has some of your genes and some of mine. It's our child. People will say, 'That's Andria's child' as often as they'll say, 'That's Peg's child.' "

She is not satisfied. "You even changed the title."

The original title had been "Actual Size."

Peter is afraid to speak up, so I call on him. "What do you think, Peter?"

He says, "You did that to my—you—to—"

The title of his story had been "A Burned Up House." B-minus title. The man in Andria's story had no pumpkins. (He was a vacuum cleaner salesman.) B. All of Peter's story was about a burned-up house and a dead crab apple tree, which were also the two main characters.

I told them, "The stories have some of my verbs, some of your nouns. You understand. Your mouth, my teeth. My subtext, your context. Your intention, my purpose."

No one said the words "ethical" or "unethical" once in the whole class discussion. We kept the analogy of genetics. It allowed us to talk about recessive characters, spiral plot structures, the mystical rosaries of literary aberration, redundant cross-generational behavioral patterns, inherited sanity, loss of.

When we were finished, we had barely talked about my novel but we were satisfied it was promising. Sure, they were unashamedly currying my favor, but I guess it was better that they do that openly than to pretend and do it secretly.

Before they could challenge me, I announced we'd workshop Peter's and Andria's stories later in the semester, maybe. "Let's be ready next class to discuss—who's next on the syllabus?—yes, here—October 2—Erminia Maestas and Susan Orstal."

Erminia's story had been entitled "Ripples" but was now entitled "August Twelve."

I felt good as I put my notes back into my attaché case and snapped it closed. "Class is dismissed," I said.

Alone in my classroom, I took off my shoes in order to look at them. It was something I had wanted to do for the whole hour. *I have not taken good care of my shoes,* I thought. It made me very sad. *I have not taken good care of you—look at you—look how sadly lovely you are.*

I carried them to the Everview bus. In my seat near the front, I had to consciously try not to talk aloud to my shoes standing empty before me atop my attaché case. *Lovely shoes. Lovely.*

"Nice day, huh?" the bus driver said. This was her way of making herself vulnerable to me.

I looked. It *was* a nice day. (I liked that bus driver!) (I liked her bus!)

Oh, luxurious, roomy, sleek, and aerodynamic limited-edition Peg! So many exciting options are standard!

4 · *Perimeters*

Pressed into you, no
imprint of my ribs
mouth, hands, no
none of my heat, none
underneath your shirt, belt, none.

None.
But on me
here everywhere
evidence, no
unscored edge, none

none fade, all
all
ask who
was I?

No.

One.

* * *

Rickee has give me this new poem. You can imagine what a lift it is to me when I'm feeling real low.

Francis looked at it and said, "She writes everything with a stutter."

"Emphatic repetition," I explained. "Pooetic technique."

"I don't know about pootry, Peg." We were in the Chemical Dependency wing of Neverview. We were probably talking too loudly.

I folded the poem back up and put it in one of my front overall pockets. We got on our knees near the buckets and brushes in order to spot-clean the Chemical Dependency hallway before shampooing it with the Dirt Mister, then vacuuming with the Rug Fiend.

Although James has always paid part of my Everview care costs (and has often offered to cover more of the cost if I will only stay on my proper dosage of medicine), I have needed to bring in income above my $7,000 annual Nontraditional Program salary. I am a natural for sanitation work of all kinds since I am unemotional about waste.

The Neverview janitor/security man came to visit us. He would tell you his first name, Larry, but wouldn't give up his last because, as he said, "You better be careful around here—they come and go when they want." Eyes so dark they had no entrance place, and short black hair; thick, dark, neck-creeping beard. His skin was pale as a white wax dixie cup. "I came by," he said. (He always bent the sense of his words by pausing in strange places.) "I came by," he said, and paused. "Thought I'd see if you were going to do the hallway which one you were going to do."

"This is the one," Francis said.

"When you look at it. Doesn't look too dirty."

"No."

"Mostly throw-up," Larry said. "Probably."

She asked, "Are things secure, Larry?"

"Never know, Francis." His butt and waist had bottomed out some, I guess, though really he was trim for middle age and he looked good in his navy blue work uniform. "Be seeing you. Later."

"You too."

I noticed how he looked at Francis and I wondered if Francis saw. She must have, but she didn't say.

"Well." He looked himself over. He was pleased. "So long."

"Later, Larry."

After he left, I asked, "Is this love, Francis?"

"With Larry?" she said. "Pleeeez!"

We hunted for spills and vomit spots, shot them with some Woolite, traded sponges, worked our way forward like a phalanx.

"Look at this one, Peg."

A good one. "Looks like a fish eating a cloud."

Her guess was that it was a porcupine cleaning its tongue, which was closer to how it smelled. In any case, it was the refuse of somebody's stomach and it had to be cleaned up.

When the water in the bucket needed changing, we did that together too, talking the whole time about how these Chemical Dependency kids wreck themselves, most of them only fourteen or fifteen. We talked about what a job it is to pull them out of the wreckage and about what part of the damage you can heal and the part that's up to a toss of the coin.

Francis said, "When you asked me about Larry? I like him some. If I'm honest with you, I like Larry."

"I thought so."

"He spooks me, Peg."

"Me too. I like that in a man." It's not true, but I think the chemicals in the bucket and in the Dirt Mister formula made me jump track.

She laughed. We worked on one last stubborn stain, which she thought looked like an American bald eagle and I thought looked like a cashew. She said, "He's real physical."

"With you?"

"I think probably with everybody. He gets real, real close. He doesn't stand still when you're talking to him, he's always moving." She moved the way he moved, her hands brushing over herself, her head bowed and lifted and the corners of her mouth shifting.

"Then it's not love?" I asked.

"It's physical," she said, grinning.

We set the Dirt Mister on low. It whipped the carpeting into a froth and hungrily roared. At first, we liked to direct it in order to clean a neat rectangular area, but then we also enjoyed the fun when Dirt Mister would just gun forward and ram a door, back off and pirouette, growl, "Ffffrrroom! Ffrrroom!" trailing or thumping its cord over the carpet.

So. We let it loose.

It almost scared the chemicals out of a few C-Ds, which made us feel ashamed. We turned the machine off and checked the rooms, tucked some kids back in. When we walked into one room where neither boy had stirred, Francis signaled me not to leave.

She sat on the edge of the bed where the youngest boy slept. She whispered, "Look at this."

He was a child, his neck still unwrinkled, his mouth formed into the shape of a need instead of a word. A child. Thirteen or fourteen. I followed Francis's gaze over his small limbs flung out away from his torso; and, wanting not to, I sat on the edge of the bed, next to Francis, so I could touch his hair, cover him better with the sheet and blanket.

"Is he okay?" Francis asked me.

Shaking my head no, I said, "Let's check the others."

Some of the rooms were unoccupied. In the two end rooms, 109 and 111, we stopped again. I read the names taped on the doors and on the beds. "Enrique Maynez, Patrick Bregan, Lucille Stollival, Tisa Kimbell." In 111, unless someone had switched the names, Tisa was in one bed and the two sleeping curled into each other, sheets pulled over their heads, were Enrique and Lucille.

They shuddered when we came into the room, and I had the feeling they awoke, signaled each other somehow, watched

Francis and me from under the sheets, listened for us to leave or to get them in trouble. Francis must have thought the same because she pulled a chair up to the side of the bed.

"You don't think there are any rules, do you?" she asked them in a hoarse whisper. She waited as if really expecting an answer.

I answered for them: "No."

"Do you know who I am?" she asked.

I thought about that. I moved a chair close to the bed but on the opposite side from Francis. "Yes. Yes, I know who you are."

"Do you know why I am here?"

"No," I said. I guess this might have been a joke, but you had to be there to be as unsure about that as me.

"Do you know why I am here?"

"No." I liked all of this as it happened because it sounded like the Q&A parts of a Catholic Mass. "No."

"Do you know why I am here?"

"Yes," I said. "I do know why you are here."

"Good," Francis said. She stood up. "I will come back. Sometime."

By now I was sure Tisa was awake too, but it was quiet when we left the room.

In the hallway, Francis said, "Beautiful children."

"Stupid too," I said.

"Plenty."

In 109, Patrick Bregan was sprawled over his bed like God's great ugly hands had wrung him out and fumbled with the rag before flinging it down. Patrick was final in his hard sleep, which I guess means he was hopeless, which means he had to be left, which is the way the Chemical Dependency wing of Neverview works, the way all battlefields work, isn't it? How are these things different?

Erminia Maestas
P.O. Box 132
Las Almas, N.M. 88005

August Twelve
(Arturo Bustamente)

Dec. 1986

Querido Sobrino,

Write more, okay? You ask to know about love, then write more. Say to me, mi querido sobrino, my dear nephew, how are things different. Things are different?

I don't speak English much. But this. Some things I *remember* in English. Will you believe I remember? Los años pasan. Means years pass.

1963.

I had spent $3 recording the song for her at the Be-A-Star booth, this was in the Las Almas Jefferson Shopping Center. If my friends see me—humiliation.

Every word I pronounce in perfect English when I sang, "Hold me close! Never let me go! Hold me close! Melt my heart like April snow." Very serious. Also, careful. Will you think about this, this Mexican boy trying if he can sound like Johnny Mathis who was trying not to sound black. My old man says, "Innocence you lose like hair, some every day you look in the mirror. So—don't look so much."

My old man, who didn't own a car, a watch either, or nothing in those days.

I took my record home and spinned it on my fingertip. This was in me and Danny's room but I didn't put one little mark on those beauty grooves. On pieces of toilet paper I wrote, "Hope you will like me singing to you" and "This is how much I feel." But on the record sleeve, what I wrote: "From Arthur for Peggy."

Man, I wrote it so careful. The little circle of paper pasted to the record, on this I write, "The Twelve of Never." After I stare at it I see "Twelve" wasn't what I mean but it might look stupid to change. See, this was our big first date, first for me, for her too, and that day was August twelve. I thought this was cool singing this. Special, original.

My little brother Danny came in, looked at me squint-faced. I'm fourteen in this story. Danny was thirteen. This made him immature by my way of looking. "Eats," he said, which was his cool way of saying mealtime and shows you pretty much what I mean about him.

The meal I did not eat too much of. I had to explain to Mom and Dad and Mr. Cool what they already knew about how Peggy and me were going to eat at Gamboa's Italian. This place was three blocks from our house. Very Italian, menus and whole works. Gamboa was a Mexican, you know this?

Mom said, "Arthur es lovestriked."

"Isss," my Dad said. "Isss lovestriked."

How many times, I can't tell even, Danny and me could've busted to bits laughing about their English. But they were determined. And you might get slapped too. They made us speak English; made each of the other also speak it. Because we were Americans. "Be American." This was what they would say if I said my real name Arturo, which I like speaking because it has this sound like the name of a nobleman on a steed charging around inside a book.

In front of us they would speak only English words. Will you believe this, if they didn't know even that we heard, they spoke only English. You had to admire. Dumb. But you had to admire.

This meant they could not—never could, still don't—talk good to each other. My dad's brothers and brothers' big families would come with cousin swarms; my mom's sister and mother, Las Ruidosas, The Unquiet Ones, would come too on Easter or like around then. They all could've been bees speaking bee language, man, because Danny and me couldn't make out one word. "Be American," my mom and dad would say to them and the swarm. They wouldn't give up, would say, "Where do you live? Be American!" This caused a fight. Many fights, much hurt.

Dumb. But you had to admire. This runs in families, I think.

Anyway, look. Dinner was about over, so they remind me to be home early from this date thing, be American, speak good. My dad said for me to straighten the tie, where did I get the shiny tie looks so slick? He laughed and hugged his hands behind my neck. "Handsome. See the looks of this handsome guy."

Danny said, "Awesome," a word we found in *National Geographics* my uncle bring us. Almost every page has this word.

Mom told again how I must show myself to Peggy's parents when I pick her up, show myself to them when I drop her off. Until I repeat this, I was not permitted to leave. "Show my self first. Show my self last." Then I go.

The walk to Peggy's house was not long. I walked first. This I remember because my tie swung across me which I never have wear no more. A promise with myself. You make these promises? Careful how many you make.

Her mom and dad came to the door together. "Arthur Bustamente?" her mom asked.

"Yes, I am," I said and "Thank you" when they invite me in. Good manners. I stood straight to show my self good to them and answered "Yes" every time when they ask, "You're fourteen?" "You're going to Gamboa's?" "Are you excited?" I wasn't sure I should answer "Yes" about this last one but I ask you could you say no to such a question?

Peggy said "Hello" when she came in. This was what I thought, which was maybe odd: that she had said hello to her mom and dad, not me.

Then her mom said, "Stand straight, dear," so she did. Her dad said, "You look pretty."

They gave her the routine. She answered "Right" every time when they ask, "Home by ten?" "You'll be polite?" "Call if you need to?"

Her dad opened the door for us and we walked out fast kind of. Her mom, little pinchy voice, says, "Come inside when you return with her, Arthur."

"Okay." I moved so I walk on her left side, this is good manners to walk there I think so in case a car jumped the curb it could kill you, not her.

Peggy walked so fast, will you believe her arms pumped she walked so fast. I ask her to slow down. She asked, "Why?"

The way she looked at me. Frozen. So I also walk fast. On the sidewalk we walked over where someone spray-painted "Eat Shit." A chance for conversation.

"You see that?" I ask.

She pumps her arms different and I thought that was her yes. This always bugs me how you see dirt up everywhere. I wanted to tell her all this but use good English. "It makes me mad, this, kind of."

"Yes," Peggy said. She was wearing one of those creased dresses like a big cooking apron you pull up to your shoulders. It showed her shoulders and arms. Clean. Elbows soft-looking. She was pudgy so she had some breasts, also some hips. Not like skinny girls, which we used to call chalkboards.

At Gamboa's I hold the door for her, jump inside to hold the other door, and told the host woman, "Two Party." I got Peggy's chair and didn't open my menu before she opened her menu. Definitely Señor Suave.

Why do girls not have so many wrinkles on their knuckles? "How pretty you are," I said because my record was hot in my jacket pocket and Johnny Mathis probably might say this.

"Thank you, Arthur," she says.

I start to ask if she will call me Arturo but think, no, my parents wouldn't like this. We order two lasagnas, two salads. I say to the waitress I wonder if they got RC, which they do. She brings the two RCs first.

"Cold, huh?"

"Yes."

"They put in ice up to the top." I see we got a table in the middle of Gamboa's. Empty booths near the windows, but we're out where people see. You get candles in orange candlejar things except if you're out in the middle. I say, "This is a nice place you think?"

"Yes," she says. She put her glass of RC down perfect on top of the first ring it made. "My dad says Mexicans are very clean."

"Yeah?"

If I only had ask her to call me Arturo. But here I am talking good English, Johnny Mathis in my pocket, scrubbed one shade lighter head to foot, so, this, it was a compliment.

So I say, "Yeah, Mexicans are clean," unsure, you know, even why I don't want to say this.

I look around for what I will say next. About the napkins and silverware maybe. What to say? See how *clean*? These clean Mexicans, they sure are clean. Nice carpeting. Clean too. I could say how these salt and pepper and sugar things are all full. Hardworking Mexicans, everybody knows how good.

Peggy don't say nothing, watches me look around me. Adult-like. Or like smug. Here's how I mean—you know about this, no? She's a girl, I'm the boy and this ball is in my court. She knows this. Somebody says to her this: *His obligation*.

So, I think, okay, you be adult. Me too. Okay, this is okay. All of the sudden, this lock in my mouth opened. "You smoke?" I ask.

"Cigarettes?"

"Me neither." If you got the ball in your court, dribble at least. "Some radio? You listen to it?"

"Some."

"You like the music?"

"Some." Peggy lifts her arms from the table, rested them kind of on her lap.

"Johnny Mathis. You like him?"

"I don't know."

"Warbles. Beautiful."

Waitress came. "Your salads," she says.

"I guess I like him. Johnny Mathis? I don't know." Peggy

moved her salad to a certain place on the table where she wants it.

I was eating already. Chewed fast so to not talk with my mouth full if I thought what to say.

She said, "We listen. My father has a favorite station that we listen to."

We ate quiet. The lasagna came which we ate quiet too. Peggy said she did not want some dessert, but maybe coffee, that might be okay. The waitress took the plates off. Very polite, puts cream in the coffee for Peggy.

A watch on her wrist, little bitty watch, Peggy looks at it when she drinks.

"What time?" I ask.

"Early," she says.

I'm thinking if I believe this. *This* is a good date? So, I think about this when we're drinking that coffee.

Real sudden, she says, "Excuse me, Arthur," walks to the bathroom.

She probably never had coffee, you know it. But this is okay because it's a break from this real good time date. Pretty soon, I get up and go to the bathroom too.

On the can, I don't go, but I read lots. Way high up: "Busted Cherry 5-9-59." "The Beaver Patrol Wants You!" Other things, dirty, some knifed in. "Ask no wht the puta can do fr u but wht u can do fr the puta."

One I stare at, didn't get only part of it: "What missile problem?" This was signed by Dick Large.

Pretty soon I'm thinking if somethings were written on the woman's walls. What kind of things?

When I pull up my pants I wash my hands. In the mirror I look like a darker Mexican, like the scrubbing wore off, all the pink gone.

Peggy is already sitting at the table. "May we leave?"

I paid. We walked quiet. Block from her house, I said I had a gift I want to give, and give her the record. "I sang this, Peggy."

"Well," she says, "that's sweet." If a person was quoting what another person says about what somebody told her, that is how "That's sweet" sounded. But she let me hold her hand, which was good except she didn't squeeze back any.

So, we're at her door. "Thank you for this nice evening, Arthur." She lets my hand go. Pecked me on the cheek, not like a kiss that lands on you, but like something like a butterfly flies its wings real close to your skin. It was okay.

I go inside to show myself. Her dad says, "You're back early." Her mom: "Will you stay and visit, Arthur?"

I stay, answer some questions. Peggy stands behind where her mom and dad sits. She watched them, you know, how you watch something you're going to memorize, how you learn walking, swimming, driving, these things?

At home also I answer some questions. "Look. Food on you," my mom said. My tie.

So much I remember after twenty-four years and after this, these sixteen when I live in Mexico. Will you believe so much? Why does Uncle Arturo remember this?

I tell you. Much loves. But also the homes of strangers, the strange homes of family, the American restaurants, the public bathrooms. I look in the mirror. More hair gone.

Write, okay?

Abrazos,

Arturo

The End

Before we vacuumed, while the foam soaked into and dried on the surface of the carpeting, Francis and I usually watched the MTV videotapes in the Chemical Dependency wing. We did that for a while, Francis waiting for Larry to show up so they could dance some, talk politely with me, and disappear, as she said, "to go just so far and no more."

When Larry arrived, he had Molly with him. He said that

some boy driving a big Lincoln had dropped her off. Peter Thompsenson.

I wanted to know what she thought she was doing coming here this time of night, coming here at all. "And make it a good answer, Molly."

She hugged me and quietly said, "Nuclear war. I'm radioactive. And pregnant. A soldier did it. Or a revolutionary. One of them shot Daddy. Hostages taken."

I held her at arm's length and told her I loved her. She always could upend me all at once and spill the laughter or tears out.

"Wow," she said, pointing at the television. "Sting. You watch Sting?"

"He's a close friend," I said. She wasn't going to tell me why she came. Maybe later. We kidded a lot when we were together; kidded and acted silly and barely ever came to the good pointy point that we both wanted.

"Hey, can't I give you a hug too?" Francis asked.

Larry said, "Sure."

"Wise guy." She hugged Molly. Then she took Larry's hand. "We'll go, okay? I'll be back in time to vacuum, Peg."

"Just so far," I warned her. "No more."

Larry said, "No less." Francis said okay to one of us.

Molly and I sat down, looked at the screen. "Jagger," she said.

"He's old, you know, Molly."

She scooted farther back on the couch and pushed herself deeper into it. She looked as though she also retreated deeper into her layers: the electric orange X-L tee shirt she wore over a man's white undershirt worn over a crisp, preppy cherry-red blouse with the collar torn off. The iridescent angelfish on her white ankle-lengths were diving toward her felt boots.

"Jagger's ugly," she said.

"Old and ugly both. Can't get no satisfaction."

"Daddy's having—you know, he's not doing too good." She whispered, "Come on, Mom. Listen."

"Look what he does to his lips, Molly. He licks them all the time. That way they're slobbery. It's a dare, the way I see it, 'Kiss *this*, Brown Sugar or White Sugar.' Whatever."

"Dad acts okay. He wants you to think some kind of way, so he acts okay when you come over."

"Good moves."

"Come on. Please?"

I do have a cruel streak. I looked at Molly, whose eye shadow was space-age silver and whose homemade hairdo was moussed and goosed into sulfur-tipped black flames. She looked splendid to me.

"Why do you do that to yourself?" I asked her.

"What?"

I looked her over again. "I've got a gut feeling Madonna doesn't wear underwear under the underwear she wears as overwear, have I ever told you that?"

"What?"

"It's a gut feeling."

"Shit, Mom."

She was trying me out with that. I hate cursing. She wore one earring, which was a camouflage-green plastic helicopter beneath her jawline. Beautiful, perfectly shaped ear and smooth, small lobe. I looked at her ear that I love so much and I thought—with amazement—how she had two. Two ears that I loved so much.

"Molly," I said, "I'm trying. I'm mean to you sometimes, I guess. I've—I think I know why."

"Look," she nodded at the set, "Phil Collins."

"Come on, Molly."

"All right."

She let me hold her in my arms. "See, Molly, think of this. If a tree that thought it was a dog mated with a dog that thought it was a tree and they had this lovely, leafy, blossoming, barking, jumping, unique creature—and then they realized: I'm a tree! I'm a dog! Well, think about it."

"All right."

I flicked the rear prop on her helicopter. *Working parts even,* I thought. "What did I say?"

"I'm a dog. I'm a tree."

"See? What's the creature that the dog and tree most love? But what's the one reminder of their mistake?"

"Me?"

"I'm saying this all wrong. I mean you can't change what you've learned to be."

"Me?"

Hell with it, I thought. I tried to be funny. "Do dogs have bark?"

"Yes."

"Do trees have paws?"

She let me off the hook. "They have pears," she said.

"Good enough."

Tina Turner was dancing so well the seams in her stockings changed course. Her lips were *real* slobbery. "What's love but a secondhand emotion?" she asked.

"Beats me," I said.

"Will you go see him, Mom?"

"I might. He's faking, though. I know him."

"So?"

"I could sleep with him. Give him some."

"God!"

"Don't curse, Molly!"

"Don't talk trashy, Mom!"

"*You,*" I said, "are not my mother."

"I know."

"Okay?"

"All right."

We made a call to Larry and Francis at Reception. I wished I hadn't talked trashy. It made me feel bad that I did that. Molly hugged me through The Bangles and Simply Red and DeBarge and Pet Shop Boys before Larry and Francis showed up.

Larry said, "If they know . . ." He paused, and looked over

his uniform as if only just then recognizing himself. ". . . I left my station. Well."

I said it for him: "You'll be fired."

"So," he said to Molly. "Ready?" They left.

"What are you grinning about?" I asked Francis. "You and Larry?"

"Please," she said.

She turned the vacuum cleaner, Rug Fiend, on and she adjusted it to low, which is like adjusting it to loud, and we roared into the edges of all those injured children's dreams again. Fffrooom!

5 · *Domino Theory*

I have worries which I think I must put on the table. They concern my student writers' lives and how they might affect my story. And they also concern how my own life might affect my story.

When I think about the Peg variables I go crazy about my own susceptibility. Right in the middle of writing this I could have a spiritual conversion of some kind, risking my whole literary aura, or I might finally read Hölderlin and the back of the Celestial Seasonings tea boxes. If the moles under my underarms begin to change color, how will I concentrate? If I have accidentally plagiarized a fifteen-semesters-ago student's three-sentence journal entry, how will I know?

My students eloquently call this "our modern world of today in which we live" where one in three tests constitutes a violation of a pact, seven of ten pacts fail, and every world leader believes she or he gets to take the final exam over. These things worry me.

My students are a variable that also worries me. While they're writing my story they might be dieting, fasting for the hungry, or hungry to take care of the Cuban threat, once and for all. They read fiction only when assigned. They each have a dish and can receive sixty-seven stations. They have remote control.

On some mornings I take a perconal and a Dayburst Energizer Vitamin Combination out of the icebox; I pump down coffee with Miracle Sweet'ner. My cholesterol count is maximum so the combination of stimulants and the glacial movement of garbage in major and minor ventricles makes my body corrosively aware of its mortality. Are my students in the same perfect state for writing?

No.

The necessary coordination between us is impossible. I try to allow only those changes in my life that will not flaw me as a writer. My students do not do the same. And, as I have explained, that is why I replace their Peg stories with my own.

So. Why have I come to James, made love with him? Needless to say, it's not easy to explain. I guess Molly's request had something to do with it. Not everything.

Who, after all, approves of consenting ex-husband-postmarital sex? I know I don't approve of it because I don't think it advances the development of Peg/me as a character and/or human being. My magician heart has been bound, locked, and chained in a box, blindfolded, lowered deep in my dark human will. But, just to show me it can, it spectacularly escapes.

I knock at the shutters of my own chemically altered brain and at the door of my room in Everview. "Who is it?" I ask myself.

My form of government and James's are different. Mine is a republic in which I write and act according to my own free will and, if I choose, against my own free will. His is a benevolent dictatorship in which Freedom is presented within the bounds of Control.

I'm sensitive to the fact that James is near my borders. No sensible person would disagree that his security affects Molly's security and mine. I do not like him and I'm not sure whether I love him, but I am more comfortable with him penetrating my body than threatening my form of government. So.

So. I give aid.

Yes, generously. I guess I should admit that it makes me feel good and guilty, guilty but good. Guilty at first, but good. Whatever.

While I'm giving aid I try not to become personally involved. At first, I let him lead. He can be a selfish lover. He can be unselfish. History has proven this.

The whole time I am escalating my commitment, I whisper into his hair things like, "I am a republic, James, a free and open democracy."

He snickers and tries to make his pleasure last, saying, "I love you, Little Peg. You believe me, don't you? You can believe me."

Most of me does not like what is happening. Parts of me enjoy. "Can't you see?" I say. "We shouldn't—"

"What?" He is barely able to catch his breath.

"We shouldn't." I say to myself: *Shouldn't. Shouldn't. Shouldn't.* But I guess I know better. It feels good to be involved, banners waving, my skin humming, all my involvement spangling through and blessing the purple majesty and brave home of me.

Uneasy bliss. Then. Bliss.

"Oh," he groans. "Little . . . Little . . ."

When it's over I tell myself, *Okay. Never again.*

How did this—James and I—happen in the first place?

Ask Susan Orstal.

She is a comic-book-crazed horror/fantasy Future Journalism Major. In her story for my class she wanted to have Peg encounter terrifying aliens. I said no. Then she wrote a story draft in which Peg wears superpower underwear at a drive-in movie. I liked it but didn't allow it. Frustrated, she wrote "Oberon Battalion," a complete-on-one-page story with both terrifying aliens and superpower underwear. Eventually, after I salvaged some of the best nouns and verbs and added twenty pages and retitled it "Duty," both Susan and I felt it did the job.

Susan Orstal
Cottonwood Apts.
Bldg. 18, #247
Las Almas, NM 88005

Duty
(Peg, 1967)

The first week in December the lead story was, *Cardinal Spellman Dies, Thousands Pay Respect*. I wrote my eighteenth "In the Service" column for the *Las Almas Sun-Bulletin*. Other stories: *McCarthy Outlines Platform*; George Romney, Ronald Reagan, and Charles Percy have *Plans For August Republican Convention*; Dr. Christiaan Barnard makes Louis Washkansky *New Frankenstein*. Also, *Banker Dies* (w. pic), *Respected Community Leader*. Mary Voorhees asked me to give her a couple letters to help start up her "Letters to Santa" column.

Santaclaus,
A perascope thing. Cheerful Tearful like my sister got. Lugige the whole sets like on tv. Thank you for them.
Annie Perez

Dear Santa,
I am Leonrad. Give me some basebals or only one would be ok to. O-K?
Leonrad Culbenten

The managing editor, Louise Wilbern, gave me another Barbara Gilliam letter from Saigon. Barbara was on detached duty from White Sands Missile Range and was writing about the horrors of the French-made bathrooms. I trimmed it back, made it readable. Louise said, "Make it respectable, Peg."

"Not possible," I wrote in the memo attached to the draft.

Barbara Gilliam's *From Saigon* story ran with Ruth Montgomery's King Features Syndicated column piece, *Experiments Could Help Hippies and Beatniks*. Miss Montgomery had been seeing a hypnotist who had given her an idea:

> What if it were possible, in wholesale fashion, to regress rioters and draft-card burners to an earlier lifetime? Would they, like many of Dr. Kelsey's patients, then be able to cast off their resentments by understanding the cause? If so, perhaps they could thoroughly rid themselves of the neurosis and hate which is now poisoning them, as well as society.

I was seventeen, a new rookie, a "gofer" really, getting weather reports, taking obits, jockeying to borrow a typewriter to get my work out. But "In the Service" was mine. A feather in my cap. Mary Voorhees, her style perfect for Editorial and Society, had been taken off Vietnam. Most of us were women except for senior reporters and boys like Robert in Composing who had a sinus deferment. Louise said Robert should admit he was a homo and get it out in the open. When he could get away with it, Robert built filler around my "In the Service" column; things like this: *A penguin can swim at a speed of thirty-five miles per hour*.

I could take a joke but that kind I didn't appreciate because of newer headlines: *M. Martinez Receives Wounds; More Non-hostile Deaths; New Mexican Toll Increases*. All this in one week. The war rarely claimed the front page, so my wire stories appeared around Section B, p. 5 or buried deeper. I didn't complain.

On December 4, my date took me to the university game where I covered the special "Patriotism Day" halftime ceremonies. (I had asked the Sports editor to give me the chance.)

I was a little ashamed to be dating Jim Aigley. He had a slobbiness to him: his straight, oily hair, the way he wore only sweatshirts from which he had torn the pouch and hood. I thought he probably had smoked dope. And then, this: my mother called him "unrefined," which was her worst condemnation.

After the game, I tapped out the names of the university officials present, the community pillars, the band conductor, but I was thinking about Jim, who was volunteering for Vietnam, and about his older brother Roy, who was there already.

Jim was waiting around the *Sun-Bulletin* for me so he could buy me a hot chocolate and try (again) to get places with me. He said, "Say 'stirring' and 'inspiring.' They're good ones."

I typed, *Halftime activities stirred the emotions of community and university people alike.*

He read over my shoulder. "Peg, you're good."

I was terrible, virtually unable to write unloaded language. *The program began with a medley of patriotic music. Band members stood on the field in the still formation of the Liberty Bell.*

"So that was a bell, huh?"

During the Battle Hymn of the Republic university thespians presented a dramatic reading of The Preamble to The Constitution. The music slowly swelled, the bell began to swing, and soon it rang from goal post to goal post.

"Goal post—one word or two, Peg?"

"Two." *When the band stopped playing and the bell held still again, this reporter witnessed many members of the audience in tears.*

Jim pretended to whimper. "This reporter witnessed many university students wipe their noses, quit school right then and there, and enlist!"

"You don't have to be sarcastic." I finished: *Bishop Sidney Metzger offered a closing prayer for our great men who are sacrificing themselves in Vietnam.*

"It's so bullshitty," he said, "all that icing."

"I'm not going to grace that with a response."

Our evening ended with him trying to get places, apologizing, trying again, driving me home, and asking, "You're not mad?"

"No," I lied. Someday I would write about him in my "In the Service" column, and I couldn't afford to be mad at him.

For the football story I had offered the headline *NMSU Patriots* but when it made the front page the next day it was *NMSU Patriotism* and was a bar against the page-bottom heading *Seabee Asks Santa For Just One Tiny Present*, a wire that Louise had held back. I had framed HMS 3 Tom Kelly's letter in an article, but at the end of the article I let him speak for himself:

Dear Santa Claus,
Santa, can you imagine the joy on my face when I open your gift and find the one thing I want most of all in the world? An Anti-Vietnam Demonstrator?
I promise, Santa, to always give him his own way for as long as he lives. Of course, that won't be very long if he insists on saying the things he says in the States.

By the end of the week, *Spellman Buried; Beauty Salon Burglary Is Hairy Affair; Washkansky Listed Critical; McNamara Gone: Was Political Liability*.

Louise handed me another Barbara Gilliam letter about the gentlemanly treatment the 3rd Infantry had offered her. I edited a war correspondent's story about *Angkor's Serenity*. More figures came in. *111 NM Soldiers Die*, 95 combat and 16 nonhostile. Communist toll now 1,800 per week, Am. casualties 13,634 between Jan. 1, 1961, and Sept. 30, 1967. They were mentioned in one column inch, Section C, p. 7.

Above these figures Robert put in a Fun Facts item: *What are fossils? How are fossils formed? Answer: next week*. Next to that ran *Dear Abby Warns: Say No With Conviction*.

Louise fired Robert.

Mary Voorhees had almost enough letters to Santa for a whole page. She came up a little short and asked if I could help.

Dear Santa,
Somthing to hold is good. Hair Grows. Spanks-She-Cries. Monkees dolls. With Davy.
Johnny put a letter.

Denise Gabriel

* * *

I am the big brothr wich wrote for Denise. 8. So nothing stuped. No chekrs or no dumb doll. I do not got a pockitnife. I do not got a Major Matt Mason.

Johnny Gabriel

I thought about poor President Johnson. In the first ten days of December: *Great Society Distrusted; Robert Kennedy Speaks at VA; Hopeful About Talks; Programs Blasted; Anti-Draft Unrest; HHH Television Appearance.*

Later in the evening when my younger brother Ben and I were watching *I Spy* I had the certain feeling that President Johnson, who sincerely cared about what he called "The Negro Problem," was also watching.

In the midst of an exploded building, Robert Culp grimly explained again to The Negro, "It's my job."

"Sure," The Negro said to Culp with perfect Negro disdain. The Negro (my mother's name for Bill Cosby) in real life was a comedian but on *I Spy* he was always Robert Culp's conscience, his Tonto.

There was a routine at the show's opening in which Culp and Cosby swung imaginary tennis rackets that turned out to be guns. Ben got up from his chair and did the whole routine.

"You're nutty," I told him.

"It's my job." He blew imaginary smoke from his finger gun.

"You're great," I said, wanting to say, "I love you, Ben" but not doing that because it would make him uncomfortable. He was a high school junior and, in a way, boys his age were not permitted to say "I love you" to their sisters, who *were* allowed to say it. "Son of Mr. & Mrs. Fill In The Blank at such and such an address" is the way I wrote my "In the Service" column. I might receive information about boys' brothers if they were military, but I never got information about sisters.

After the commercial, the two television actors made eye contact. "I just do my job," Culp repeated.

"Look, forget it," said Cosby. Then the credits flashed, the men swinging their rackets, their guns.

Once, earlier in the year, my parents drove forty miles to El Paso in order to see Bill Cosby perform at a dinner theater. My mother made them leave. At home, they fought about the sex jokes. My father kept saying, "It's not just Negroes, Marcella."

"You can't tell me," she said.

"It's not just The Negroes. Get off it. Look at Joey Bishop, those Smothers Brothers."

But you couldn't tell her. And, after all, they agreed about most things.

All these items were on my mind, tickering like the AP wire, tickering and never turned off. Ben and I had some graham crackers and milk and we talked about Jim Aigley and the Aigley family. They had lived next door to us in '65 but had "fouled their own nest" my father said and lost their house, ending up in some apartment somewhere.

"Did you know Jim is going to be a soldier?" Ben asked.

We never talked about the war. Ben usually pretended it didn't interest him, and I didn't bring it up.

"You think he'll end up going?" he asked.

"I don't know, Ben."

"But if he—"

"What are you asking?"

"Nothing." He put his arms on the table but leaned his body back.

"Well," I said, "the war can't last. It's about over, everybody says."

I felt he wanted more. I felt he wanted me to open the back of the ticking mystery and explain about war, how war worked. As if I could explain or knew how to say what our parents and the politicians and all the journalists and soldiers couldn't or wouldn't say. How could I look at Ben, his slender hands and wrists on the table before me, and picture him a platoon leader?

When I went to bed, I fell asleep but had no dreams. Or no memory of dreams, anyway. In fact, I think I hadn't had dreams for weeks. I woke up in the mornings and tried to remember. Nothing.

December 10. My story, *Las Almas Fighter Pilot Has First Mission Memories,* which should have been five hundred words, was eight hundred, then it was edited down to three hundred. I found out, and I asked Louise not to run it. She ran it with *Uniform Changes Since WWII* and gave three full columns to an AP, *Vietnamese Gals.* When I read the article, parts of it made me angry.

> This is a country in which not every woman is a refugee, not every woman wears a coolie hat, and not every housewife lives in a thatched hut with shooting at her doorstep.
>
> In government and business as well as within the family circle, their influence is considerable.
>
> Vice President Nguyen Cao Ky said he wouldn't have run for office if his wife hadn't okayed it. Insiders say she made the decision.
>
> South Vietnam also has two women senators, women who run banks and big businesses, women who hold hamlets together in the steaming jungles, women who direct the best-run program in the country—the midwifery clinics.
>
> As for the Western beauty influences, Mai Ky, beautiful wife of the vice president, flew to Tokyo under an assumed name to have her eyes widened by cosmetic surgeons—"To make myself beautiful as possible for my husband," she said later.
>
> Three doctors in Saigon specialize in eye-widening and bust-enlarging operations. Girls pay about $125 to have their noses made smaller, about $90 to have the skin at the outer corners of the eyes slit. The doctors do a thriving business.
>
> Western beauty ideas have brought two more changes to a Vietnamese woman's life: brassieres and beauty contests. Both are immensely popular. Black brassieres are preferred, being easily visible under a lightweight garment.
>
> The wealthy Vietnamese woman probably speaks French and English, has been schooled abroad and will send her children abroad. She counts calories, frets over her figure, exercises to keep her waistline.

* * *

Dear Santa, I wrote, *shoot my editor Louise Wilbern somewhere bad.* Mary Voorhees gave the letter to Louise, who threatened to give it to the publisher, Mrs. Bonte.

Jim called to tell me his induction information came and to ask if I dated Marines. Because he had enlisted they were going to send him as soon as his brother Roy returned.

For our date that night I powdered my breasts like crullers. I tried my blouse on without a bra but I'm bosomy so that looked trashy. I knew that they didn't need to be packaged like prizes for him to try touching them. But since I was finally going to offer them I wanted him to understand that I would be offering them as gifts and not as grocery store produce. Standing before the mirror, I adjusted them in the brassiere and wondered whether I would want to help him unhook it or would unhook it for him. I buttoned the blouse up to the top because that drew it more tightly over my body.

On the way to the Aggie Drive-In Jim told me where he had hidden the beers all over the car. *I don't go out with boys like you,* I thought. *What am I doing?* I sat close to him in the car, slid my hand behind his thin, wiry back.

Dead Heat on a Merry-Go-Round was the first feature. We talked about James Coburn, how much he talked compared to Clint Eastwood. Earlier in the year, *Hang 'Em High* had been filmed at White Sands National Monument, and we all admired Clint.

He had his arm around me and his hand touched my stomach, then caressed my right side. "See that?" he said. Coburn, who had killed a bad guy with a knife, was gazing down at him with distaste for the victim, but for himself too. Jim untucked the right side of my blouse from my skirt. Clint would have done it more coldly. For Clint it was more like shooting cans. His hand touched my side and hesitated. We did not kiss. We were both watching the screen.

I would not let him take my bra off until *The Chase,* which was the second feature, starring Marlon Brando and Jane Fonda. By then, I couldn't avoid it. Because he was concentrating so hard on me, he only vaguely noticed Fonda, whose outfits exposed both her well-developed virtues. Her breasts were pushed up and together so that, to me, they looked like a bare butt jutting out of her front.

Marlon Brando reminded me sadly, ridiculously, of President Johnson. Marlon's body and his powerful neck made the comparison impossible, but I couldn't help myself. My blouse was untucked and unbuttoned and Jim was impatiently exploring the two hooks of my bra.

"You better, you ought to kiss me," I said before I helped him unfasten everything.

By now, we were hunched very low in the car seat but I worried that a security guy or prankster would shine a flashlight on us, so I wouldn't let him completely remove my blouse or bra as he stroked and stared at my breasts. "Calm down," I said when he pressed his cheek against my left breast. "Hey."

"Oh," he said.

"You should kiss me, Jim. Come on." I certainly didn't want his lips all over my chest. Though I understood that it was possible for me to enjoy this, I apparently wasn't ready for that pleasure.

He took the underside of both my breasts and tried to close his hands around them. It hurt. "Jim! You can't—don't." He didn't seem to understand that it wasn't his body.

"Okay. Enough!"

He stopped, finally, all at once. "Wow," he said. "I got carried away, huh?"

You stupid boy, I wanted to say. *Child.*

He disentangled himself from me. We both gazed down at them. I pulled on my bra, untwisted the straps, and hooked the back. Smoothing the scalloped foam petals on the undercup, I realized how much he had bruised me. "Damn," I said. "You jerk."

I think he had anticipated my reaction because he said, "You're right, Peg."

"What?"

"You're right."

He might have said it sincerely. I couldn't tell. Before I had let him touch me, he was ordinary to me, another boy who wasn't even my kind of boy. Now, he had kissed and held my body. He had bruised my body. And it is still inexplicable to me how much more complex that made him when it might reasonably have made him only a jerk.

Driving home, he talked about when he thought he would have to leave for Camp Pendleton. He was going to be a Marine. He was going to be a good soldier. "You think so?" he asked.

The more he talked the more he tried to make himself sound like one hundred and fifty words of print for my "In the Service" column. I already knew how it would read.

> Marine Private Albert James Aigley, son of Mr. and Mrs. George Aigley of Las Almas, will complete two weeks of training under simulated combat conditions in the fundamentals of day and night patrolling, employment of infantry weapons, survival methods, and assault tactics at the Camp Pendleton Marine Corps base.

"You don't even know what you've done," I said.

He drove the car up my parents' driveway. "I hurt your—" he said, "you. Look, I know it, Peg." But I was mentally doing my job.

> This individual combat training is given every Marine after his graduation from recruit training. Taught by combat-experienced noncommissioned officers of the infantry training regiment, it prepares the young Leatherneck to become part of the Marine air-ground combat team.

"You don't know anything."

"You're right, Peg." He was sincere. "You're right."

> While in the field he will be taught how to use hand grenades, a compass, and the principles of map reading and land navigation. He will learn how to detect and disarm mines

and booby traps and, while being exposed to live machine-gun fire, he will learn to advance safely from one point to another.

He asked if he could call me.

"Is that what you want, Jim?"

From December 10 to December 20, these headlines: *Humphrey & McCarthy: Already Squaring Off; Phnom Penh A Paradise; Johnson Says Informal Talks Could End War; Pioneer 8 Heads For Sun.*

December 21 I submitted a story, *Injured Soldier Undergoes Surgery*, about Army Second Lieutenant David Raymond, 2nd Battalion of the 199th Light Infantry Brigade's 5th Infantry near Long Binh. I edited the information I received from the Army, but I also did some homework, and gave a conscientious description of what happened in the explosion of a cartridge booby trap. The disintegration of David Raymond's feet. The burn treatments preliminary to surgical procedures at William Beaumont VA. I gave two hundred words more than the standard one hundred. I think I knew what the results would be.

Louise sent it back, a memo attached: "You want off Vietnam? You're off." Then she came to the desk where I was taking an obit over the phone. "You got my note?"

"Excuse me," I said to the woman on the line. She continued talking into my chest where I held the receiver.

"You're on notice, Peg."

I said, "Yes. I'm sorry."

The woman on the line asked, "Are you even listening?"

Louise returned "In the Service" to Mary Voorhees, shuffled some others so I could cover the Amazin' Aggies and "Letters to Santa." That beat gave me time to think more about the newspaper news, the softness of half-stated facts. If we wanted, we could make even the letters to Santa lies.

By the end of December: *4,000 Police Halt Demonstrators in NY;* 15,654 Americans killed in action; *Doctor Says Rejection Not Wash-*

kansky Death Cause; 97,678 wounded; *Wallace Targets Ohio*; 472,000 military personnel now in Vietnam; *Reagan Says Morals Form Umbrella, Protect Us*; Jim sends in letter to Santa.

> *Dear Santa,*
> *I want a Jungle Jim and a knit-o-matic and live ammo and some silly sand. Also, I want Peg to marry me before I leave for basic.*
>
> *J.A.*

I called him and said, "Ho, ho, ho."

Then, a few days later I agreed to go to Elephant Butte Reservoir with him to watch the satellites pass over. We borrowed a small outboard which we moored in The Breaks. We lay next to each other, our heads on the seat cushions, the rest of us miserable. At 2:10 AM., right on schedule: Echo I.

All our layers of sweatshirts, sweaters, and jackets didn't help either of us against the cold on the lake or the sharp edges of the boat bottom. I took Jim's right hand and put it on top of where my breast might be. He laughed and said, "You're so easy."

At around 3:30 A.M. when Echo II came, I woke him up. "Watch," I said. But neither of us was interested.

He gripped the collar of my jacket and sleepily kissed me. When I kissed him back I liked the warmth of his nose next to mine. We stopped kissing, pressed our chins together, and giggled and kissed more.

"Here," he said, "put your hand here. Please, Peg. Feel me."

I thought of this as a self-evident truth: I should. *I should.*

Besides, it was romantic to be in the darkness on the cold lake, our bodies in pain, confused about and rightly afraid of each other, but embracing, convinced we were protecting each other with our arms.

We wondered even then, in 1967, if it was a just engagement. We wondered, but we committed our lives to it.

The End

* * *

Paula talks with me one more time about my readiness for discharge. One more time, we review my decision. She asks when I am scheduled to leave.

"8:30 A.M."

When will you come back?

"Once a month. The last Thursday of each month, for an examination."

Where were you when you made this decision?

"Underneath a man. Cleaning a rug. Writing a book."

And?

"All of the above."

She turns her glasses in her hands and cleans them with a tissue. Paula ———. I can't remember her last name. No matter how hard I try. She is half real to me.

Close your eyes now, Peg. Imagine me here in this chair. The room around me. Are the curtains open? With your eyes closed can you see if the curtains are open?

I am sure they are. Lustre Glaze Chintz. "Always open," I tell her. Maybe the curtains don't work or something because I never see them closed.

We have done this exercise before; it is called the window exercise. I like this.

How close are you to the window? Can you see through the closed curtains?

"They're open, Paula."

Good. Is the window open, Peg? Can you hear the sounds in the room?

"I can."

I imagine myself as my fictional self on the outside of the room, looking through the windows where the curtains are open. I see Paula stand up. She asks, *Peg, will you hold me?*

I see Peg wrap her arms above Paula's waist, locking her hands over each other on Paula's back. Not much of you to hold on to, Paula. So slight. Your hands could be leaves or the skeletons of leaves fallen over me.

None of this happens, of course.

"That's all?" I ask.

We're done, Peg.

Paula has typed up a schedule of our monthly appointments. The first is two weeks from now. Attached to this is the step-down schedule which I will use to wean myself from Prolixin. Possible side effects are indicated on a notecard.

All three sheets list her four phone numbers and all are signed with her name.

She does hug me but it feels reflexive, like someone handling a drinking cup. My bet is this hurts her too, this careful, professional detachment from me.

In our room, Francis was waiting. She was sitting at her typing table, her hands joined on her lap.

I said, "Francis, you okay?" and pulled a chair up to the table. "Francis, I have big news that I have to give all at once, okay?"

"No," said Francis, but nodded her head yes.

Then I explained how I had made my decision to leave Evview; that it was a judgment call and I wasn't sure about it but I was going ahead anyway.

Francis asked, "Did you tell Molly?"

"Molly knew it was coming, I guess."

"Paula?"

"I already had an exit appointment."

"Your husband—James?"

"Loves the idea. He says I get the side of the bed near the alarm."

Francis looked down at the keys of her typewriter. "Kind of sudden." Her lower eyelids pushed tears over her eyes, then drew down and took the tears back. It seemed to take a long time for me to scoot my chair even an inch closer to her.

"The students?" she asked.

"You think I should tell them?" I hadn't thought of that. "I guess I should, shouldn't I?"

"It wouldn't be fair—if you didn't."

I put my arms around Francis's shoulders and asked, "Did you know I was going to do this?"

"I knew."

"How did you know?"

"Honest, Peg, it's a side effect of the Elavil: you know the future."

Though Francis meant to be funny, I knew she was being truthful. I remembered how certain depressants had made me so placid that the twitching world vibrated against my solid stillness and sounded notes I had already heard inside myself. "Look, ask if they won't let you take less of all that stuff."

"Okay."

"I'll miss you, Francis."

"You will," Francis said. "See? I knew that."

Later, Sergio played soothing music for us. Throughout the hour he assured us he welcomed all requests.

Francis set her pillows up behind her shoulders. She lifted up to twist her long-sleeve dress straight on her body. She did it again, twisting everything askew.

"You're messing with yourself," I said.

"I am? I am?" She was maybe a size fourteen or sixteen, and her dress was well worn at the shoulders.

In our seventeen years of friendship, I never saw her receive an outside visitor. Once, however, at six in the morning on a Sunday, she asked me if I'd like to see her ex-husband. Until she walked us to the picture window at the C Wing lounge I thought she meant to show me a photograph. Instead, she pointed out the window to a Coachmen fifth wheel trailer hitched to a Chevy truck. "That's his." I knew I could believe her. I had to.

"He's at the nurse's station," she said. "Twice a year he makes a boating trip to Elephant Butte. He stops to ask about me."

"I don't get it," I said. "He doesn't come to your room?"

"No." We looked out the window at the clean, well-kept trailer. "He asks about five minutes' worth," she said, "and goes fishing."

When he came outside to get into his truck, he bent to check his tires. He had a thick neck and strong shoulders and upper arms, but bending did not come easy for him so he only slightly inclined his whole upper body, turning his head slowly right and left. I remembered how my mother would characterize all men as having some animal in them if you looked close. I guess I'd say that if you looked real close you saw a burly old owl.

About then, Sergio asked if we ligked inzdrewmendtal.

I said, "We ligke."

"Gooood," said Sergio and Francis simultaneously.

No one can imagine the binding pleasure between Francis and me at such times. Those are the times when I am in His hands again. I see Francis's self-satisfied grin; I hear Sergio say, "Liszen." I believe again that God made it all. But I cannot believe any of it was good on that seventh day until He laughed.

Sergio offered his own personal favorite. "Very zsimple, calm, and is, I thingk, no zo very zsad. I like ezspeshul."

6 · *Air*

I awake two hours after I lay down. Five-fifteen.

The bus driver picks me up for an airing-out drive. This is the day she opens all the bus windows and bus doors front and back and tears up Highway 28 to Hatch then back again in order to air out the bus. It is a gusty October morning, the night blackness stained with dust that has the smell of guttering church candles.

"Boy," I say, "this is a good ride." I am nervous with her, I guess.

The legend about her is intimidating. Supposedly, she is supremely stable and always has been. No depression. No psychotic disorders. They say she has Doubt, but mostly Driver Doubt, on the order of "Room to pass?" "Will I make this hill?" "What's my braking distance?" Not "Can I go on?" "Am I screaming downhill?" "Should I end it?"

She manages never to parody herself in the way she dresses or wears her hair or talks. She doesn't mess with herself. You won't see her having medicated or unmedicated tics, somatic delusions like touching to see if she has lips or panicking, checking whether the front of her hair has been conspiring to mislead her and she is really bald in back. These are things I do, have done. They're harmless things but I know they make me "harmless," while she is neither "harmless" nor "harmful."

Awesomely normal. In novels, people like her are often powerful elements of subplot but are almost never major characters.

We've talked about her here at Everview. She's heard us talking about her and is not bothered.

"Her past is pristine," we say.

"Every day?"

"Sixty-nine years of days."

We have figured that out. It comes to about 25,250 normal days.

"Nights?"

"Nights too," we say, because we believe. We believe in her: her mind a glistening, lively, delicate web in a human spirit impregnable to the gusty wind, the night hauntings, the danger in speeding forward.

She doesn't talk very much. To be truthful, she almost never talks. Once we thought this betrayed other curtains behind the first curtain. The current thought among us is that not talking is probably how the normalest people stay normal. We have talked and talked about this. We have tried silent contemplation of this.

Talking makes you vulnerable. Small talk, party talk, bed talk, business talk. And what does writing do? We have decided: waving a flag from a hilltop makes you vulnerable; writing, planting a flag on a hilltop, is suicidal.

We had a bet that the bus driver didn't write anything.

Letters?

"No," she said, "not much."

Notes to herself?

"Why?"

A grocery list?

She said she had a good memory.

We slowed down to fifteen miles per hour as we came into Hatch. I had not been there since the Hatch Chile Festival a summer ago.

"Look," said the bus lady. White smoke poured through side streets and onto the main drag. The farmers were burning the Russian thistle and salt cedar along the Rio Grande, blackening all the unplowed land on the town's east side. In minutes, the stink filled the bus.

Someone had repainted the English words of the sign on Loya's Lounge, but let the Spanish words go to hell.

DANCING EVERY WEEKEND
Bailes Cada Fin De Semana

Next to the lounge the Good Mexican Food Restaurant had its lights on, and a woman inside waved to us without looking up from the table she was cleaning. The main drag, running south to north, changed from East Hall Street to West Hall Street. We passed The UpBeat Resale Clothing And R.V. Park and the Hatch Mercantile. The Mercantile's sign—GIGANTIC SHOE SALE—made me laugh because somehow it conjured up images of Hatch's thousand residents lumbering through the smoky streets like dinosaurs.

The bus lady bought me OJ at the Kountry Kitchen.

Back on the highway, I admitted I couldn't get warm.

"No?"

"Sorry," I said.

"Here." She indicated I should take the wheel.

"What?"

"Here."

We did the transfer at sixty-five miles per hour.

She helped me put on her plum-colored corduroy jacket. "Fits," she said. She closed every window in the bus.

When she nodded for me to shut the bus door, I did, with one pull of a handle. Then she took a rag and spray bottle from the dashboard and she cleaned and polished every window.

"Okay," I said finally. "Thanks." But she let me drive the entire way back.

* * *

Two hours later she took me and my luggage from Everview to James's house: a big brick cottage with a painted concrete porch and white iron railings; with an unrusting white iron fence completely encircling the yard; a knocker and a nameplate on the front door; a picture window magnifying its own brightness; a goliath stone chimney; and a stone fireplace wide and deep enough to burn all the houses of stick, all the houses of straw ever built by all the little pegs everywhere.

PART TWO
Stone

1 · *Stepping Down*

(NOVEMBER 1988)

For eighteen days now I have been a woman living with a man. This is something I haven't been for a while, so I'm often awake, trying to assess my alien inalienable rights.

I hear James putting on his Mr. Vendor clothes at the foot of our bed. He has a slowly inflating tire around his waist, but owns the same old gray chino uniform pants, so his zipper closes slowly. He rummages around in one of his top drawers for the ironed handkerchief that will go in his left pants pocket. Last, he puts his watch on, checks his neat, close-trimmed hair again and licks two fingers to press down anything on his head that might have a mind of its own.

On his forehead two jagged vertical wrinkles are incised above the eyebrows; once they appeared only when he frowned, but now they are permanent. He brews coffee. When the timer dings, he says, "Good." If my eyes were open I might see him pacing, holding his cup just so, soaking his upper lip in his thick coffee. I might see him reach into his pants to rearrange his shooters in their pouch.

Following are some facts I had forgotten.

A woman living with a man gets to hear him talk to himself on the toilet; gets to see him with his pants down around his ankles; and, if the man is James, the toilet paper is neatly folded into five wipers on his knees. Always five. If the man is James, he is mumbling to the bigger James crunched inside himself, "Okay. Okay, man. You got it. Right?" His voice like a small ceramic tile ricocheting against the tiles in the bathroom. "Right? Okay, man."

When he leaves, he shakes his keys in his hand: his way of weighing the responsibility of all those locks he has to open on candy machines everywhere in Las Almas. He has worked for Mr. Vendor for many years.

"Bye, Molly," he says. He is talking to the house—it's 3:45 A.M. and Molly's asleep.

"Bye, Little Peg." The door shumps closed. As he backs his Nova into the street, I remember his face, which he shaves so clean and scrubs so hard that his pores are wide open. He scrapes at his whole body with a handbrush. I have seen him use the brush on the backs of his ears. Truthfully. The backs of his ears. Probably all the pinkness of his skin accounts for the strange white prominence of his jawline and the boyish brightness of his pupils, the scored depth of the wrinkle lines at the corners of his mouth. I think he must be a handsome man, this uncrooked forty-year-old man walking the uncrooked path along his uncrooked life with his half-crooked daughter and loop-de-looped but unlooping little wife.

Standing in the shower, rinsing my skin with my palms, I picture each part of James circumscribed in a razor-sharp edge he has traced around himself. To cauterize the places where he has honed himself against me, I make the water almost scalding.

The closet I take my clothes from is dark and chilly, so the sweatshirt and the jeans soothe me, and even my shoes are cool. I might have thanked all my clothes for their kindness. A week ago I would have.

Sitting on the toilet, I misfold the paper into origami gooses, rockets, and spiked suns, but regain myself and unfold them into efficient squares. It is 4 A.M. I pull up my jeans, which are the new much-televised expensive ones. James, who has bought them for me, has chosen a size too small because he is hopeful. And thoughtless.

The strong coffee James has brewed is okay drowned in two percent milk and a big puff of Miracle Sweet'ner. I let it harass my gums before I swallow it. The same old argument I have with myself is really over when it begins.

No one has ever seen you.

"But I shouldn't."

Has anyone ever seen?

"No."

Ever? Even once?

For eighteen mornings no one has seen me even once. So, I pull on the bus driver's loaned plum jacket and venture out into the good fortune of my dark neighborhood. The Vagrant Queen.

The Vagrant Queen likes to trespass against those who have never trespassed against her; she likes to push her nose against all the sleeping bellies in her neighborhood and she likes to sniff. Okay, it's a manner of expression. The Vagrant Queen likes prayerful manners of expression because they are needed to describe the night on her block: always hallowed, His kingdom already come, His will done on earth as it is in heaven.

Tonight the moon is full but pared of its skin and rubbed thin. The Vagrant Queen levitates on her back atop the hedge Mr. Klish trims so conscientiously that all the branchtips are ice picks. It is difficult to get up there.

She nestles her head inside the sharp green fingers in order to fine-tune her perception. Around the dull moon is a luminous nimbus; the lower curve extends almost to the horizon; the upper curve knifes the sky's azimuth; but the whole lens focuses on her own block, the dull eye of God peering through. "Ooooo," she hears Him say, or Her say, or hears Herself say, as they trade stares with each other.

She rolls in order to plunge herself off the hedge. "Ooof!" All the mulberry trees slump over their moonbent shadows as if to help her up from the curb. The VQ rubs her left arm and massages her legs bound in her prewashed, high-style jeans.

She tightens the string on her sweatshirt hood. "You all right?" she asks, but forgets to answer herself when she sees the trebled moonlight on Mrs. Maynez's front yard and stands at the base of the pines in order to look up through the branches. "Oh, Mrs. Maynez," she says, "you should see." The farthest branches quiver from the November cold darkness underneath them and the wavering silveriness pressing down upon them. It dizzies the VQ how the limbs hang more from the sky than reach out of the tree trunk.

In Mrs. Maynez's backyard her cinderblock walls have kept the mulberry and poplar leaves captive. The Vagrant Queen has a sudden notion. *I shouldn't do this because I shouldn't just because.* She chews the fading green blood out of a poplar leaf and says, "Come on now. You shouldn't."

Then she hangs leaves, stems up, from clothespins on Mrs. Maynez's lines, and wherever the design makes the whole clothesline rosary look right she also hangs up a withered pumpkin leaf.

"Don't be stupid. More to see," she says, finding herself in the Pefermans' backyard where the skeleton of a century plant has shot up like Jack's beanstalk. Its slim secondhand shadow twitches on the Pefermans' ten-foot-high cinderblock wall. "Look at you," says the VQ, planting herself on the patio. Then and there she would make herself rocket out of herself, like the century plant, her cells nascent thirty-eight years and then, not having to wait, self-multiplying their joy to the highest power. But her toes are cold, and that ruins that.

Walking the alleyway, she notices even the alley litter has changed color with the season. It worries her that Mrs. Hahn's lawn is deader than the Methuams' lawn. Missus Hahn, Missus Hahn, sorry, missus. She remembers swingset singing, "In Maine they bicycle against the wind / No one's bicycle moves anywhere in Maine. / In Oregon the birds all grin / Birds have gorgeous grins in Oregon." Ahead, Mr. Imwalley's chinaberries have been blasted off his trees in only one quiet storm a week before. The golden berries avalanche up and down the alley;

the sound of them over a smooth morning is like talons clicking against ice.

Someone might be watching. If anyone saw her, what would they think?

A block south on Branson, a truck door slams shut, the truck roars, then runs quiet. "This big," says someone, probably from up the alley. Someone else says, "Sure?" "Really," the someone says, "this big."

In front of her own house again, the VQ is almost hit by a newspaper flung from a hand and arm pitching fastballs through the open windows of a narrow van. The wrens and grackles flutter up, settle back on tree limbs, gaze down at the newspapers. The wrens seem to murmur, "bleakbleakbleak," and some, hitching their wings, have no comment, while the grackles burst into hacking, hysterical, manic laughter at it all, at the whole neighborhood, or at the first traces of daylight erasing the moon from the middle to the faint edges, then erasing the edges. What kind of birds stay even in the winter? How do they survive?

She crosses the lawn of her house, walks around to unlock her own back door. *No one has any idea,* she thinks. *So.* More coffee. And one pale yellow oblong tablet.

The withdrawal from Prolixin is a steep staircase of maybe ten flights, maybe fifteen. Tumbling down it backward, The Vagrant Queen knows she must not look over her shoulder.

I ask myself this question: *What is wrong with you?*

I throw away the letter I have written. I have another cup of coffee. I bring it to my kitchen table and do not allow myself to look past the table edges. I spread my newest draft of Mike Burns's short story before me.

Inspired by Susan Orstal's story, "Duty," Mike has decided to outresearch Orstal's research. So he has included the personal history I've offered and has also featured Woodstock, Apollo 11, the first single gene ever isolated, the second and third, the active-duty GI war protesters, with the refrain to "I've Gotta Be Me." He has built in curtain calls for original members of the 1969 to 1970 cast of characters: The Beautiful People, The Chicago Seven, Manson, Muskie, Nixon, Twiggie, Arlo, Agnew, and doses of The Tijuana Brass, Mike Douglas, Westmoreland, Claudine Longet, and of course, Le Duc Tho and Arthur Godfrey. He has killed off everyone but Claudine.

Single-spaced, his story is sixty pages long. Was. Poor Mike Burns. I have hardly kept a word of the original.

Michael Burns
3693 Brangus Place
Las Almas, N.M. 88001

Second Hands
(Ben, November 1970)

I think the worst coward can ignore fear even when it sweeps over and over you like the second hand of a clock. I'm platoon leader, and pretty much the worst coward in my outfit, so on a mine sweep operation I'll try to think of something that I can picture whole and concentrate on completely. If it's something stupid like a horny fantasy or a basketball game or a two-pound boring book I've read, that's okay too as long as it will stretch itself out in me, block the twitch of that second hand so I don't mess up.

That's how it is that lots of times I imagine my sister Peg keeping me company on sweeps. We're just two years apart in age so you could say we grew up soldiers in arms. I'm lucky how I can be on day ninety-two in country but, thanks to Peg, not actually be "here" as much as I'm in New Mexico. If it's 1300 hrs. here in Phu Bai, right now in Las Almas, New Mexico, it's one day earlier and four o'clock in the afternoon.

"You don't understand," my dad said, "about radio. And you don't know about loyalty either."

"I wish he'd give it a good blow," Peg said.

We were talking about Arthur Godfrey's nose and the lifetime supply of congestion which filtered his voice.

"But he wouldn't sound the same," Mom said.

"It'd be a shame," said Dad. "Nobody'd listen to him."

I really couldn't stand Arthur Godfrey. It's no credit to me how much energy I could put into hating somebody who played ukulele, sang with a full nose, and called people "bub." But, man, I hated him and Hope and Welk and Benny and Gleason and that whole gang of the radio-era living dead.

"Mr. Godfrey cares about people," Mom said. "You can tell he does."

This all happened one afternoon a year ago on the last Friday in November, the culmination of Hawaiian Week Bargain Days at the Albertson's Grocery in my neighborhood. Peg and I had a cart with bad wheel alignment. Mom and Dad's cart had the same problem.

Grocery shopping as a family was not something we regularly did. But I was leaving soon for Basic and my older brother Anthony was due home from Nam in three weeks, so Mom was feeling sentimental, remembering back when Anthony and Peg and I used to go with her, me in the cart seat, Anthony pushing, and Peg riding the sidebar.

Peg had talked me into going with her and Mom. Then the three of us had ganged up on Dad, who agreed to go with us on the condition that we'd buy real food, lots of it, and not the pinchfuls of crap that were his usual high-blood-pressure curse.

We didn't have a list or anything. The way I thought of it, our job was to move real slowly close behind Mom and Dad's cart and look for something like what they were looking for but which they might have missed. To keep Mom happy we would have to buy some milk and cheeses and a few nongrocery items, though the real challenge was to discover the carcinogenic, high-cholesterol, sugar-laced stuff that would be so good it could actually kill my dad and might at least do hidden damage to the rest of us.

Peg said that Dad liked root beer, we should get him some Hires. He overheard us and said we should get Dad's, it was better. We put a carton of six bottles in the cart, and when Mom looked over her shoulder to see what we bought, I held the carton up to show her. She pretended to frown at me, pushed her wobbling cart forward.

My mother is beautiful. But over here in Nam I have some problems picturing her as being more complete than my wallet photo of her. She doesn't always wear her hair that way, whipped up into a firm, sticky Lady Bird wave. Still, that's all I can see. Dark, penciled Kodak-gray eyebrows; Kodak-black eyelashes and eyes. Grim grin. And I can't see her hands. Sometimes I'll try to remember her hands and her arms and legs where they ought to be somewhere on either end of her photo. Useless.

Peg looks a lot like my mom in ways. So, when I'm trying to think of things about my mom, I'll think of Peg's Mom-type smile, which is, at its best, a compromise between her emotions. You can't see her teeth when she smiles. And Peg has light blond down along her chin that you can make out in a certain light and which I think Mom has also.

While Mom bought some eggs and cottage cheese and things, Peg and I leaned into the tall closed refrigerators next to all that. Dad whispered, "Careful!" covering Mom's eyes when we pulled out some Budweisers.

"John," Mom said, "you don't have to act so goofy. We're in public, don't you know."

Peg did a pitch-perfect mimic: "Really, John! You're embarrassing us, don't you know."

We were enjoying ourselves, Mom included. I'm not a deep guy, I don't think of myself like that, but this was near to the time I was going to leave everyone, so I was constantly looking for the story in the lines on my own palms. I wondered about why we couldn't always be as happy as we were on that Albertson's expedition.

The next two aisles were Housewares, School, Misc. Supplies, and Hygiene, Health, Paper Goods. We looked at the shelves, at all the extension cords and clotheslines and boxes of Empire pencils, Elmer's glue, and the different brands of toilet bowl cleaner, the roach motels, the roach sprays, the roach and pest bombs. Mom sailed us past the douches and tampons, the other hygiene stuff. Mom was what people would call "prudish," though we wouldn't razz her about that because it was ingrained in her. The way we thought about her was that she was "refined," a word plenty different than "prudish."

My dad had his hands right next to hers on the cart. His nails were ugly and knuckles uglier. For twenty years he's been making cinderblock for Oscar Rado & Sons, Co., and he has his job tattooed onto him. His skin on his arms and neck and face is pitted; if you look close, you see the grit trapped under it even at his forehead and around his mouth. His blond-turning-gray hair is Brylcreamed; he finger-combs it straight back. You try to find something in him that relents and you almost can't. Except, he has a big, hard gut that goes about to the center of his chest over which he wears silly-looking white Mexican wedding shirts. And, here's another thing: as if to punish him for his unique style, Mom has made all his white socks washing-machine pink. I can see that. I can look right through my own fear at that.

When we turned the corner of that aisle, a nine- or ten-foot cardboard Koa-Koa Sauce palm tree with motorized limbs swayed before us in a pretend tropical breeze. Mom said, "That's nice. They didn't have that last year."

Ice Cream & Novelties, Breakfast Entrees was the widest aisle in the store, with a long freezer box running up the middle, shelves over it, and shelves across from it on either side.

We decided to split up, Peg and I taking Ice Cream & Novelties and Mom and Dad, Breakfast Entrees. I asked Peg if we should get the frozen brownies, the blintzes, or the Pralines 'n Cream ice cream. She put all three in our cart. "Mom," she said across the freezer, "I'm going to pitch in some money for these things." Peg was working for the *Sun-Bulletin*, had her own apartment but never much money, so it was a nice thing for her to offer.

Mom said, "Well," and looked at our cart, "if you're going to be silly you might as well pay for it."

"What'd you get?" Dad asked.

I held up the ice cream.

"Wow," he said. Like a little boy would say it. Beautiful. You have to know that we just never much saw that side of him. Like a boy in knee pants and suspenders.

Peg touched my hand and nodded at him. "Yeah," I said, but

didn't say, "Peg, I love you for being so great." In my family you left that unspoken. Of course, you could find ways to show it. Eskimo Sandwiches, Top Whip, Mrs. Hibble's Peach Custard.

At the end of the freezer aisle, on a display all her own, was Little Debbie. Dad stood next to her, gazed down where shelves of Little Debbie cakes and brownies and rolls were arranged over her cardboard skirt. I genuflected before her to choose Dunk 'Em Sticks, which would have been his choice exactly. I knew that even in Aisle 5 (A—Mexican & Macaroni; B—Salad Dr. & Pickles) you could find ways to show how you felt: Vienna Sausage W. B-B-Q Sauce and Vlasic Hot Pepper Rings and Teeny Weenies.

My mother was getting into the fun. She was going to go along now, do this for Peg and—probably—especially for me. But I had a suspicion that at home she would hide or throw away every junky, wonderful gift.

I directed us to the back of the store, where Quality Meats were in a freezer box stretching to almost the whole width of the Albertson's. The butchers were working, so you could see them behind their sliding windows, spinning the hooked carcasses like dance partners, sawing away at the ribs, chopping at the stumps of limbs, and wrist-flicking the parts onto white Formica tables. Each of their butchering knives was more perfectly suited to its purpose than any weapon ever tempered for war.

We bought pork ribs because they were one of the mortalest sins of all for Dad's diet. Peg went to the palm tree, returning with two jars of Koa-Koa Sauce. "Hot Style or Medium?" she asked.

"Medium," Dad said, "and Hot Style."

I have separate photos of Mom and Dad. They took an anniversary picture but neither liked it; the separate ones satisfied them better. They have twin beds, his with a shamrock-green corduroy bedspread, hers with a kind of churchy comforter that has blossoming camellias on it. On the weekends when they take naps, he sleeps on her bed, she sleeps on his. If it's Sunday, 1100 hours here, then in New Mexico it's Saturday, 2 P.M: my parents' nap time.

We did two passes of the meat freezer. It impressed me how the rows of tongues and feet and brains merited their own small but carefully crepe-decorated section in the freezer box: a place of honor; as if the butchers wanted to acknowledge the grace of these body parts, separate them from rumps, flanks, shoulders.

In the next three aisles we bought Cheez-Its, Cardinal Potato Chips, Oreos, and Windmills. Mom also bought coffee, grapefruit juice, saltines. Candy & Nuts & Baby Supplies were on the same side of Aisle 2. Dad picked out some malted milk balls and red-hots. Peg and I followed after, tossing some Butterfingers and Circus Peanuts in our cart.

Mom pointed out the cost of diapers to Peg. "Three dollars for the disposable kind," she said, and when Peg ignored her, she added, "Babies get more expensive all the time, don't you know." Peg was married to Jim Aigley, overseas already; by Mom's reckoning, Peg should see that marriage and diapers went hand in glove. But Mom wouldn't say that. Her sense of propriety made her say "purkie" instead of "fart." The *Evening News* body counts and the black and white footage were "deplorable," don't you know.

I'm wrong, I know I'm wrong about this whole way of thinking, but just because I can't shoot my anger straight doesn't mean I don't have to shoot. We'll be on a sweep like this through a grove of trees where the aboveground roots can confuse you and, even after defoliation, the damn shadows stream everywhere. I'll get a mental picture of Mom and Dad and Arthur Godfrey and Gleason and Hope and the gang turning off the radio to watch the TV. Before long, Hope makes a crack about some beauty queen whose "body (wink, wink) counts." Gleason jabs his arm out for an uppercut at a gook and shrieks, "One of these days—right in the kisser!" Welk asks if they can bring on the bubbles. And Godfrey, his poor beat-up nose dimming, says, "Deplorable, eh, bub?"

If it's 1300 hours here, then in New Mexico Mom and Dad are waking up from their naps. My dad's hair looks as though he dreamed in trenches; the pillow-sunk side of his face is older than the other. My mom puts in her bridge, which she calls her "partial." I'll bet she looks different without her molars and eyeteeth, but I've never seen her without them, not once.

On Aisle 1A Mom bought bananas, celery, carrots, none of which were compatible with the Fritos, Bacon Puffs, and shoestring potatoes we bought on Aisle 1B.

The bakery was in that same part of the store. Dad chose a pecan pie, still hot, from the pie rack.

"Enough is enough," said Mom, making him put it back. He gave her a chin-out, frowning look. She stuck her tongue out at him—propriety right out the window. We all laughed. We made fun of her; I wish that wasn't true, but we did—we poked fun at her.

Then, after everything was rung up, Dad had the bag boy bring him the pie. It must have been hot on the bottom and hotter on the edges because Dad shifted it in his hands, rushing us to the car. By now it was five-thirty in the evening.

Driving through the neighborhood, I slowed down to have a long look at everything. Mrs. Rado's new backyard wall was higher, her windows barred since the burglary a month before. Across the street from her house, the oldest Armenterez boy was raking leaves; he was a weight lifter, making his body molten, cooling it down, all the sheaths of muscle angrily glowing, becoming larger and larger by the day. We figured him—the whole neighborhood figured him—as the kid who burglarized Mrs. Rado, and we knew how it satisfied him to see her changing her home, frightened of her own home because of him, just him.

"She can't move," said Dad. "She can't afford to sell."

Mom said, "It's so sick."

The car got quiet. When we parked in my parents' driveway we could hear both the high school and university bands practicing for the main campus homecoming on the next weekend.

We took the sacks in our arms, listening to the boomcashinking and bleating. The brass sounded purer than it had on other, warmer winters. Maybe the chilled metal of the saxes and cornets made crisper notes, or maybe in the cold the players' lungs were less overeager, their tongues more agile on the reeds and mouthpieces.

We took the bags around the house to the back door because Mom didn't like us tramping the living room carpet. On my second trip, the jar of Hot Pepper Rings bumped out of my bag and shattered everywhere on the ground. I started to clean it up but Dad asked Peg and me to put groceries away, said he and Mom would be the cleanup crew. It was a mess, I said, and since I made it I ought to clean it up. But Mom said it was their job. They took an empty coffee can out with them and got started.

Looking at them through the kitchen window, Peg said, "Today was fun, don't you think?"

"Can you believe Mom?" I said.

Peg stuck her tongue out and did her imitation: "Enough is enough."

We had at least six bags to unload. "Peg," I said, "you think we made too much over Dad?"

"They're both—you know—they're scared, Ben." I felt she was saying that she understood how scared I was too.

She handed me the Bacon Puffs. "Want some?" she asked. We opened the bag and chomped on some. We drank root beer; decided Dad was wrong, that Hires was better than Dad's; we talked about our brother Anthony, how he would be out of Nam in a few weeks and come back to make them feel okay. No one was better at that.

I asked Peg about Mrs. Rado; whether or not the old woman would be able to keep up the business with Mr. Rado dead now and the sons gone; whether she thought Dad's job with Rado & Sons was in trouble. We both knew Dad was planning to retire early. So, I don't know why I asked Peg all that, except—hell, I don't know why I asked.

Peg said, "She'll have to back out or have it all blow up in her face."

"Goddamn," I said.

It didn't surprise us how long Mom and Dad were taking to clean things up outside. We stopped unloading bags in order to watch them. They were on their hands and knees, picking up the slivers of glass, putting them in the coffee can between them. Their shoulders and hips were close, so sometimes they touched, but they never bumped. Though they might both reach for the same piece of glass, they instantly knew who would take it. In about the same way, I knew my sister Peg's fakes and feints and she knew mine too, the way good soldiers have to know these things. I always really did believe we could read each other's thoughts.

This is what I think; this is what I know Peg thought: Mom and Dad would search out every shard and sliver. In the morning, they would get down on all fours together in order to painstakingly check the same place, because Anthony and Peg and I once ran barefoot through their yard and because they believed what might have hurt us once could again.

The End

"The jar of pepper rings is like a symbol," said Andria Charley. "Jars can be symbols."

Through the hand he held over his face, Burns asked, "What?"

"Wombs," Andria said, then, more shyly, "You know: uteruses."

"Is class dismissed?" I asked. "Have I dismissed class?"

"Fuckin' right," said Burns.

Blake said, "Good story, Burns."

"Yeah," Norm added. "Real original."

Andria raised her hand. "Is it okay to write a grocery store story?" She was always asking about what was permissible and what was not.

"What's that, Andria?"

"I mean, like a whole story?"

"Yes?" I meant to say "Yes" rather than "Yes?" in order to avoid her asking more.

"In a grocery store?"

"It's a superstore, not a grocery store, Andria. And anyway, Fauknerald did it," I said, "and Steinwelty, Dos Equis, Upbellow."

She reached her hand under her funny bird's-nest hair, and she rubbed the back of her neck. "Oh."

Gotcha! I thought. *Right in the old left frontal lobe.*

"Mrs. O," asked Norm, "how come Francis didn't come with you?"

Did they care about the story? Any of them? "Peter," I said, "what about the story?" His eyes were dull, but his mouth and lips were expressively yearning.

"Well," Peter said, "you couldn't see where—if you—it was good, I think, but until the end you couldn't—kind of—you know—get it exactly, or very exactly."

Through his worn yellow shirt his collarbones showed. His mom gave him awful mixing-bowl haircuts. Overall, he had an emaciated and saintly appeal. I could picture how Francis used to fix her eyes on him, and I could almost understand.

"Well. Okay, what about Francis?" I asked. But now they were interested in the story again.

It was supposed to be Burns's story. Of course, it wasn't. Burns, who as a matter of principle never raised his hand, said, "Here's the thing. You don't get a climax in it."

"What about the hot pie?" said Norm. "That's a climax."

"What pie?" Burns never liked seeing Mitchey's arms and hands so close to Norm's on the table. "What fuckin' pie?"

"Are you blind?" asked Blake. His quiet firmness stopped discussion. "The pie's a bomb."

Finally, Andria said, "You can't do that. Pies aren't symbols. Are they?"

All The Invisible looked down. I was actually tempted to call on one of them and ask just how he felt about pies or dominoes or perimeters or bras. I might even ask about Francis. But no one's opinion about her really mattered.

Francis, I thought, *you're my friend. I know you are.* I half-listened to some of the argument between Burns and Norm and Andria.

Where are you, Francis? What curb of what block are you standing on? Where are you being jeered at now?

In my mailbox, Rickee had left me a note. "Will you post this?" It was her new three-stanza flier (dittoed, no doubt, in the English Department).

R & R Real Estate
Apt. & Storage Rental
Space

Comfortable & Affordable
Limited No.
Available

Messages
523-6036

Anthony telephoned me to ask if I'd get together with him at the Jerry's 24 Hour Restaurant. That meant he had just gotten a letter from our parents in Chicago.

We both ordered pie. Apple pie. The Dessert of the Day.

He put the letter on the table before us. I knew what it said. *And how is your sister? Is she doing better? Do you visit her? Do you send our love?* I pushed it back toward him. "Anything new?" I asked.

Anthony said, "Yeah. She's got him talked into both of them seeing some psychoanalyst."

When the waitress served, us, I noticed his piece of pie was bigger than mine, and I told him so. "God," he said, "it sure is," and we switched the two plates. "Mom and Dad sent a check for you, Little Peg."

One hundred and seventy-five bucks. Every two months. "Does this mean I have to pay for the pie again?" I asked.

"*I* didn't get a check!" he said. That was enough for us to laugh at together. We both wanted more times like that.

2 · *Permanence*

The Beauty Bee fit me in for a one o'clock appointment today so I could do something normal with my appearance. I wanted that normal look in which the wind or air, in flawless harmony with my needs, is supposed to have styled me. Molly says that the normal look is a little disheveled, that normal but defiant is multidisheveled, that weirdsville is fakey, shaped and hammered.

When Jen said, "We'll have to cut some," I let her make me lighter on the top. The hair on her arms smelled like perm, and her own head was in transition of some kind. I handed her tissues for the curlers.

"Heavy people have to watch out," she said. "Hair means lots."

"Yes," I said.

"Not everybody's got God-given looks." She asked about her son, Peter, who was in my Introduction to Making Fiction class.

"Exceptional," I said. In my opinion, a lie of four or fewer syllables is venial.

"Peter says you're scary."

"I am."

"You are kinda big."

I handed her a tissue.

"I work faster if I'm talkin', but I talk too much, huh?" She slowed down. Whenever she turned me to the mirror, I closed my eyes and said, "I trust you," which I didn't.

It was not a tight perm, so I felt comfortable with the dryer over me. Better Living Through Chemistry, I thought, thankful to have such a normal television jingle in my eely brain. I called Jen over. I reminded her I didn't want anything moussey because my daughter used mousse and it looked like bacon fat. I couldn't hear her, but I think she said either "Who?" or "So?" That should have been a warning to me.

At the end, she had to explain. "The whole perm just didn't take, hon." She recommended I not shampoo it too much, said some mousse and a hair pick would give me Windblown anyway, as long as I stayed out of the wind. I looked in the mirror. On the top of my head I had lighter hair and less of it; the bands of hair around this were frothy in some places, plaited in others. Normal But Defiantly Fakey is how it turned out.

Jen was apologetic about taking the forty-five dollars. "You got a difficult head," she offered. I bought some Catching Fire mousse and a Zu-U hair pick. She showed me her signed picture of John Glenn, which looked authentic. *Thanks for the cut!* it said, autographed with a gravity-defying ink pen.

In my visit with Paula Analyst, at her office downtown, I explained about John Glenn and my hair, and Jen, and the feeling I had that I was rocking or swinging. "When I swing up, everything looms, brightens, or shrieks. I swing back and all the sounds, the brightness, everything makes me want to reach my feet down and stop. But then I can't."

Where are you now? she asked. She had changed the frames of her glasses. Her new glasses were the overlarge kind businesswomen were supposed to wear, that looked like a businessman had lent them to you.

"Where am I? Up."

And?

"I'm up. Up." I wished she had gotten a pair of ugly, functional glasses. I told her so. I said I was okay, that I was coping with all the swinging up and back but I just wanted to report it.

For the next half an hour she grilled me about my step-down schedule for the Prolixin and the lithium carbonate. We went over every stage. She handed me a set of notecards identical to the set she had given me two weeks earlier.

She said, *It would be dangerous to alter this schedule.* Her perfume, an animal-sex-gland scent, smelled like chalk and coffee grounds and face powder and lint and Lysol. It makes sense to me that men would be excited by all the smells of first grade. It stands or at least slouches to reason that animals carry that classroom odor in their glands.

"Henry!" I remembered her last name! "Paula Henry. Dr. Paula Henry."

Yes.

"Yes. Well, I never can remember your name."

She thanked me. She said, *Okay then. You have your schedule.*

We talked about my problems with having absolutely no appetite or voraciously wanting to eat anything, whole tubs of butter with a spatula, anything. We reviewed the old problems with sleeplessness. She said we should avoid a prescription for now; that we should try a "phase advance."

On crisp, new salmon notecards, she made out a schedule for phase-advancing me. I would go to bed earlier and get up earlier. I would go to bed that week at ten and get up at eight. The next week I would go to bed at nine and get up at seven. I would ask James and Molly to remind me about meals. Eventually, I would go to sleep at seven and get up at five. I would not break routine. Routine would give me structure. Structure would give me orientation. Orientation would give me confidence.

She advised that I continue writing. If I could, I should keep written self reports of the swings up and swings down. She apologized for not letting me use her word processor since I had left Everview. Another client knocked on her office door. A businessman type. I thanked them both, and left.

Is anything harder to remember than a woman's last man-name? As I walked away from her office, I forgot her last name. I was too stubborn to turn back. Was it Paula Gordon? Paula Adams? Daniels? Michael?

I took the one-ways running between Espina and Solano streets. At every streetlight I was sure I would see Francis, who by now understood that I was avoiding her: a hurtful thing to do. I crossed Lohman, rehearsing my excuses about my step-down problems with the Prolixin, and how she hadn't wanted to see me yet or she would have called, and how James had said I'd better "shrug off that world if you want to live in this one," and how, anyway, in a few more weeks I'd be in the kind of shape to show my new self off to Francis.

"Peg!" From the parking lot behind The Pecan Tree restaurant and the COAS Bookstore her voice called to my back. If she didn't call out again I could go on as though I hadn't heard. I rushed away, silently thanking her for letting me go free.

Somewhere near the Furr's grocery store and the fire station, her steps echoed mine. "You don't want to see me," she said calmly. "I know. It's okay."

"Damn!" I said. I turned around and hugged her. "You were going to let me—damn me—you were going to let me go right on." I grabbed half of her coat collar and pulled her into my arms.

Hugging me with her cold hands on my neck, she said, "I miss you."

"Me too."

"I mean it," she told me, as if she was saying, "*I* mean it," and asking, "Do *you*?" She said, "I don't have a roommate, you know. I don't have company."

"It's been three weeks."

"That's not so long, right?" The fleshy tip of her nose looked painfully wind-chapped.

"Forever to me, Francis."

"Well," she said, not letting loose, "you have to go, I suppose."

"We've got time before you catch the bus." We leaned back from each other's embrace.

Looking me over, she said, "Okay. Is it really okay?"

We held each other's hands and walked. She asked, "Would you like me to repair that hairdo?"

"Is it that bad?"

"No, no. But it makes a statement. I'll have to tell you that."

When we crossed Boutz to Chaparro, I said in my best Welcome Wagon voice, "Welcome to my neighborhood!" I knew that in all Francis's rambling around Las Almas she would not have roamed in my neighborhood. The "walkers" in any town learn which main streets to wander, which dying part of downtown and which obsolescent, emptying malls. We have our police, security people, our Neighborhood Watch programs. Though Las Almas is not cruel to walkers, long ago it drew uncrossable boundaries that it redraws with each new real estate development.

"Is this where it begins, Peg?"

"About right here," I said. "A square block is what I guess it is. Boutz intersects Chaparro here; then Chaparro to Alamo is a block; and Alamo goes west a block before it runs north and south back to Boutz. An alley runs north and south through the middle." We were standing in front of Mr. Petrillo's where the untrimmed hedges collared his house all the way around to the back. "Look what the Millers—they're old people, lot of old people in the neighborhood—look how they built a little container kind of wall around the edges of the yard here."

"That will be peed on." Francis scraped the toe of her shoe against it. "Dogs in the neighborhood?"

"Some."

"Loose?" She shook herself in her coat and grinned.

"Some."

"They'll pee on it."

"Well, I hope they plant honeysuckle or something to kill the smell. This one here is the Walters. And this one is Mrs. Punicinski. Thirty-five years on Chaparro. Her husband, Tom, died last summer."

"Old," she said, her voice polite.

I moved us along, talking about how some of the houses went up in the thirties, the rest in the late forties. Nervous blabbering.

"All the trees," she said, "pruned and trimmed, huh?"

"Yeah, I guess so."

"Nice. Warm."

Inside James's house, Francis asked for a tour. I took her into the small galley kitchen, where James had replaced the old tiles with Armorcoat, the kind that has two layers of shine beneath a microthin sheen of bright perfectness. Can cause dizziness. Do not look. Professionals must install. "Congoleum, Francis. Straight from the Congo. Never needs waxing. Self-mopping."

Our refrigerator, lemon-colored (quieter, for some reason, than the white ones), refrigerated things, and froze without buildup. "James bought it because it makes ice the shape of orange slices," I said. You could adjust temperatures. But you could not make it stop producing ice. "Look at this, this is something you don't see much, I bet. A *blue* light inside. 'Arctic Blue.' Says so on the bulb."

We walked through the dining room and living room. "His mother gave us the rocker. No arms though." In our bedroom, I showed her the bed with the hand-turned bedposts. Neatly made. "An ugly comforter, don't you think? I mean, that drooping branch design. Bad omen, don't you think? Just joking." The leafless branches bent over the two mounds of our pillows.

I said, "The Prolixin is a problem, I guess. I have bad dreams sometimes, Francis."

My worst was about the dream refrigerator. The dream refrigerator was making ice. She was not able to not make ice. Glutting herself with it, bursting her doors open, spilling it out. Every piece rocking on its curved back or sledding over another piece into another room and another.

"This is the master bathroom."

Francis and I sat on the edge of the tub. We looked at the smoke alarm on the ceiling. "Yeah. I asked the same question, Francis. But if you think about it, you could put alarms in worse places, I guess."

Sometimes the dream ice changed shape. It looked like human ova look under a microscope. I wanted to stop the dream in order to stop the ice from looking like ova, but I couldn't. The ova were knee-deep in the house; drifts were peaking against the walls, peaking and then spilling their smooth peaks off. Icy, dream-deep, drifting human ova. Ivu ova. Ova in trillions. Clacking, crunching ova. More than the house could hold. Anyone who knocked at the front door could be killed. Death by ova.

"That's a picture of me he likes. He says he likes looking over at it when he's shaving." In the photo, I was pregnant with Molly, caressing my swollenness, romantically gazing at it, my eyelids closed. We put the photo back on the bathroom counter.

We filled crisp celery pieces with marshmallow creme. At the dining table—walnut, three leaves, a brand-new table pad—we had strategy session about my hair, deciding finally that embalming would be wiser than risking further damage by trying to repair my head. The shears, in any case, would have been hidden away somewhere where I couldn't find them.

We talked awhile about my problems in stepping down from the medications. I told her how I probably only imagined it, but I guessed that I was in some kind of passage between absolute rigid control and self-immolation. Francis asked, "And what about Molly?"

"Her too," I said. "Only with her the cause is Love."

"Since when?"

I would have liked to keep the confidence Molly had asked, but I never could win in an argument with Francis's eyes. "Ten days now. She and Peter Thompsenson."

"Peter!" she said. "Well, of course. Right. He is beautiful, isn't he?"

"Nerdy."

"And beautiful." Francis grinned. "Better watch out for him. He's The Kind, you know."

I knew. "Exceptional." And what young girl would not be willing for someone as vulnerable as Peter? I'd rather she take up with some cocksure boy who would give her enough reason to say no only by expecting her to offer herself. A boy like Peter would offer *himself* to Molly, and she would want to gently guide him through his difficult virginity.

"Molly will make love sooner or later," Francis said.

"Thank you, Dr. H. Panky," I said, "your expert opinion has helped me painlessly raise the hood on my daughter's maidenhood."

"You're welcome." Until she smiled, I would hardly ever be conscious that Francis was twenty years older than me. Her face had less resistance to expression than mine, so a faint smile folded the rings of lines under her eyes, darkened the deep wrinkles around her mouth, and rounded all the cragginess at her cheeks and chin.

She still looked hungry to me. I said, "I've got some blueberry muffin mix. I'll make it if you want."

It was the add-water-only kind and it took us longer to find the muffin tin than to mix and bake the muffins. In twenty minutes we ate nine of the twelve. We put the last three in foil because Francis said she would enjoy them later.

"This is real food," she said.

I appreciated what she meant. "Yeah, it is, isn't it?"

"I'll have to catch my bus."

I asked, "Are you sure the bus lady's coming back at four?"

"You know her," Francis said. "You can be sure of her."

We picked up our plates and silver. Francis pressed some of the cake onto her fingertip and ate. "I wonder if I could visit in your college class?"

"Well, it might not—" (I didn't have any notion why it might not be a good idea. None.)

"I shouldn't come. You're right," she said.

At the front door, she pulled her coat on and put the wrapped muffins in an inside pocket. As roommates at Everview, we had had a clever thing we always said when we were saying good-bye. "Don't be stranger."

Francis screwed up and said, "I miss you. I love you, Peg."

I said, "Don't be stranger," because I'm an asshole. That's a good enough explanation. This friend I loved so much would be slogging the fringes of my neighborhood in a few minutes and would then be on a bus to a room in the bug zoo where the bugs obediently ate prescription Raid and stayed out of the breakfast cereal and the knife drawer, and where only Sergio ever kept his promise to visit regularly.

When James came home at four, he knelt by me where I lay on the sofa. Very quietly, his voice like a small boy's, he asked, "You want to be held?" I resented needing him. But he let me cry in his arms, and let me swipe my nose clean on his work shirt. He stroked my closed eyes with his thumbs while his fingers smoothed my forehead. He asked, "Do you hurt? Couldn't they give you something?" He knew, without my asking, how to turn my head so that it rested on a less bony part of his chest. "This crying," he asked, "all this crying all the time. You're not stepping down off your medicine the right way, are you? You're not following the schedule."

Softly, I said, "Shut up." I repeated it as I fell asleep, certain that whatever truths I brought back from my sleep he would say were only dreams. An absolute truth is never absolutely acceptable, is it? That's something I had heard my father say.

Lewis Blake
375 Sangre de Flores #3
Mesilla, N.M. 88005

Map of Rivers
(Peg, 1971)

I still think everything my father did he did more for himself than for my younger brother, Ben. He could have visited Ben at the VA when he was medivaced there in early March. He could have seen for himself that Ben could not stay alive long.

He made himself believe Ben would leave the hospital and need a place to start recovering. Without so much as consulting my mom, he took out a loan in order to buy the Rado house two blocks away.

In a week, he had heaped up a pile of timbers, plywood, and other supplies; he set up a band saw in the backyard. He sketched some plans. Then he telephoned my older brother Anthony so he could take the two of us on the grand tour.

Mom and I were both angry with him, and angrier in each room he showed us. We saw the clothes closets, two spacious bathrooms. In the third bedroom she said, "Enough," and turned her back to him. But, as always, she followed after him again.

He pointed out how much nicer it all was, the fixtures and appliances, the carpeting, the solid construction and generous insulation, than in our own home. Molly, afloat inside me, had dived into the deeper part of my pelvis, where she now swam more gracefully than she had in the months before. I was twenty. My husband James would be coming back from Vietnam in July. I should have been able to say to my father—but I didn't—that the money was wasted on Ben, that here was all their retirement money locked inside Mrs. Rado's walls.

Last, he took us to the master bedroom, where the south and east walls had floor-to-ceiling shuttered windows with iron framing and bright, new panes, each the size of your palm. He asked Anthony to open the shutters all the way, but it was late morning and the light didn't suit my father. "In the evening," he promised, "this'll be great."

He made us go into the walk-in closet to show that all four of us could fit. He showed how the closet light went on when the door opened, then shut off when it closed. In the dark, he said, "Nice, huh?" and, in the light, "What do you think?"

"Nice," Mom said. "A bargain."

"Let's go," said Anthony.

"Look," my father said. "Hey—"

Mom said, "We should. It would be better if we would just go."

Anthony took Mom's arm. "All right then." He led her out of the room.

"Hey—come on, Anthony, don't."

Anthony's dark hair was ungroomed around his ears and neck. If he chose to look straight at you, he would shift his shoulders forward while drawing back his grimly handsome head and powerful neck. He came back from Vietnam two months before Ben was inducted, one month before my husband James went there. In James's family he and one of his two younger brothers were enlistees. Both his father and mine were World War II veterans. When you think about it, the odds were probably diminished for someone like Ben.

My father had rolled his navy blue work shirt sleeves just above his elbows. "Lots of work to do here, Little Peg."

"Sure is." I walked with him down the hallway to the dining room, then out through the kitchen to the backyard.

"About here," he said, losing his train of thought. "This. About here." He traced through the air with his hand and said, "I'm going to put a little patio down so he can get the sun." If you didn't look carefully, you'd have thought my father looked all right. But closer up, you could see the brick grit embedded in his face and arms and hands. Sometimes I would imagine my mother's body honed against that grit, which had become a part of him in his twenty years of work at the Rado & Sons brick factory.

"I was thinking," he said, "how you could move in here with Ben when he gets here. You know—help out until James gets back, and the baby comes, and you two move somewhere else."

I didn't answer him at first. Because of my blessed maternal state, I had constipation and gas and bad nerves compounded by a cruelly indecisive bladder. I asked him for water.

"Right," he said.

He called from the kitchen that the house didn't have glasses yet. He came out with water in a baked bean jar that had probably held nails. "It's clean," he said. "I rinsed it out."

I guess I was going to say no to him about moving into Ben's house. I think I might have if not for the worried way he looked into the water and then back up to me, holding the jar a second after my hand had closed around it. The dirty-rain taste of it was good.

At six-thirty the next morning, Mom and I brought my luggage, clothes, bedclothes and towels, and a box of borrowed silverware and cooking utensils to the Rado place. My father unfolded a cot in the living room. Before he went out in the backyard to work, I made him move the cot into the room that he said would be Ben's.

Mom neatened my bedmaking. She had always folded bathroom towels and ironed pants and made a bed in the same respectful way we were taught to fold the flag. One hand drew the sheet tight, the other expertly tucked it under a corner. "He's happy you'll do this," she said.

"Stay, you mean?"

"Mm-hmm." Beneath her ears she blushed. At a certain part of her face her cheeks met the loose skin under her eyes and formed lines, definite as scars. "He's buying some furniture this afternoon. He's picking up a hospital bed somewhere in Chamberino, from a family, some people we know at church."

"In charge, isn't he?" I said.

She put her hand and arm inside the pillow to straighten the pillowcase. "Don't be snide, Peg."

"In the center ring, Peg and Mom—ferocious beyond—"

"Please, dear."

"—beyond imagination."

Her teeth almost emerged through her thin white smile. A warning.

"You know what I mean." I offered my version of her smile. "Not really, huh?" I handed her my pillow, and went into the bathroom.

Afterward, I sat on the closed lid of the toilet and thought abut Mom, and about how all the circusgoers admired the tigers more than the tiger tamers. Jumping through the hoops, posing on the platform, and bounding gracefully down on command. When the tamer's whip cracked, it wasn't his control but the rage the tiger held back that we watched. That's what I saw, anyway: the muscles moving in her face like crushing undercurrents.

When I met James, I was determined not to be like my mom. Then, the first time James circled me and commanded, "Do this for me, Little Peg," "Wear this," "Don't talk like that out in company," "Make me this one promise," I heard him shouting, "Up! Up!" and—how do I explain this?—I wanted to be good for him. When my skill was perfected, I wanted to be better. *"Good girl!"* I imagined everyone, my father and older brother and the whole penis gallery applauding. *"Good girl!"*

After James left for Vietnam and assumed I would stay with my parents, not rent an apartment; and when he asked me not to take a full- or part-time job; and when he questioned whether I really felt I needed so many girlfriends; or if I really wanted to take courses at the university; when he asked all these things, I was the good housesoldier. *Make me just this one promise,* he said in letter after letter. What I did was what my mother would do. I followed all lawful orders. Patriotism.

I found Mom in the kitchen, where she had removed the grate

from the bottom of the refrigerator, and she was sweeping lint out with her fingers.

I stood over her. "Are you going to hang around until Dad gets back with his whatever-the-hell-it-is?" In so many words, I moved her out of the way, as Anthony had done the day before.

In some ways, I could not believe Mr. and Mrs. Rado and the Rado sons had ever lived in that house. In the mornings when I awoke I heard and smelled the empty house's perfectness: no odor of uncleaned cabinets or recooked cooking oils, no old carpet breathing years of spilled coffee and greasy ground-in bits of potato chip and popcorn; no burbling of drooling faucets or light fixtures humming like thumbnail locusts. Every board in the floor behaved and every door hinge and faucet handle noiselessly obliged me.

As the walk-in closet light came on all by itself, I smiled into the full-length mirror at my chunkiness, only some of which was pregnancy. I pulled off my silver-blue silk nightgown. I gave myself the quick once-over that James would give me if he were there. He never looked close. He preferred touching me, his uncomprehending hands trying to read me. After lovemaking, he was even less interested in looking. So, though he wasn't there to speak for himself, I felt I could put words in his mouth. "Solid woman," I said. "Head to toe."

I'm not sure why I did not masturbate while he was in Vietnam, except that I somehow assumed it would have been a kind of dereliction of duty. I did permit myself body hair. I let my underarm hair grow, and the hair on my shins got shaggy. If he were there, James would ask, "Are you just going to let yourself go?"

I'm not an expert on this, but I think in 1970 housesoldiers did even stranger things. At least four days a week I devoted whole afternoons to writing him. I had imaginary conversations with him. I remember that when he eventually came back from

Vietnam, I was disappointed he could not talk with me as intimately as my pretend-James had.

The sound of a snarling truck engine outside made me look again at myself. I dressed there in the closet. When I shut the closet door behind me, I appreciated the automatic darkness.

My father unlocked the front door and quietly came into the house. He handed me a paper bag with a box of doughnut holes and a pint carton of chocolate milk inside it. "Well, Little Peg," he asked, "is it a good morning?"

True to our family custom, I answered, "Set sail!"

He blew the powdered sugar off a doughnut hole and ate it. "Mr. Aigley's coming over to help me set up the bed, get the place ready. Can you make him coffee?"

I said sure, that it would be good to see him. A half truth. Andrew Aigley was my father-in-law and, while I didn't know him too well, I could have figured that if he were asked, he'd help out.

My father had also called my brother Anthony. He said he didn't think Anthony would come. "You never know," I offered. The men in my family had been one strong woven rope; now that a strand had been destroyed, the others had unbraided.

The coffee made, we walked outside to the dismantled hospital bed piled in the truck. "The bed's a good one," he said, "I hope I can remember how it goes together. Needs a new mattress. But look, you've gotta see this." He drew a large black cardboard cylinder from the open window of the truck cab. He set his coffee on the truck hood, pulled the cap off one end, and unsleeved the shiny, rolled-up vinyl. "Come on inside. I ordered this through the mail. I tell you, you can't believe it."

He carried the map inside to Ben's room. "You know how these places take forever. I ordered this thing for Ben in December."

"Okay," I said, "show me."

He unrolled it on the bare floor, and we knelt down to look it over. About four by six feet, the Mercator world map was named The Map of Rivers in grand turquoise lettering at the bottom. All land was the lightest gray, with topographical variations rendered in only slightly darker shades so that the mountains, the land masses, the poles, all the geographic awesomeness of earth, even the oceans, was insignificant compared to the cerulean claws everywhere: the blue, slender branching arms and narrow, shell-blue curving wires. *S* upon *S*, the narrower threads branched out in pale, gnarled fingers or fanned into deltas, or sprayed into lines that the sharpest fingernail could not trace; they vanished and reappeared, always more important than the pale gray world beneath them. The Mississippi, the Murray, the Amazon, the Congo, the Nile, the Rhine, the Volga.

No nations, states, or cities were named on the map; no monuments or ports or peaks were marked; the land was cleansed of highways and railways. The map's legend explained how the ten different shades of blue defined Stream Order, "the ranking of river systems in size and complexity." In silver lettering it said, "Streams of the first order (deepest blue) are spring-, rain-, or snow-fed brooklets without tributaries. Streams of the second order (lighter blue) are fed by those of the first order, and so on. A great river may have a stream order as high as ten."

The map had twelve eyelets at the top and twelve at the bottom and, as my father knocked tacks into the map on the wall where the foot of Ben's bed would be, I joked that it always fell to women to hold up the world or hold it down while men hammered it in place.

He pretended to knock my forehead with the hammer. "You're overeducated, you know that?"

When Mr. Aigley came, we traded news about James. Whenever the Aigleys and I discussed my husband, I had the notion that we were sharing only a portion of what we knew. I felt it was fair enough for me to be stingy with them, but it angered me for the Aigleys to believe they should not let me know everything.

My father had been leaning against the truck with us in order to listen in on our conversation, and that angered me too. I know it all makes me sound immature.

We discussed again the gum disease that James had contracted in An Loc, which made it painful for him to eat. Since February, he had lost ten pounds. Mr. Aigley said, "So. Anyway, what can you do?" He turned to my father. "You know the drill, John." I guess that's true of VFW buddies like them: they know the drill.

"Yeah," said my father.

As far as I could tell, I didn't know any of it as men knew it. Who—a woman?—could know what they knew? A wife?

"I bet Mr. Aigley could use some java, Little Peg."

Mr. Aigley said, "Sure. You already got it on?" From the pocket of his work pants he fumbled out his leather gloves. "Black's fine. I could get it." He smoothed the gloves onto his fingers.

"No, no," I said, and fetched.

When I came back, he had closed his hands, and was holding his leather fists in front of him. "So, where do we start?"

"First, you gotta see something," my father said. He took his buddy inside to see the map.

By 10 A.M. they had neatly spread the skeleton of the bed over the front yard and then sensibly, systematically figured out how the contraption went back together. The gusty March morning sky brightened. I looked through the iron grates of the picture window, and I sized them up: Mr. Aigley, the flab of his arms and upper body quivering as he assembled the pieces he stood astride; my father, with his face asquint in concentration as he worked or, more often than not, as he stood apart from the whole mess and gave instructions. I took measure of the two men, because I liked little instances when I could promote myself to some imaginary military rank. Lance Corporal Peg O'Crerieh Aigley, SP3, IC, SU (In Charge of Sizing Up). There. That's how I was. Am.

I grinned openly at their bellies swaying in the sling of their shirts, and their fifty-year-old backs and awkward hands, and I decided I was (overweight—pregnant—nauseated) stronger than either of them.

And, later in the evening, when Mom and I visited Ben at the VA in El Paso, at first I coldly assessed the small part of my brother lying before me without his right leg, without his arms, without his slender, bony wrists, his almost unwrinkled hands. His narrow chest and his neck and face were drowned in bandages stiffening from drying blood. When I said his name, I was surprised to hear it come from me. *Ben.* Like a shutting door, the word sealed me off from everything but what I felt inside. I descended into myself as though I was made of cavern floors and could descend a level at a time to call a signal word out; then, a level deeper, a longer message; then, deeper yet, echoing sentences making nonsense out of the ones they overlapped. Outlined beneath the sheets, his body reminded me of a root pushing up through the earth or trying to claw deeper inside. His chest made a cooing sound, the murmuring of water flowing close under rocks.

My mother would have been helped by my tears if I could bring on tears, but here is what I did instead. I held her so she couldn't escape my arms. I said, "If he doesn't—can't—die before we get him to that house. Mother, listen. He's dead already if you look close enough." She wanted to get away, but I was too strong for her. If I was going to make her cry I wanted her right in my arms where I could feel what I had done. "I'll do it if I have to. If he can't die. If nobody else will."

On the drive home, she was still crying. My baby tumbled, plunged deeper, and surfaced, and I could almost hear our shared blood splashing inside me. Instead of consoling my mother, whispering that everything would be all right, and walking her from the car to her home; instead of that, I sat and watched her fumble with her front door. I thought of the pretend trips Ben and I took as children, sitting in the front seat of my parents' Olds, reaching L.A. in five minutes, only turning left once to be in New York or, for that matter, Asia.

When I came to Ben's house, the perfectly clean windows seemed to me like shiny black marble panels placed over the fathomless darkness inside. I went into his room to sleep, but I chose Ben's bed rather than the cot so I could look at the map. The dams also were unnamed.

At first my father and Mr. Aigley had planned to do all the remodeling themselves. They did succeed in assembling the bed, constructing the front- and back-door ramps, lowering certain counters and shelves and tables. Then they unwisely tried to remake Ben's bathroom.

A plumber friend, Joe Pruszcak, had to come out to repair the damage. The new toilet he brought was fabulous, the men agreed, a beauty of a can. The tank and toilet were all one sculptured unit. The lid and seat were padded. You think about a toilet, they said. What a thing, huh? You gotta see this.

"A beauty," I said. Despite myself, I was won over again by their adolescent enthusiasm. Still, Liberty Vitreous seemed like a bad name for a toilet, and I told them so.

We all laughed together then. Mr. Aigley read the bill (he had insisted on paying half), and said the price of freedom was three hundred and fourteen dollars and ninety-five cents these days, and we even thought that was funny.

Before the three men muscled and sealed and bolted the toilet in its place, they brought a chair into the bathroom so they could rehearse the transfer Ben would have to manage from wheelchair to toilet. To figure out placement of rails, they had Joe Pruszcak, a tiny man, move from chair to toilet and back again until they scratched brace markings on the wall. I watched from the door of the bathroom. Though Ben's build had once been twice Mr. Pruszcak's, there was logic now in adjusting things differently.

For determining the placement of the bath rails, Joe also pretended to be Ben. My father marked the walls with chalk and said, "Sit in there, Joe."

Joe sat in the tub. "Like this?"

"We've got to put handles in there," said my father. "Where—" Looking down at the little man in the deep tub, he could only make enough breath for the one word. "Where . . ."

Mr. Aigley leaned near his buddy. "Hey, John. We'll take a break."

Kneeling down, my father looked again into the tub. "What? Yeah. Okay, yeah." He handed the chalk to Joe, who made the marks where they needed to go. Helping him from the tub, my father almost lifted him completely up and out. When Ben and Anthony and I were very little, he would lift us out of the tub like that, and ask, "All right there?" He took his hands from Joe's waist.

Joe said, "I'm outa time, guys. If I don't get home, I don't *go* home."

They knew what he meant: a wife's tyranny. Anyway, they avoided the whole shipwreck into intimacy that might have happened if my father had cried. After Joe left, they installed the handles, swept up after themselves, asked what I wanted on the pizza.

"I don't want pizza," I said.

"I'll bet the baby wants pizza." said Mr. Aigley.

"Oh God, I hate that."

My father asked, "What?"

"When people talk to my stomach."

"Our momma's crabby," my father said.

Mr. Aigley took our orders for soft drinks and said he'd be back in a jiffy.

When I was fifteen the Aigleys had lived near us. In one of the milestone scandals of the neighborhood, their home had been repossessed and they had completely packed up and moved out between midnight and 8 A.M. on a Sunday in December 1965.

I don't think a house light went on anywhere in the neighborhood that night, but probably no bedroom window was left closed. We were so obvious, the Aigleys must have known we all were watching. My father had characterized them as a family that fouled its own nest.

Five years later, on the night I announced that Albert James Aigley had proposed and I had accepted, I imagined windows gliding open from one end of our neighborhood to another.

On our honeymoon, James had told me, "See how things turn out? After my dad lost his job, and we went through that repo thing, we were white trash. That's how my parents thought of us after that. They fought a lot about my mom looking for work. We had fewer choices and we knew it. And once I accepted it, I could adjust myself."

We were fishing, our bobbers very far from us, too far to watch them on the glittering lake. I had asked him how he had adjusted, what he meant.

"We didn't talk about money. I didn't listen when kids told what they got—the bicycles and tennis rackets and things. That's part of what you do, you don't listen or look or imagine too much. I bet our bait's gone."

"I guess you got pretty mad sometimes," I said. We held on to our rods and reels.

"Nope. You stand far away from all the crap and you hit an Off switch. You know the things that make you mad are right in your face, but they can't reach you."

I listened carefully to him, my husband of two days. I looked out at the lake, out where my bobber might be, and I imagined just exactly where it was. I said to my handsome red and white bobber, *You have an Off switch. You don't listen or look or imagine too much.* I said it over and over. *You have an Off switch.* I did not yet understand how exactly that described the perfect soldier.

When he returned with pizza, Mr. Aigley and my father talked about how they were going to hook up the television in Ben's room and what kind of remote control they would need to run the radio, room lights, television, and bed. This conversation went on forever. At first I heard both men; then I heard gibberish. At a certain point, their voices seemed clarified by distance, so that I could identify each word but no longer distinguish the men, even though I sat near them.

"It would be something if they could get one remote for all that, wouldn't it?"

That would be neat, but probably impossible, said the other.

"What?" I said.

"Yeah," said one. "but they order a satellite out in space to shift a quarter of an inch or spin slower and change orbit if they want."

Ben has no hands, I wanted to say.

"Problem is, the Pentagon doesn't buy its equipment at the Radio Shack."

"Hell if they don't! They just pay ten times what we do. Right?"

"Right."

"Peg?"

"Right," I said.

The men took slices of pizza with them to Ben's bedroom. I heard one quietly say, "She's awful upset."

A little before six the next morning, my brother Anthony stood at the back door, knocking lightly, probably unsure that he wanted me to answer.

When I let him into the kitchen he perfunctorily hugged me and said, "They've whipped the place into shape, huh?"

"You can get what you want from the icebox," I told him. "I'll dress and be back."

I went to Ben's room. The baggy maternity jeans I pulled on were softened by fine dust. Hitting the knees and butt clean with my palms, I heard Anthony say, "You're mad at me for not coming around."

"Me? He might be hurt some about it. Not me." The dirty tube socks I pulled on were stiff, so I took them off. "He and Mr. Aigley have been remoting stuff—their favorite thing to do. The doors, the bed, lights, radio. They're coming this morning to remote some of the windows, start building a deck."

"I'd like to, you know, be better to Dad." Anthony's voice was deep, fake.

I tucked my sweatshirt into my pants. That looked bad so I untucked it, held the waist of the pants out, and asked my bump, "Well, Baby, is it a good morning?" No answer yet.

Anthony said, "I've been talking with Mom, you know."

I nudged a brush into the front of my tangled hair. "You seen Ben?" I looked at The Map of Rivers. The Ganges, the Niger, the Thames, the Yukon.

"Mom says you hurt her feelings."

The Rio Grande, the São Francisco, the Khatanga. "Hell with the socks," I said and returned to the kitchen.

He asked for toast. I popped it in, asked him again, "You seen Ben?"

"Not yet." He asked for coffee. I put the coffee can, the filter and brewing equipment in front of him. "Put in five table-spoons," I said.

"Mom says Ben's about ready to come here."

"What?" I sat down at the table. "What did she say? What did she tell you?"

"Settle down, okay? She says Ben could, you know—"

"My God. Are you that cowardly?" When he pushed the brewer at me on the table, I said, "Look her straight in the face." I leaned across the table. "Okay, look *me* straight in the face."

Anthony set his elbows and arms up to prop his head, but then he lowered his hands on the tabletop and looked at them. "I bought a bunch of rose grafts. I've got a shovel. I told Dad I'd make a rose hedge out around Ben's deck. In the back."

"Anthony," I said, "he's—you go—you go see. He's like a shell something horrible has shed and left behind."

"It'll make Dad happy." He brushed the knuckle of his thumb against one heavy eyelid. His voice lower, he said, "Okay? You have a problem about it?"

I sized him up in a clownish, dramatic way—my head cantering up and down in order to show him I was sizing him up. I could have been helped by his tears if he could bring on tears. But he stood up. He looked down at me, and said, "You're a miserable bitch."

I'm not much for denying the truth. I let him go outside and get his shovel and rose grafts out. He had dug the first hole by the time I brought water to him. I uncoiled the lawn hose so I could soak each hole as he dug it.

Mr. Aigley and my father drove up an hour later with doughnut holes and milk. My father shook his prodigal son's hand and held on to it. He made Anthony eat. He showed him the map in Ben's room, then took him on the house tour again, asking his opinion of their work.

Standing in the backyard with the two men, Anthony was enthusiastic. "You're a miracle worker, Dad. You guys are something, you know it. Has Mom seen all this? Wait'll she sees."

After that, they knuckled down. They worked from ten to five, almost without a break. Mr. Aigley and my father conducted remote maneuvers in which they tested the probable sequence of commands. Timed lights operative? Inside and out? Garage, television/radio, air conditioner and heater remote functioning? Master bedroom remote operative?

When they tested the fire detectors, they let the warning alarm ring in every room and then in each room separately. Above the din, they shouted, "Functioning! Functioning!"

Anthony patted the mound around another green stick, and smiled at the two old soldiers. " 'Functioning'?" he said.

"Yeah. They sure know the drill, don't they?"

He spoke to my face without looking into it. "They've been there. You haven't."

I thought of James, who was "there" now, while I was not. Because I didn't spit something back, I guess Anthony felt he had told me everything I didn't know and, now that I understood, I would shut up. "Water here," he said.

The three men eventually worked together to start making the little backyard deck. They stained the boards, rubbed them, restained, and varnished. Maybe they shouldn't have varnished them yet, they said. They wanted Anthony's approval to strip off the varnish right away. He gave his approval, then got on his knees with them in the strong fumes of the acetone stripper, stain, and varnish. Before the boards were dry, the men began framing the deck.

At five, I drove to the DQ to get us all big malts for dinner. When I returned, Anthony and Mr. Aigley had their arms around my father, whose own stained arms helplessly enfolded my mom. Ben had died. All their arms would never be able to console her.

At home, Mom took some kind of prescription downer. She was pale but calm as she lay down, and when she started blubbering, "Ben Edwin!" she was already asleep. I left as soon as that ended. Mr. Aigley walked out the door with me, promising my father and brother he would telephone them in the morning. He offered me a ride.

"I have a car," I said.

He walked me to the curb, his eyes about to spill. "Nothing I can think to say. Wish there was."

"It's better to say nothing." For his sake, we hugged each other.

In Ben's bed at the Rado place that night, I took the remote control from the nightstand, but had to press four buttons before I got the shutters open to let moonlight into the room. It was a button with a tiny "L" sticker on it.

The next morning, just after dawn, I heard them banging around in the backyard. I dressed and tried to keep myself hidden from view as I watched through the kitchen window. Anthony was yanking the rose grafts from their tamped mounds.

My father was ripping apart the frame of Ben's deck, throwing boards toward a corner of the backyard. The noise seemed to awaken the baby.

"What the hell are they doing?" I asked her. I dressed quickly, telling her, "That's enough," then saying it to both of us, and then shouting as I buttoned my blouse, "That's enough!

"Stop it!" I came out the back door. Neither man even unbent himself to look at me. I stood behind my father, and I said, "Stop." He pivoted to throw another board. "Listen to me," I asked, but he looked past me to make his aim true. I shouted beyond him and Anthony, "You make me sick! Stop. Some other family will want this. Some other soldier is going to need this and you know it."

Anthony said, "Little Peg. Come on."

"I'm—what is it with you pieces of shit and your stupid hands? Hammering away or tearing down—not happy if you're not hammering—and marching in your stupid parades—crying like goddamned babies at the cemeteries and heaping Honor on the graves." I kicked my father hard in one leg, which made him stop and which brought Anthony to his side.

"All the Bens—my Ben, my James—what do you purple hearts do about them?" I tried to slap my father but missed and hit him in the neck. He stepped forward as if to invite me to make the next slap count. The tears in his eyes streamed out.

"So stop," I said. "You make me puke—so just stop—because somebody's going to need all this—you know it—don't you?—some old vet will have to buy this place for his son." I made a fist and punched at the weeping, pitiful little man. I tried to push him down on the ground.

"Please," he begged, "for God's sake, don't."

Anthony grabbed my shoulders and held me back.

"Get away from me." I taunted my father, "You're too damn puny. I should pick on somebody my own size." Running back into the house, I was vaguely aware of them following.

* * *

An hour later, when I left the bathroom in which I had locked myself, they were gone. I perched on the edge of Ben's high hospital bed and looked at the map. The Song Hong, the Song Da, the Mae Nam Chi, the Mae Nam Mun, the Mekong. I was thankful Ben did not live to look at all the healing transpirations of this gray world, because he would have wanted to live then, and his dying would have taken longer. I rocked myself on the bed as I sang to my baby—some swingset song, the kind in which you're gulping air on the swing back and, on the swing up, singing yourself out past gravity. Out, far past.

Later that week when I committed myself at the Everview Residential Treatment Center they assigned me a nice room with an older woman named Francis. She warmly welcomed me, calling the building "the bug zoo." And that seemed so right to me that it instantaneously established the basis for our long, close friendship.

The End

"Right on time," I said as I opened the door to Lewis Blake. I closed it behind us. I had three designated "fresh student fiction" desks in the narrow office I shared with two other Nontraditional teachers. It was almost impossible for me to navigate by the middle of November when the piles of undone work tilted to the point of crashing down. "Come in," I said, sidestepping through multiple drafts. I had two "ancient fiction" chairs in the back of the office, and I removed the layers of long-neglected typed pages so we could sit.

"A question," he said. He pointed his chin up, as if to make the scar on his neck what I would have to think about first. The purple heart badge, the place where someone must have opened his throat with a slash.

"So?" I looked at his dark, overbold eyes, and saw that just below them but also around his whole face his skin was eroding from what he had already seen.

"Mrs. O," he said, "what about my story? We going to discuss mine or this 'Map' one of yours?"

His own story had been called "Story Math." I found it unacceptable because it had been his version of Vietnam and not mine. "Blake, your story was better than mine," I said, "more bombs and heroism and beery brotherhood and other stuff, I guess. You know—more catharsis than mine."

He had expected lies, I think. His shoulders rolled forward and his neck relaxed when he said, "Shit."

I offered the thought I had just then. "I'd make a bet only men say 'shit' that way. Women say 'shit' more directly." I noticed a peculiar way Lewis clutched his right hand in his left. "A woman will look you right in the eye and say 'Shit,' but if you won't look at her she won't waste the word on you."

"Shit," he said.

His eyes were darker in my office than in my classroom. "Shit," I said back. I had so much to ask him. Why did he wear fatigue pants? The shirts with his nametag?

Instead, I asked, "So. How are you?"

"Great."

We both nodded as if drawing words in the air with our foreheads.

"Mrs. O," he said, "what've you got against me?"

"Me?" I asked. "Okay. I don't like the way you look at me, Blake."

"Yeah? Yeah, that's it. Sure. Know what? I got the exact same problem with you."

The answer was easy. "Solved," I said. "We won't look at each other."

As he was nodding yes, we looked.

I took his blasted right hand and turned it in my own hands. He leaned forward as if I had drawn all of him toward me.

I said, "You left some fingers somewhere."

"In my story."

"Is that where you left them?" I asked.

His hand grew warmer right there in my hand. I touched the three fingers left him, and I heard him whisper, "No," withdrawing. "That about your brother? He died for real in Nam?"

"He was killed there. He died here."

Blake straightened his back. He moved his head, answering no to some question he left unasked. Then he said, "That must've been twenty years ago."

"Seventeen," I answered. "What about you?"

"Seventeen."

"And?"

He said, "A long time."

"Right." I already knew how this conversation went. "You've got it all switched off. Nineteen seventy-one. The whole six o'clock news just switched off, I bet."

He breathed in once. He tried not to breathe out. He pressed his one whole hand into mine, the tears coming to his eyes before he could stop them.

I cried with him. We didn't look at each other during the little time we cried; still, when he brought his half a hand back into the cradle of my fingers, we might as well have been embracing. "I'm fucked up," he said.

"You sure are," I said, and I could tell he heard me really say, *Me too*, because he laughed the last of his tears out of his eyes and looked at me straight. Just like that, we were sitting apart again.

"Mrs. O," he said. "Your story. I liked it okay. It's not fair, but I liked it."

"Thanks."

"I don't think I knew what I expected from you. But I got it. I'm not stupid."

"Shit," I said as a man would say it, my shoulders rolling forward, the word spit at my shoes.

"Anyway," he said, "this was enough. Let's say this was—okay, Mrs. O?"

"Peace?"

"No," he said. "Retreat."

"And no hard feelings?" He wouldn't meet my eyes again. "About the story, I mean?"

"You screwed it. No question about that."

"Good?"

He nodded yes. "Real good."

"Thanks, Blake." We saluted. We laughed, and saluted a little better.

"See you in class, Mrs. O."

My office door closed so quietly I could tell that he had guided it back instead of only letting it go.

I sat in my favorite office chair. It will rise as you spin in it counterclockwise and will descend in the reverse. I spun. I rose.

I spun again, down to eye level with the middle drawer of my file cabinet. All the five drawers were empty except that one, which contained the three shoeboxes of Ben's things my parents had given me. Among them once were some of his rank insignia and his medals, but I had given them to my father and Anthony.

I pulled out a box marked "Papers" in my mother's retraced square lettering. What I wanted was at the top: a wallet-size laminated card. I really cannot explain why I have gone back to read this and dumbly look at it so many times. I have photographs of Ben that I have never looked at as often as this stupid pocket card.

MACV POCKET CARD, "The Enemy in Your Hands"

As a member of the US Military Forces, you will comply with the Geneva Prisoner of War Conventions of 1949 to which your country adheres. Under these Conventions:

You can and will:
Disarm your prisoner
Immediately search him thoroughly
Require him to be silent
Segregate him from other prisoners
Guard him carefully
Take him to a place designated by your commander

You cannot and must not:
Mistreat your prisoner
Humiliate or degrade him
Take any of his personal effects which do not have significant military value
Refuse him medical treatment if required and available

ALWAYS TREAT YOUR PRISONER HUMANELY

KEY PHRASES

English	*Vietnamese*
Halt	Dúng lai
Lay down your gun	Buỏng súng xuõng
Put up your hands	Dua tay lên
Keep your hands on your head	Dua tay lên däu
I will search you	Tỏi Khám ỏng
Do not talk	Dùng nói chuyện
Walk there	Lại dang kia
Turn Right	Xảy bên phai
Turn Left	Xảy bên trái

"The courage and skill of our men in battle will be matched by their magnanimity when the battle ends. And all American military action in Vietnam will stop as soon as aggression by others is stopped."
21 August 1965 — Lyndon B. Johnson

THE ENEMY IN YOUR HANDS

1. *Handle him firmly, promptly, but humanely.*

The captive in your hands must be *disarmed, searched,* secured and watched. But he must also be treated at all times as a human being. He must not be tortured, killed, mutilated, or degraded, even if he refuses to talk. If the captive is a woman, treat her with all respect due her sex.

2. *Take the captive quickly to security.*

As soon as possible evacuate the captive to a place of safety and interrogation designated by your commander. Military documents taken from the captive are also sent to the interrogators, but the captive will keep his personal equipment except weapons.

3. *Mistreatment of any captive is a criminal offense. Every soldier is personally responsible for the enemy in his hands.*

It is both dishonorable and foolish to mistreat a captive. It is also a punishable offense. Not even a beaten enemy will surrender if he knows his captors will torture or kill him. He will resist and make his capture more costly. Fair treatment of captives encourages the enemy to surrender.

4. *Treat the sick and wounded captive as best you can.*

The captive saved may be an intelligence source. In any case he is a human being and must be treated like one. The soldier who ignores the sick and wounded degrades his uniform.

5. *All persons in your hands, whether suspects, civilians, or combat captives, must be protected against violence, insults, curiosity, and reprisals of any kind.*

Leave punishment to the courts and judges. The soldier shows his strength by his fairness, and humanity to the persons in his hands.

(September) 1967

3 · *Accords*

After half an hour of discussion completely clogged our appreciation for the story, we experienced literary arrhythmia. As always, this led us to discussion of symbols.

"The story's got good symbols," said Mitchey Shultz, Future English Major, in white turtleneck and new navy cashmere.

Andria asked, "What? Do you mean the map?"

"Well? Isn't it a symbol?" The earnest ignorance with which Mitchey could ask that question impressed me. She would be a good English teacher someday.

"So," Norm said, "I think the thing means something. I think you've got some Real Themes in there. A whole pod of them."

"The map?" asked Andria.

"It's a symbol," said Mitchey, very sure. Peachy face cream. Fresh Peach fingernail polish. Peach Blossom or Peach Blush or Peach Something lipstick.

Andria asked, "Is the hospital bed a symbol too?"

"Come on, Andria. What're you, stupid?" Burns penetrated his fist with his pen. "Beds are always symbols."

Norm said, "Fuck the symbols, okay? I've been trying to tell you there's Big Theme Whales in this one."

Burns said, "I got one! 'War Sucks.' "

"See?"

Peter Thompsenson muttered something. If he hadn't pushed himself so hard and close against the table, he might speak more clearly.

"Petey," Norm said, "go ahead."

"Maybe you could, you might think this is a story in which, where, a woman, a man—"

"A Sex War!" Burns said.

"It's depressing," said Hutto, one of The Invisible.

"Good!" I said.

Burns said, "That's always good, huh, Mrs. O?"

"Hey," Norm asked Mitchey, "you see what I'm talking about, don't you?"

I said I thought we might be missing the point. "What else?" I asked. "What about the author's technique?"

"You definitely got some of that going in there," said Norm.

Lewis thanked him.

I said, "We have to look close." Sometimes I insincerely offered coy invitations for them to actually think. "Look closer." If they wouldn't accept my offer, I would forge ahead. After all, I had my own notions.

"See all the commas?" I asked. "Have you ever seen so many commas? Every page."

I asked them to take out their notebooks. None did. "Okay," I said, "but this is crucial." Mitchey took out her notebook. Then, Peter.

"You can draw a line. On one side you can put the great comma users—the Jameses, the Hawthornes, the Porters, the Woolfs—the standards of correctness—and on the other side, the slobs, the losers in the war between correctness and magic —you know, the ones who write well but don't make it into Norton's Standards for Post-Mortem Literary Measurement Anthology. The Dos Passoses and Hurstons and Caldwells. Always Anton Chekov before Kate Chopin; always Hemingway before Stein; always Sinclair Lewis before Katherine Mansfield.

"Everything, sooner or later, comes down to comma laws.

Hundreds of them. But I want you to know this, because professors in The Department of Real English will not have covered this in your literature surveys: In literature and life two questions are important above all others. What is restrictive? What is not restrictive?"

Mitchey raised her hand, absolutely certain of answers.

"Put your hand down, Mitchey." Sadly, she was just outside slapping range. "I'm going to give some examples. I want me to make up your mind about what restricts meaning and what does not. Write these down. Take them home. Choose."

1) *"The woods are lovely _ dark _ and deep."*
"The woods are lovely dark and deep."

2) *Her real name was Frances _ with an e.*
Her real name was Frances with an *e*.

3) *The time of day _ she thought _ was morning _ after which she couldn't think again.*
The time of day she thought was morning after which she couldn't think again.

4) *"Men create war in order to compete with women _ who create life."*
"Men create war in order to compete with women who create life."

5) *Norm? Put your hand down _ Mitchey.*
Norm? Put your hand down Mitchey.

6) *Please _ Norm _ more.*
Please Norm more.

7) *How _ she wondered _ when she put the commas in _ where unrestricted meaning ended!*
How she wondered when she put the commas in where unrestricted meaning ended!

8) *"We soldiers of all nations who lie _ killed _ / Ask little."*
We soldiers of all nations _ who lie killed _ / Ask little."
"We soldiers of all nations who lie killed / Ask little."

"Mitchey. You have a question? Save it."

Burns asked, "Do we get Mitchey's story now?"

"No." I opened my attaché case, looked inside. A new letter from Francis to Molly—where did that come from? A new poem from Rickee.

Mitchey's lovely, compassionate story about a neighborhood eccentric named Golly would have to wait until I could write one to suit my own purposes, to follow Keats's advice and cram my life onto the naked foot of Poesy.

Attached to Rickee's poem was a note.

> May I read this aloud to you? I am alone in my office this afternoon.

"Rickee," I said as I knocked, "it's Peg." She would never answer it if I only knocked. She took my hand and led me to a chair at her desk where old tissue-paper dress patterns were covered with poems and what looked like germinating diary entries. Her fine gray hair was like moon-silvered fog lifting from her head. She had unwomanly shaggy white eyebrows. Another woman might have plucked them, but she seemed to have cultivated hers. She leaned against a bookshelf. "I like how that tissue paper takes ink," she said. She unfolded a front bodice. "Can I read it?"

To the left of the center of the bridge of Rickee's nose was a small mole, the color and size of a peppercorn. That and the afterimage of her hair and of her eyes layered in leaf-greenness wouldn't let you look away. "Go ahead, Rickee."

She put the bodice before me and recited.

DAUGHTER

Sleeping, or
near sleep, we
are broken
apart when she
creeps between us

We
curve in on her
like closing gates she
opens with her
arms, her shoulders,
hips

We
close back,
close shut, close but
unlocked, our
bodies only far
apart as our
blood

Too small to grip
a cup, her
fingers clasp my
throat, latch my
breath, fasten my
voice closed

I
should wrench my
neck free, wake him,
unhinge us

I
should unclench her
strange, strong fists,
I should, I
should, I
should
I

Rickee admitted me into herself that completely. She had no daughters. I asked her to read the poem again to me. Neither of us really knew how to talk to each other, so she read it twice more. I liked how she read, as if she could barely dare to pronounce the words.

She read another.

I WILL

fit you in
a cardboard box.
Tape up
everywhere where light
might come.
Kick down on my
shovel.
Dig
deep.
Round out
cool walls.
Hide until
dawn.
Sing songs.
Change
all the words.
Bury you.
Pray
a prayer for you.
Chalk the truth
on wood.
PIGEONS
I KILT.
Pound the stake
in hard
to make
it stay.

"They're no good, are they?" she said. I disagreed. I told her they were her best yet. In fact, I thought her poems were better and better, which gave me new hope.

She handed me the poems. "Think of something to do with them, will you?"

I couldn't think of a thing in the world you could do with poetry. Still, it would have been wrong not to have accepted them.

At six-thirty Molly met me on campus so she could drive us home. Before we left the parking lot I asked her to read the letter from Francis/me. I hadn't read it, or even signed it.

My Dearest Molly,

I'm thinking about you. I like writing to you when I'm thinking about you and you're not here right now.

Do I seem better to you? I seem much better to me, even in the mirror. I laugh less but that is actually very good because anything could make me laugh before. What I mean is that I have control. I am adjusting myself.

Have you been reading about those Russians? Did you know that Am. medical experts say Russians statistically have more red corpuscles than Ams, except for jobless, homeless Ams, who have more red corpuscles than they know what to do with? Keep up on your current events.

Where you live makes a difference, doesn't it? This is a small matter, but I guess I like having no signs in your father's house. Our doors do not have decals that say OPEN or USE NORTH ENTRANCE or LADIES. We have no name on the mailbox. Do you think much about that? We do have a number on our house, I know, but James says that can be taken off anytime I want.

A block any direction from us we can find traffic. I miss the bus lady, but I like traffic. We are all so identical in our different vehicles, aren't we? Four legs or two. Going the same speed. You're an '86 Porsche, I'm a '68 Pinto, but the same cop is clocking us at the school crossing. He has 571,008 red, rotating, whooping corpuscles, give or take a few. "Nothing in school is more important than Civics." Walt Disney said that, or Joseph Stalin.

I do not see Francis, and I suppose that is for the best. If I wanted to see Francis, I would not know where to look. She left Everview. Checked herself out. Maybe forever.

The healthiest person you'll ever meet would like to know how a burning building feels and smells and sounds. Am I right? So, I do miss being with Francis sometimes. She loves us—you and me. Who knows how she feels about James? But she cares about us.

Did you know Francis will have her fifty-second birthday next week? This will be the first time we have not celebrated with her since you were born.

She was thirty-four then, and I was twenty-one. She had just had a third late-term miscarriage. My brother Ben had just died. I never considered the symmetry of that, until now, seventeen years later. Our lives, as we have poured them back and forth into each other, have distilled.

If Francis was in trouble this very moment. If Francis could not tell us about what the trouble was. If all her rooms were burning, her doors and windows were closed. I would find her.

Face to face, I do not think far enough, or see near enough. Writing you this letter has been good for me.

Wherever she is, she will not just disappear, will she? And when I'm better, we'll see her. Won't we?

I love you, my dearest child,

Peg

Molly handed me the letter. "You haven't read this yet," she said. She started the car, gunned the engine, and had pulled into our driveway before I finished reading.

"Where do we start looking for her?" she asked.

"Wait." *I do not think far enough, or see near enough,* Francis's/my letter said. I/she wrote, *I guess I like having no signs.*

"Where do we look?" Molly pushed away tears with her fists.

I told her we would do best on foot, that Francis might be somewhere in our neighborhood.

When Molly and I had walked our own alleyways and peered

over cinderblock walls into all the yards, we crossed Boutz. The Garden Arms Apartments and Press Room Bar were unlikely places for Francis to be, but we checked out the locked apartment pool area and rec room and laundry. In the bar, we walked past every booth, and Molly asked the bartender, "Have you seen Francis? Fifties. Neat, and worried-looking? Walks a little stiff?"

He hadn't seen her. "Remember us," Molly said. "We might check back here."

He grinned at me. "No prob."

"If she comes in here," Molly said, "tell her we're looking for her."

Outside, Molly asked me, "Did you think he was cute?"

"Him?" I said he looked okay, the Snoopy earring was a good touch, and I liked his gold eye shadow.

"Tasty," she said. This and "Nasty" were the kind of things Molly said to me to test her limits with me. I liked that. I liked how she had grown less afraid for my mental health since I had rejoined her and James and had begun stepping down from my medication.

We crossed Montana to the Furr's grocery store. Behind it, we watched an old Mexican dismantle cardboard boxes, flatten them against his chest, and pile the tied bundles atop others in his pickup truck. His dark arms worked like sharpened scissor blades; in the way he flexed his knees and gave himself no allowance to pause, he seemed to have set his own rules.

"He words hard," I said.

"He reminds me how Dad does things." She was walking close and just a little ahead of me, so when she stopped I had to stop.

I said, "You're right. James has always worked like a—he's always done honest hard work." I had started to say that James worked like a "little beaver" or "like a lifetime bulb" but, for once, I checked my cynicism. We watched the man stack and shift his bundles so they reached above but could not spill out of the homemade plywood walls of the truck sides.

Across the wood he had handscripted HOMBRE DE CARTONES. The box man.

I said, "Francis shouldn't have left Everview. Something could happen to her. If she gets off her medicine—I mean, she couldn't have taken it with her—she's already in trouble." The only time the box man looked at us was when he waved as he clunked away in his truck. "I guess we'll go to the Furr's and walk up Boutz to El Paseo, the Albertson's, the Alpha Beta, where people are."

"You're right," Molly said. "Francis has a thing about hanging out."

"I guess so. I wouldn't call it hanging out. You could call it something else."

"Sorry." She walked a little ahead of me again. The way she glided forward without even slightly rotating her hips and shoulders was one hundred percent James. That nodding of her head, as though she was quietly saying thank you to the streetlight and curb and cars and all of it; that was me.

At a streetlight with one of those buttons for the crosswalk, I pushed the button. She pushed the button too. We both had pushed it once. I asked, "What if your push cancels mine?"

She said, "Mom."

"I'm not being funny. Do you know how these things work?"

"Mom." She pushed the button. I pushed it also, and finally we crossed.

When she was eight, she insisted on pulling me in her wagon. I was too tall and too large to sit in it, so I stood while she pulled me in drag-car bursts that made me lose my balance. "You can do it," she said, and helped me back into the wagon.

See what I mean? I was a mom on training wheels. I've never taken them off. Without needing to pretend, we really did love her dolls. But they lived their whole lives in the same unlaundered clothes.

We didn't mop and rinse; we only mopped. We never once preheated an oven.

She gripped my hand as we crossed the street, and she held it along El Paseo on our way to the Albertson's. "I'm going parking tonight with Peter Thompsenson," she said, "and, look, it's no big thing, but—"

"Parallel?" I asked. "Park-ing?" All my lewdest *ing*word aching thoughts bayed in my poor contracting head. "Oh, Molly," I said.

She said, "Mom, come on. We know the syllabus. Rules and regs. Cruising, parking, maybe touching. No bruising my fruit or his, you know."

The pressure in my head would not equalize. Cruis-ing. Touch-ing. Ing! Ing! Ing!

She said, "Nothing nasty, I promise." She guided us onto the sidewalk in front of the Albertson's. We looked through the large glass windows for Francis. Hawaiian Week Bargain Days were advertised in soap lettering from the top to the bottom of the panes. In its usual place at the end of the long freezer aisle the Koa-Koa Sauce palm tree waved back and forth, spinning blank side to paint side. Cutout clouds and volcanoes hung from the ceiling.

"See anything?" Molly asked.

"Not Francis," I said, but I looked longer because she might be there, after all; it would make sense for Francis to be pushing a shopping cart with me, to have her hands right next to mine as my mother and father did once.

The fluorescent lights sharpened the leaves of the cardboard trees atop the display shelves. I could look in on the jungle, hold on to my daughter's hand, and anchor myself with her. My memory is a confusion of limbs, like shadows fallen across water. All my emotions about Ben and my family seem to exist on the surface but also at the bottom of me and, always, wavering in a place between surface and center. I want to follow the shadows back to the branches they are reflecting. But following them leads me back to Vietnam, where I believe that in every moment of waking and sleeping I walked every day next to my husband James, and where, for every moment, I know I breathed inside my brother Ben's skin. How can that be only a dream?

Inside the store, people's full carts did not seem to me to make them any happier, "Look," I said.

"Huh?"

"A jungle, isn't it?"

She said, "What?" and looked harder through the big windowpanes. Then, slowly, she fixed on me. "Mom," she asked, "did you ever, you know, worry? About ever going to Neverview?"

"Whew! Molly. I— The Big House?"

"Yeah."

"Honestly?" I wanted to be inside the Albertson's, my own cart full, talking with some stranger in line about how I had bought everything but the things on my shopping list. "Honestly. Here, this is the truth, Molly: no."

"Honest?"

"But you don't know. God. I should tell you this. I've worried for Francis for years."

"Yeah?"

I wanted her to understand. "It's the same thing," I said. "I love Francis. So. Honestly then. I've worried plenty about Neverview."

We gazed into the store again. "See anything?" Molly asked.

"I'm thinking."

"Mom." She straightened the collar of my blouse, and pulled at it to try prying me away from the store window.

"Molly, do you think much about Grandma and Grandpa?"

"Well. Of course I do."

In 1971 my parents moved to Illinois to live in my mother's childhood home, a lovely stone two-story. Anthony and I both discouraged them from visiting, and they were satisfied to come only once a year as long as James brought their only grandchild to them on Christmases.

Like everybody else, I own a revised version of my life with my parents. All the other drafts, the ones closer to the truth, are gone. Dennis Tiber, out of kindness to me, tried a spin on the untrue version I gave to him. He is one of The Contractual Invisible. One of those student whose obsession with the grade makes it necessary for me to promise an A just so that neither of us has to pretend he really matters.

When I threw his draft away last week, I said, "Tiber, you might have gotten the story right. But that wasn't the assignment."

"Do I still get an A in the class?" he asked.

Dennis Tiber
P.O. Box 1399
University Park, N.M. 88003

Pinkville
(Peg, 1959)

One summer morning I walked through my parents' neighborhood in my pajamas. My father was with me, wearing only his boxer shorts and his Cards cap. His shorts had dime-size silver-blue crowns on them.

He had thought he heard me cussing my pain. My brother Ben was actually making all the noise; but our father sat on the edge of the bed and whispered to me, "Come on, Little Peg." His face was completely shaded under the baseball cap. I knew Ben was awake, even though he didn't say anything or move in his bed.

We walked out the front door. We closed it matter-of-factly behind us.

"So," he said. "Charley horses?"

I lied. "Yessir."

"Painful, I guess." It was probably 2 or 3 A.M., a chilly time in the valley if you have on only undershorts or pajamas. He had his own slow pace, and I could keep up with him if I strode out. We had to duck under the low branches of the Armenterezes' two mulberry trees. If he had wanted to we could have walked around them into the street.

Next to the Armenterez house was the Meadlos' tiny place with six giant cedars. What do you call that color of green so black and deep?

The two Meadlo boys had their own basketball hoop. My brother Ben resented how they still couldn't make a lay-up but they had their own hoop on a pole sunk deep in concrete.

"Lookit," my father said. He nodded at a rock swift on the

white backboard. He knew Ben and I liked to catch them, and he said, "Lucky lizard, huh?"

"He's safe." I thought for a second about shaking the pole.

"The dark time must be his favorite part of the day," he said. If I was curious right then about why we were walking the neighborhood at that hour, with his explanation he had helped me understand—kind of. Who knew we were there? Who could catch us? I looked at him, appreciating him. His boxers were twisted a small turn, so his left leg had less room to move than his right. His Cards cap was way down over his forehead, putting everything but his mouth and chin in moon-shadow.

At the Dursis' he asked, "What do you do with the lizards?"

Nothing too bad. Ben wouldn't let us do anything really bad. "Experiments," I said.

"You hurt them?"

"Nah." Ben and I used rubber bands to fit tiny bells around their necks, or painted codes on them with Magic Markers before we let them go. You might see one a month later dragging its bell. Once, we saw one we had marked B&P, Inc. I always wanted to fit little clothes, overalls or sundresses or bow ties and belts, on them, but Ben saw to it we were naturalists instead of Nazis.

Walking there next to me, my father smelled like a postage stamp, like paper and glue. I saw how the dark hair on the tops of his feet and toes was thick. Going past the Bustamentes', then the Parrujos', I told him, "They owe me two months." They always owed for the *Sun-Bulletin*. You had to go back all the time.

"Chuey Parrujo's a mechanic."

"So?"

He didn't look at me. "He works hard."

And doesn't pay when he owes, I thought.

He said, "Watchit," and guided me by the shoulder to keep me from stepping into the Turners' hedge. He might have held my hand. If I had reached out for his, he would have held mine for a little while.

At Gruver Street we turned around to walk on the other side of West Street, and we passed Mrs. Barker's, who was a certified clown. She had bright orange brick trim around her yard. On her mailbox was the glow-in-the-dark orange name GOLLY. Mom had said to be especially good to her because she was alone in this world. And look what can happen, she added.

When you collected for the paper, Mrs. Barker would give you candy circus peanuts, then make both her hands into puckered mouths which would politely say, "Thank you!" and "Oh, dearie, thank you so *very* much." She was not old. She was probably my parents' age. In 1969 after his tour of duty, my brother Anthony moved back to my parents' neighborhood. He told me he wasn't surprised to find Golly still there. The Dursis, the Turners, Meadlos, Huttos, Sledges, Mitchells, Parrujos, all still there.

"Charley horses better?" my father asked.

"Plenty," I said. "Pretty good."

I felt bad about what I was doing. Back in my room, Ben was having real charley horses and real nightmares, and here I was pretending I had his problems. I wanted to get back to the house. "I'm kinda cold," I said.

"All right. It *is* cold, ain't it?" We crossed the street, headed back toward our house, but he stopped at the Medinas' driveway. He said, "Watch." He blew his breath into his hands, closed them, and then leaned down to let the white breath out in front of me. I tried, but couldn't do the same thing. Bending to a catcher's crouch, he pushed his cap up high on his forehead. This time, after he blew into his hands, he pitched his breath out of his hairy fists.

"Neat," I said. I had believed I saw something where there had really been nothing.

Like almost all the houses on our block, the Medinas' was a rosy pink adobe over cinderblock. I think that sometime or other people must have felt pink color brought warmth to the neighborhood; and, after that, making or keeping your house pink was a way of showing you wanted some permanence and commitment, you needed acceptance.

Even the big Rado house was stained in rosiness. "That's my boss's house," he said, as if I hadn't heard him ever mention it before. Rado & Sons was the brick company my father worked for. If you ever asked him what his job there was, he'd say, "Monkey," bending forward, doing a spooky monkey grin. "I'm a monkey." We kept walking right past the bright, dark windowpanes where our reflections were silvery traces.

The Rados had tree experts prune their poplars front and back each fall. Just about the whole neighborhood turned out to watch the three experts, who wore identical gray work jumpers, and who earned twenty-five dollars each. We knew what the cost was because every year somebody asked them what the job was worth. Their billcaps had Tree Team Co., Unit 4 printed on them, which to me meant they were a big operation, taking care of all the Rados everywhere.

When we got to the front porch of our house, I was anxious to see Ben. He was going to be mad at me, I figured, for getting something from my father that my father just never offered. His time, I mean.

Inside, he took off his cap. His whole face was pale from the chill. The brick grit under the skin of his forehead was darker against that paleness. "Little Peg," he said, "sit down and let me rub those charley horses out."

I started to admit to him that I had lied about the pain. *They're Ben's leg cramps. Ben's got them real bad.* But I said, "Nope. No. I'm—the walk did it for me."

He didn't offer again. He took my hand, closing all my fingers, my thumb and wrist too, inside his palm. With his other hand he shifted his boxer shorts around his waist. His head moved only slightly left and right, as if he was saying no to himself about something known only to him. I wondered what it was.

No. I should do more for her. Or, *No. I bet she's lying about the leg cramps.* Or, *What am I doing walking my neighborhood in my damn boxer shorts?*

He asked, "You need anything?"

"Nah," I said. His eyebrows were bushy and tangled-up curly. "Thanks for the walk." Around my mouth and in my toes and fingers I was beginning to thaw.

"Bear down. They really hurt awful. They hurt. But they go away."

"Yessir," I said, kind of talking to his gut instead of him.

"Walk 'em off." He put his Cards cap on me. "Lookit," he said, to show me how the cap came down over my ears and almost covered my eyes.

"Yeah." We both were happy about it.

That was that, except for him asking me, "What day's today?"

"Thursday. Friday. Thursday, I think."

"Good night," he said, already in his and Mom's bedroom before I could say, "No. It's Friday."

In our room, Ben was sitting up, bumping his raised knees together so they made a fist-and-mitt-smacking sound. He didn't act mad, which made me feel even worse. He asked, "So?"

"We walked all around."

"Huh?"

"We walked all over."

Ben's head moved that same way my father's head had, answering *No* in some deep cavern of him where I could not go. Everything went quiet between us. Inside my own silence, I made up what happened next.

Ben asked, "He gave you his cap?"

I said, "Yeah. But, look—here, you take it."

He put it on his head. "Hey, thanks," he said. Everything was okay. Inside me, I pretended that he said, "You're all right, Peg."

"I'll tell you what," I offered. "You ever seen him out of his shirt?" Then I told about his big stomach, the black hairs there, like metal shavings arcing over a magnet.

But it was all just pretending, because Ben and I didn't really say a thing. I fell asleep with my father's cap still on my head.

The End

> The village we went into was a permanent-type village. It had hard walls, tile roofs, hard floors and furniture. The people really had no place to go. The village is about all they have. So they stay and take whatever comes.
>
> Sgt. Michael A. Bernhardt, My Lai trial, 1969

By seven o'clock that evening Molly and I had walked around the old downtown area and through the barrio before circling back to the six blocks of the El Paseo strip to look for Francis. We started at the Circle K on Boutz Street and walked north to the Sonic and two auto parts stores parked next to each other, then to the Thrifty and other shops in the Brazito Plaza. It was cold outside the shops, so we went into and through each one.

At the edge of the plaza an abandoned Hardee's was being remodeled. Light filtered through the scratches in the black-washed windows so that the building resembled the dagger boxes magicians use to pretend murder. I stood inside the yellow lines of a parking space and howled, "Francis! Francis!" I didn't really believe she was inside, but I had needed to shout for the last two and a half hours of walking.

I was gratified when Molly joined me, staked out her own parking space, and hollered. No one came out. We hollered louder.

She said, "Dad would freak, if he heard us."

"Truer words were never spoken," I said.

"He's got like a low freak threshold." In just that way, Molly had always tried to educate me about her father. When she was ten or eleven, one day she asked me whether I knew that he liked flower gardens. No, I answered, I hadn't known. "I teach," I said. "I have nothing against gardening. But I teach."

Insuppressible, she said, "He likes geraniums."

"Well?" I asked.

"Francis isn't in there, Mom." She led me to the Jerry's 24 Hour Restaurant, where she could call Peter and we could warm up. After her phone call, she scooted next to me in the booth.

"So," I asked, "Peter all right?"

"Yep."

"Ready for your date?"

"Nope."

Our hot chocolate came. I admired her orange vinyl miniskirt worn over startling nylon neon-blue bicycle pants. Her preppy navy sweaterjacket had a homedrawn glitter peace symbol on the back, and I was glad to see that come back in style. "What kind of car does Peter have?"

"His mom's. Sixty-nine Lincoln Continental."

"Oh God," I muttered, "Holy Mother, a Lincoln. With a queen-size backseat."

We both laughed. She said, "Intimate. But roomy."

"Okay, Molly. I like to joke. But let's stop, okay? I don't like you parking with him."

"Mom." She put her coffee cup in the center of the dish. "It isn't something that's up to you."

"Well. I guess so. But it should be."

"Well," she mimicked. "I'm seventeen. In half a year I'm going to college and you have to show some trust."

We both drank hot chocolate and watched each other. Her lovely auburn hair was in an unmoussed, unterrorized simple jaw-length straight cut. "You," I said. "You have a clever way of being a maternal daughter."

"Sorry. But you ought to trust me by now."

"Why? Because you're seventeen? Listen, Molly, by now I

ought to know what I ought and ought not to feel about how I am or I could—or when— You know what I mean."

"You don't trust me. That's what you mean."

That was it in a nutshell. I said, "Okay. I don't trust you. You're seventeen and I don't—for this one thing with Peter and his Lincoln and your body and his—trust you."

"Too effing bad."

"I hate that."

"Huh?"

"Cussing. I never taught you that. James never taught you that either."

She grinned at my lie.

"Smart aleck."

"Come on, Mom. He's picking me up here. Chill out."

I was thoroughly unchilled out. I said, "He's changing into fresh underwear about now. He's clipping his nose hairs. He's putting his mom's cologne on his pits." I could actually picture Peter doing all this. I remembered his journal entry about his fist. "He can't get the part in his hair right. He's decided on another pair of underwear."

"Gross."

"I'll say." An important question occurred to me. "Is he uncircumcised? You'll have to—"

"Mom."

"Badly circumcised? Does he know how to use a condom? Do you know how to use it? Have you bought some?"

"I'm on the pill, remember?"

I had helped with that, against James's will.

"There he is." She stood up and leaned over me. "I already told you. We're not. We won't."

"You sure?"

When he walked to our table I said hello to him. I used my classroom voice, but it didn't faze him.

"Good evening, Mrs. O. Hi, Molly." He had chapstick on his lips. He smelled French. He held my hand too long when he shook it. And what was he doing, shaking my hand?

I said, "You two have a nice evening."

"Are you going home?" Molly asked.

"No. I have to find Francis. Don't worry."

She hugged me. "Be careful," she said, as if I were the one going out with Mr. Concrete Fist. Clever girl.

When I telephoned Everview, the receptionist Marva said, "Everybody's acting like it's okay, you know, like she will wander home."

"Right," I said. "Like a stray dog."

"What do you think?" I asked.

"I don't know like what, Peg." Marva ate a whole lot of Seconal. She had walked untethered in deepest inner space beyond the flimsy craft of family and home and the simple divisions of time into sleeping and waking and working. On Seconal she had seen the tiny blue aborted earth from distances NASA wouldn't know how to calculate. She was a good person to ask about the future.

"What do I think?" she asked. "I, you know, I think—I don't know—but I think you can see this, see Francis out there. Oh, Peg—you can see her out there somewhere where cars are going too fast and she's waving to the little children in the cars. You seen her do that? And, you know, you know, she leans too far. You know that. She never stays on the curb."

I said, "I'm going to find her, Marva. Count on it. Have they telephoned the police?"

"Oh yes," she said. "And I've got messages for you. Paula Henry called—you're supposed to call her back right away."

"Home or office?"

"Office," Marva said. "And the bus lady called. You have to talk to her. She says it's urgent."

I said, "Marva, I'm going to telephone you when I find Francis." When I asked her to give me her home phone number, her faint giggle was spooky.

"I live at Neverview, you know," she said. "You didn't know?"

I thought she only worked at the place, that she had graduated: Neverview to Everview, Everview to Mr. James's Neighborhood. Like me. After we hung up, I telephoned the bus lady, who said she would meet me at Jerry's Restaurant, where I was calling from.

She wore black high-top tennis shoes and some kind of sweat suit, I think it was a softball uniform, with lettering on the shirt: Shickkitters. Without saying hello, she took my wrists in a firm grip. "You're hunting for Francis?" she said.

I explained where I had gone with Molly, and admitted we hadn't turned up a clue. "Do you know something I don't?"

She rocked my arms forward. "Peg, nobody's going to tell you this, so I am." We moved onto the little padded bench in the lobby of the restaurant, and she smoothly sat us both down, our knees pointing at each other, her hands releasing me. She said, "Francis has got a few dozen bottles of meds with her. Her boyfriend, what's-his-name—"

"Larry."

"Larry. She must have stolen some of his tools to break into the pharmacy. And she's got plenty. Enough." She touched my knees with her fingers and knees, looking at her own strong hands, and not looking up. "You know what I mean?"

I said, "I have to call Paula Analyst."

"At home?" she asked.

"No."

"It's ten at night. She won't be in her office."

"Right," I said. I had hardly been aware it was already evening.

After the bus lady left I walked to James's house. I always called it James's house, though it was my house too. When I was not living at Everview I lived there, slept there, showered and shaved my legs there. I had closet space, drawer space, cabinet space, kitchen and counter space. And yet I knocked at my own door before I entered. As always, I asked myself, "Who is it?"

My fingers gouging the eyes of James's brass tiger's head doorknock, I thought of the bus lady. She could always hold her mouth closed when she listened. She listened only once to what you said. And she heard.

James was not, of course, surprised to see me. "It's you all right," he said. He held the door open, looked closer at me, and stepped aside. His perfectly shaved face and calm expression mediated whatever vulnerability we might have shared.

"Look at you," I said.

"Yeah?"

"Never mind."

To tease, he backed away from me and put up his fists. He stuck his jaw out and said, "If you really connect, it'll be awkward for you to ask me to go look for Francis, won't it?"

"How'd you—"

"Mrs. Libby called." He lowered his fists.

"And who—" But I already remembered her whole nametag all at once. Libby Lawrence. "The bus lady."

"Yeah. Urgent, she said."

"I've already talked to her." I told him about Francis and the medicines she had stolen. "Please, help me find her."

"You've called the police?" When I nodded, he said, "They'll find her."

"Please, James." I stood closer so he would look at me. "Please?" No compassion surfaced in his eyes.

"Okay," he answered, so flatly that I guess I didn't really hear him.

"James," I said, "I'm asking you." They weren't my words, but I owned them as surely as a wedding band or bed or credit debt is mutually owned in marriage. All James's first letters from Vietnam were sounded in me by those three words. From memory, I knew the three to add: "I'm asking you *this one favor*."

"Okay," he said. "Give me a minute to get ready." I followed him to the bedroom, where he stripped off his robe and dressed in his white work uniform. He said he would take the Mr. Vendor truck and look for Francis until his shift started at four-thirty in the morning. He said I could take the Nova so we could split up two wide areas east and west of Espina.

When he handed me the keys to the Nova, the bitterness was lost in me every bit as suddenly as it had possessed me. Like a murderous nurse wounding and then bandaging the same man, I asked, "Can we hug?"

"Hug?" he asked. Standing very close to him, I dropped my shoulders forward to imitate his amazement. "Okay," he said. "Sure."

I held him and felt his hands on my back, his fingers spreading over my shoulder blades. "We don't have to be enemies, do we?" I asked. "This is a good thing you're doing for me. It counts. I won't forget it."

In the driveway, he went over our plan. He would take her to Everview if he found her; I should do the same. We should each call Everview periodically to check; no sense in trying to find each other. He reviewed our designated areas again, making sure I had it clear, saying, "Let's not overlap our areas. You take east. I'll take west of Espina."

I straightened the crisp collar of his white uniform. "Thank you," I said. "I won't forget."

I revved up the Nova, and sat still inside the increasing roar, watching James drive away. My assigned area began at Telshor, a street parallel to Espina but about twenty blocks east of it; I was supposed to work my way west from there; on his side of Espina, James's strategy would be the converse. This is how seriously I took my assignment: though I thought a cup of coffee might refresh me, I worried about crossing one block west of Espina to get a cup at the Circle K on Espina and Boutz. I finally couldn't think of where a Circle K might be in my own designated area, so I drove the one block. I accelerated right past it when I saw the Mr. Vendor truck already parked there. I figured I would wait until James left to pull in, so he wouldn't catch me overlapping his area even for a second.

I saw him come out with a large mug of coffee. He backed the van up. Instead of pulling onto Boutz or Espina, he drove into the narrow alley between the Circle K and Gino's Pizza & Subs. He turned the van off, and he stayed there. Fifteen minutes later he slowly drove out of the alley and onto the street.

I stayed for a long time where I was parked before driving by James's house to see about my hunch. His van was in the driveway. The lights in the house were turned out.

An hour before sunrise, I telephoned Anthony. "Look," I said, "maybe you can't—won't—do this. I need your help." I explained how Francis had been missing overnight from Everview.

"Well," he said. "You need me then." I knew that was his way of acknowledging that I was truly desperate or I would have called absolutely anyone but him.

When I picked him up in the Nova, he leaned forward in the seat and turned his head to look at me straight on. He said, "You still need me?"

"I already said I did, Anthony."

He stopped grinning. "That's something brand-new."

"So?" I asked. "Where are we going?"

"Your neighborhood. Circle it."

I told him I had common sense enough to have already done that.

"Circle it," he said. "Start about ten blocks away—on Lohman, west to Main, Main south to University, University east to Locust, and north to Lohman. Then circle in closer to yours and James's place. A little at a time."

"It's James's place, not mine."

Anthony snapped in his seat belt. "You're moving out again, huh?" I could tell he answered himself yes; he fell silent. Hunched down in the car seat, he stared out the window, already sure he could see what I could not. Ironically, when he looked straight at me it was as if he was still only trying to look through so many closed doors. I think that had something to do with his six-foot-four height, the solidness of his upper body, his large dark eyes and wide forehead that, all together, made him seem both physically and emotionally distant.

For sixty days of his duty in Vietnam he was a mole; his job was to enter one of the thousands of Vietcong tunnels and abort it. He was supposed to avoid the booby traps inside and the enemy as he encountered him. Or her. He went only a few yards inside sometimes, but other times he crawled very deep to set explosives in place, then retreat from the mazes.

I know what he did because he wrote my parents about his duties there, and my mother shared the letters with me. Neither he nor my father has ever once spoken to me about their wartime experiences. So, I have had to imagine how Anthony has been changed by crawling himself through that darkness and sealing shut the exit and the entrance to things that might have hurt him once and that could again.

"Molly and I walked over all this a few hours ago," I said. "What's your strategy?"

He asked, "Where have you looked exactly?"

When I explained how we checked inside neighborhood backyards, the Brazito Plaza, the Albertson's superstore, and other places, he said, "She won't be inside a building. She'll be outside somewhere. Look for a place outside where she can see but not be seen. Drive slower. And turn your brights off."

At Main and University avenues we circled over and over again into the shadows under the I-10 overpass. To the east a few blocks, the Dairy Queen at the University Plaza had a good view of much of the valley. He said, "This is too far from James's house—or the Everview place. It's worth a try, but it's too far." As we pulled back onto University Avenue, he said, "Come on. Don't look that way, Peg. Trust me."

It was one of the few times in my life he had not called me *Little* Peg. "I do. I trust you, Anthony."

"Good." He nervously laughed. "This is all scary, I know. But I like it. I know what I'm doing, and I like that."

"Right."

"I can't explain to you," he said. "All this—you don't know about perimeters—I know about them. If Francis was running away that's one thing, but if she's hiding that's another. Something about people hiding: if they can, they always hide within view of their own perimeters." He unsnapped his seat belt and turned his body toward me in the seat. "That way you can always kind of spy on yourself—on where you might be if you were still safe." We drove quietly for half an hour up and back on a two-mile strip of Lohman Avenue.

At the Pep Boys Supply on Solano and Lohman, he said, "Hey there, Mannie, Moe, and Jack." We waved at the giant fiberglass boys standing in their work clothes, looking astonished at the world's inexhaustible auto supply needs. By now, Anthony's concentration was diluted. He seemed to be watching me, trying to find *me*.

"Peg," he said. "We're closer. I can feel it."

"Where to?" I asked.

"Keep circling in toward James's neighborhood. Take the next left on Espina."

"Yes sir." I saluted.

"Okay," Anthony said, saluting back at me. I asked him to drive past James's house. The van was still parked there. What James had done was a kind of desertion. And desertion was a choice of survival, after all. Leaving someone like Francis under fire in order to let yourself live: I could understand that.

Anthony said, "In Nam. In Nam— Is it all right? Can I talk about it?" He waited for me to nod yes. "I figure the guys who we lost on perimeter watch were guys who looked in, not out. Hugged the edge too tight. In my platoon if you got wasted that way we called it 'getting salted.' Like Sodom and Gomorrah. Biblical justice."

"God," I said.

I pulled into a Circle K on Espina so I could buy us each a candy bar. We pulled back onto Espina and went south.

He put his candy bar on the car dash. He said, "The thing is, you'd be safer if you'd patrol beyond camp perimeters. It makes sense to put yourself on the one-point ring instead of the twenty-point ring of a dart board."

"Don't I know it," I said. "I'm going to eat your candy bar if you don't."

He unwrapped it for me and handed it to me in sections as he tried to explain better. "Night's the best time for us to look. You know: the unconscious part of you sees farther in the dark."

We drove up and back on Espina, which goes slightly uphill as you drive north. From Espina and Mesquite we could see down several streets and alleys. It was almost 6 A.M. when we reconnoitered Boutz Street.

At the corner of Almendra and Boutz we saw the parked truck of the box man, *hombre de cartones*. Anthony said, "Go a block up. Pull over." The very moment I pulled over, I saw her. She was sitting atop the precarious high peak of folded cardboard in the box man's truck. Her best white Western blouse with the black pocket stitching was the kind of rayon that almost glowed in the dark. She had turned up her collar, but she had no sweater or jacket.

Anthony said, "Target practice."

I didn't have any idea what he meant. Then I saw that she was taking pills and capsules from an open bottle and throwing them. The alley where it all landed was already littered with hundreds more and with broken syrup bottles and crunched paper medicine packets. I started to get out of the car.

"Wait a second," Anthony said.

"Why?"

"Let her show us if it's all right to approach. Keep your lights on."

She didn't give us a signal. The moonlight silvered the white woman's down at her jaws and her silver pageboy-cut hair, but her nose looked more punished and vulnerable than ever.

More pills rained. Two or three small plastic bottles. Finally, I drove next to the box man's truck. Anthony pointed his hand

and whole arm out the open car window as if he were pointing a rifle at Francis. "Pow," he whispered. Recoiling from his own strangeness, he called out to her, "We're friends, Francis."

She climbed down immediately but calmly, as if all along she expected I would find her at just this time and place. "I'm sleepy," she said, "I'm too sleepy. Don't make me talk, okay? I can't do it."

By the time Anthony drove us to his house in my parents' old neighborhood, she was asleep and we had to wake her up to get her inside. I called Everview to report that we had found her.

Marva sounded unconvinced until I told how and where. She said, "I asked God all night, you know. You know, I just asked, 'Don't let this happen.' But I didn't believe. And I was wrong, wasn't I?"

"You were wrong," I said.

"And that's good, isn't it?"

"It's great, Marva. We're at my brother's house for now. Call Paula and tell her. Let everybody else know." We said goodbye.

It was the first time I had been in Anthony's home in over fifteen years. I sized it up: heavy glass end tables, a glass dining room table, and etched glass stereo cabinet; the kind of clean-to-the-creases cleanness in the drapes and covered furniture that a housemaid would have to do for him.

Francis slept on one of his soft, deep sofas. Her legs were indecently splayed wide, her hands rested low on her stomach. And she snored. I lay on the floor near her. I heard Anthony rummaging in the kitchen and refrigerator, probably checking to see what he would offer us for breakfast before he went to work in the morning.

The trade his service experience had so wonderfully prepared him for was to be a hod carrier. In the eighties few people in the Southwest built with adobe; almost everything new was brick. Between injuries, he made good money.

"You live real nice," I offered.

"I'm safe," he said. It sounded as if he set a bowl or pitcher down on the glass dining room table. Then I thought I heard him breathe differently, as though he didn't want to be heard breathing.

I could tell what he was doing now. He was setting the table for the three of us. "Peg," he said, "thanks for calling me. I know you think I'm an asshole. I *am* an asshole." The silverware rattled in his hands, as if he was pointing the fistful of forks and knives at me. "You're an asshole too."

"Anthony," I said, "why aren't we more compatible then?"

We laughed. I didn't move from where I lay. I heard him sit down at the table, and I believe I heard his chair give a little, and I imagine that his head was resting on his folded arms as he wept.

Why didn't I go to him and hold him? Because I know that he did not want that. He wanted to cry. He wanted me to hear him cry. No embrace we could possibly have offered each other could be as healing as that.

Norm Navares
976 B. Milton
Las Almas, N.M. 88001

Oceans
(Marcella O'Crerieh, 1971)

In New Mexico were deep, wide oceans long ago—
Oceans wide and deep and long across New Mexico.

Marcella and John rose from bed on the first ring of the telephone in the kitchen. 4 A.M. On the evening before, when Peg had gone into labor, Marcella had driven her to the hospital.

She heard John say the baby's name: "Molly Ann." He asked, "You called her husband?" Marcella stood near him, but he pressed the receiver close to his ear. "Molly Ann?" he said into the receiver. "At two-twelve. She's okay? They're both okay, then? *How* much? That's big, right? Yeah? Yeah. You called her husband's people? Good. Nice of you to call us, ma'am. Okay! Tell her at eight. Tell her we love her. Would you do that?"

He hung up. "Went great. Everything went great. Molly Ann!"

"Molly Ann!" she said. "My granddaughter."

"Healthy and all."

She knew he wouldn't have thought to ask about how long Peggy's labor had been. "You said Peggy's all right?"

"Great." He put his left arm over her shoulder and his right hand at her back. "Nine pounds and eight ounces." They box-stepped and pivoted, and she kissed him on his grin.

In bed, he spooned himself around her. "You shouldn't be crying," he said, his forehead nudging her shoulder.

Later, Marcella felt him spread his rough fingers over her neck, trace the top of her ears, and brush through her hair to the back of her head. He cradled her head in his hands as he had done almost every morning for twenty-six years. He whispered, "You okay?" His face and his breath smelled like the moist November farmland in Illinois where she had grown up.

"I should get ready," she said. She broke herself away from him, shed her nightgown, then stepped into the bathroom. Since Ben's death, she used the shower as the only place she could go to cry without John hearing her.

At the dining room table, they sat close, next to instead of across from each other, and finished eating breakfast.

"Great news, huh?" he said. "We should get Little Peg and Molly Ann something. Let's get a toy or something."

She said they could buy sleeper outfits. "And Peg will need blouses if she breast-feeds. We could buy her one or two nice blouses at Penney's tomorrow."

He asked if she wanted her orange juice. When she answered yes, he stole the full glass. "I'll get you some more," he said.

From the kitchen he asked, "Will you be okay at the hospital?" This was like John, to be in another room, staring into the refrigerator, when he asked her something important.

"What kind of question is that?" She gathered her bowl and his, the spoons and glasses and cups, and brought them to the kitchen sink. He was looking at three of the children's preschool drawings, taped onto the refrigerator door during the fifties, and repaired and retaped, but never moved except to be placed on new refrigerators. The children's rooms had eventually become empty "guest rooms," but many of their toys and books and drawings were still everywhere in the house.

The one John seemed to be looking at had dark green crayon figures, the shapes of milk spills, free-floating inside a house under a roof twice its size. There was a Mom germ, a Ben germ, an Anthony germ, a Dad germ, and the biggest germ, the only germ with arms and eyes and a roaring smile: a Peg germ. Marcella watched John bend down, his hands braced on his thighs, his face very close to the drawing. Ben had drawn it when he was four. In 1956. He had gotten his interest in germs from one of the silly swingset songs Marcella had made up for her children.

She would get Ben and Peg swinging out and back on the swingset, her hands clapping, and she would sing, "In Texas they say ma'am and missus / in Texas, out in Texas. / In Tennessee they all drink tea / in Tennessee, in Tennessee." Ben quickly memorized the whole song. He liked it so much he would even show off and sing parts of it for relatives and guests. "In New Jersey gentlemen are germy / everyone's a germy gentleman in Jersey."

"Germs. You gotta wonder," said John. "What was Ben thinking?" He rinsed and dried the plates as she brought them out of the scalding water. He remembered the expectant silence building between Ben and him before Ben left for Vietnam.

John dropped Marcella off at the hospital. He'd see Molly Ann when they brought her home, he said. He couldn't go inside. He must have thought at first that he wanted to, because he had put on a new navy tie and drawn the knot tightly against his throat.

"Kiss that little girl for me, okay? Kiss the both of them." He tugged at his tie but it didn't loosen. "Don't forget your supplies," he said, reaching into the backseat for the sack. His goodbye was the slightest sad nodding of his head.

At the nurse's station, she said, "I'm Peggy Aigley's mother." She held up her paper bag as if it were her ID. The nurse said, "*You're* a grandmother," and that made her less nervous.

Molly Ann was in a bassinet next to Peggy's bed. Peggy was asleep on her back, her bed propped up, her shoulders slumped forward slightly. Tubes were threaded into her arms; her hands were held out, palms up, at her sides. Marcella arranged the sheet, blanket, and comforter in their proper layers and pulled them up to Peggy's waist.

She rested one hand on the bedrail and one on the edge of the bassinet so she could look closer at Molly Ann's bandaged head and left eye. Her closed fists were mittened in her sleeper shirt.

Peggy's skin, which usually seemed suffused in pinkness, was slack now, tender around her eyes and mouth. She was chafed where her chin and the flesh of her neck overlapped; Marcella wished she could wash her with warm water and her own warm, soapy fingers, then rub lotion on her neck.

I'll do that, she thought. *When you're awake.* "You too, Molly Ann," she said. A velvety patch of vernix along the edge of the baby's scalp was the only unscathed part of her face. She must have clawed her mouth and cheeks as Peggy had done in her first few hours of life. Like Peggy's, the outer bones of Molly Ann's eyebrows were bruised by forceps. John had nicknamed Peggy "Champ" when she was an infant because her face looked like a prizefighter's mug for so many days.

Peggy's thick, auburn hair was oily and had been pushed back from her temples, drawn down behind her ears. It needed washing. It should be combed out and brushed. In this room where the morning light was softened by the closed curtains, Marcella could imagine her daughter beginning to heal deep inside, now that she and her husband had a child.

The stuffed chair that she sat in near the bed smelled as if someone had just cleaned it with one of those lemony ammonia formulas. The curtains had the same odor. In her bassinet Molly scratched one side of her face back and forth against the cotton sheet under her, and turned her head to scratch the bandaged side. Quietly whimpering, she tensed her small mouth in determination.

From her paper bag Marcella brought out ribbons for Peggy's hair, a compact, eyeliner, and lipstick, a new belted cotton dress that had been difficult to find in Peggy's size, and some boat shoes, bright white and brand-new. She also brought out the two Minnie Mouse terrycloth jumpers she had gotten for Molly. They could talk about new clothes. *Do you know what this ribbon is called? When you look better, you always feel better, don't you? It's called spidersatin. Feel. Has the nursing staff been good?* She might help Peg put on some makeup. *You really don't need makeup, Peggy. You're one of the lucky ones, don't you know?*

No. Maybe not. Maybe not this visit anyway. They would talk about Molly. How beautiful she was. How proud James was going to be when he came back from Vietnam. *All of us. For all of us, Peggy, it's so wonderful.*

Or. Or it might be a good time for them to talk about her babies' births. Difficult deliveries. Unruly babies for their first months. Peg and Ben, the unruliest. No.

She kissed Peggy's eyelids, as cool as stones under streams. "Dear Peggy," she whispered. She bent over Molly Ann's bassinet to kiss the top of her head and hum into it as she had done with her babies. Molly's small fist hit her square in the jaw.

It was the first thing she told John. "She smacked me!"

"Well," he said, "she's one of ours, all right." They drove around downtown so she could tell him everything. She lied about the physical details.

She cleaned his sunglasses for him, and put them on his face. "Remember Peggy's birth?"

"You bet," he said. "Those were some days, weren't they?"

They were, she thought. They were some days. Why did it take more effort for her to remember them now in the same nostalgic ways he remembered them?

They received a call from Peggy's in-laws. John talked to them. Anthony called to ask if he could bring dinner. He said, "You can tell me all the particulars, Mom."

"You could visit her yourself, don't you know," she said.

"I should. Listen, I know I should."

"You could—"

"Come on. Let me buy some barbecue. Some champagne."

She let it go. "That will make your father happy." They agreed that Anthony would come over around five o'clock so Marcella would have time to visit Peggy again at seven.

John telephoned his father in Nevada to congratulate him on being a great-grandpa. Marcella telegrammed a message to her parents in Illinois. "Start it, 'Mom—Dad,' " she said into the receiver. " 'Her name is Molly Ann! More info soon. Peg fine. All of us better now.' "

On the living room sofa, she and John divided the Sunday morning *Albuquerque Journal* between them. Her loafers pinched her toes, so she slipped them off. She swiveled to tuck her feet under his left leg, and she burrowed each foot deeper under and then between his legs until she could feel the inside of his thighs with her toes. Late morning sun bathed their shoulders. She looked at John, wishing his barber would shave that gray stubble low on his neck.

The Trends section feature was about irises and the New Mexico Iris Society, which was planning The 50,000 Living Flowers Memorial for Flag Day in June. You couldn't put Vietnam out of mind. It was as if you weren't allowed.

The members had selected the irises from their private collections. They had determined how they would synchronize the rhizomes so the plants would all start blossoming within the same three weeks on one hillside near the college campus. In August they would dig them up again and take their own back. Then, each June the same rhizomes would be used again. She wondered if the Iris Society had considered that they would need more irises and more hillside every year the war continued.

"John," she said, but then decided against asking him to tell her. She wanted to know how he felt now; whether he was only pretending outer calmness for her sake. Instead, she asked, "Would you like my section?" and tossed it onto his lap. She poked the paper up with her toes so that he looked as if he was trying to hide some private happiness.

Without meeting her eyes, he smiled, reached under the paper, and held her toes, fisting them like coins in his palm. He continued reading. She thought she felt the muscles in his thighs slightly contract around her ankles and feet. When he finished with the front page section, he handed it to her and took up the Trends section.

"John," she said, "can we?"

The grittiness of the skin on his face made his frown look as though it had been drawn on him with a stick. "Goddamn," he said, "I don't know. I think I want to."

In the bedroom she unzipped him, pulled his pants and boxer shorts down around his ankles, and whispered, "John . . . let me . . . let me put these on a hanger."

"What?" he asked. She hung his pants up.

She unbuttoned each button of his shirt without touching his skin until she reached his heavy belly, on which she drew a rippling circle that soon included his testicles, and then only them. "Hmmm?"

"I don't know," he said.

They both laughed, and she let him undress her, though she retrieved her blouse and slacks to hang them up. She always felt she looked heavy when she was naked. Hefty. Hefty was okay, she thought, as John smoothed the wrinkles of her neck with his hands and brought her into the bed. He shifted himself to his right side; she lay down, their combined weight rocking the bed forward and back, making the broken headboard creak.

She wished her legs were shaved. She wished a filmy, silky something covered her body, which she wished was glowing in youthful, muscled healthiness. But she looked at John's body, almost half the air let out of him, his chest hair coarse and dirty gray, and the thought of them as walruses having splashing, blubber-bumping, buoyant sex was fine to her. More than fine, she thought. Real fine. Her hands smoothed the backs of his rough, hairy legs, smoothed him behind his knees to under his buttocks.

He kissed her hairline, from her forehead to her ears to the back of her neck. He kissed her chin and around but not on her mouth. He asked if she was okay. Then, "You angry?"

She knew he meant to ask whether she had anger left in her about Ben's death. "Yes." What a strange question for him to ask now. But, yes, she had been angry beyond expressible rage. "Oh God, John, you don't know."

"I wish you wouldn't hold back," he whispered.

Right now, she had the chance to be happy and she didn't want him turning her back toward anger. "I want a kiss, John."

"Marcella. We're both angry. I'm—I could kill something."

"I want— "

He barely spoke aloud. "I can't understand."

He moved his head up, and she saw his tears. "No," she whispered. "Here." They kissed for a long time, their hands together near her head while he moved her hips and his so that she could finesse him very near but not inside of her. Her tongue moistened his lips and he kissed her shoulders, breasts, and the insides of her arms until her skin felt the pulsing in his penis and thighs and the tops of his feet. "Marcella," he said, "you can cry. Why are you hiding when you cry?"

She said, "Stop. Don't."

He pressed her against the bed mattress. "Goddammit, what are you thinking?"

She pulled her hands free. "You're cruel. You don't know." She was welcoming him inside her, taking his shoulders and back into her hands, and lifting her body from the mattress. "John, I want it. I couldn't show you. I want it. Deeper."

"I don't know anygoddamnthing. That's how it is." She locked her ankles around his lower back. "Deeper," she said as he pushed her hips back and down with his own, then pressed her against the headboard.

She lowered her ankles and feet so she could jab him with her heels. If she could hurt him, she would.

He muttered, "Come on. Come on!" The headboard made a cracking sound. She rocked with him against it.

"Here!" she cried. "Please!" His cheek scraped her jaw as she ground her left temple against his.

"Can't," he said. "Help me. Come on."

Slowly, she felt a kind of heated stinging move from her face to deep inside her head and then to her stomach and bowels; and the awful stinging became pleasure, and, in an instant, the pleasure rushed outward through her body. "You'll break the bed," she said, "do you want—what? What do you want—do you want to break it?"

He said, "I'm *trying*!"

The laughter lasted through most of the crying. Afterward, she could not remember that they had wanted anything more than only to cry together.

"He didn't know me," John said. "I think—I thought being his dad was a job or something. That's what Ben saw. Me doing my goddamn job."

"You stupid man." She tucked his head between her own head and shoulder. "You're a stupid man."

"I thought my job, you know, was to know *him*."

She believed him. Hadn't they both thought that? How had they loved their children so unconditionally, and still loved them wrongly? Through all those years of marriage they had never confessed one deeply private grief or admitted even one profound confusion about themselves to Anthony or Peggy and Ben. Since when was that part of the job of a parent?

And Ben. As a teenager, how many times had he asked to be told about the Second World War? Was Dad ever afraid of being a coward? Did you have to plan for Dad dying? When he lived, did you have to change plans? Then, when Ben would not ask anymore, in how many ways did he show that he wanted and needed to know?

John trembled as he curled against her. If they were not lying on top of the bedclothes, Marcella would have covered them both. Instead, she reached behind her to open the window blinds at the head of the bed. If someone looked in? Let them look. The sun felt especially good on her calves and the bottoms of her feet. Two old, sweaty walruses, out of the water again, sunning themselves.

Later, she woke at the sound of the headboard quietly cracking, like a small, dry bone. The bed collapsed to the floor. She was not surprised he slept through the crash, but she woke him up, kissed his sticky lips, and said, "Congratulations!"

Their feet were slightly uphill. His eyes opened, but he closed them against the glare of the afternoon light. "I did it, didn't I?" he said. "Broke it." His eyes were still shut.

When Anthony arrived with the barbecue and the champagne, he was in a hurry to hear about Peggy and Molly Ann. She put paper plates and napkins in his hands and silverware in John's so they could set the table as they talked.

John was enthusiastic. "Two-twelve in the morning. A big baby." He remembered her weight and length exactly. "Perfect health, too."

Anthony asked, "What about Little Peg?"

"She's good. She did great."

"Well," Marcella said, "she's going to be okay, that's the important thing. John, look where you've put the forks."

He looked, without comprehending. "We can see Molly Ann after dinner. We'll all go see her, okay?"

"And we'll visit Peggy," she said. "Forks go on the left; knives on the right."

He stared at the arrangement. "Right." He picked up a fork, apparently forgetting what he meant to do. She guessed he was thinking about Peggy, and knew he must be afraid of seeing her.

Anthony said, "I got the baby a squeeze toy. It looks like a hot dog in a bun. Pretty stupid—but it should make her laugh, huh?"

John put the fork back where it had been. "You know what goes good with barbecue? I'm going to run to Albertson's to get that three-for-fifty-cents fresh bread." He must have seen she was going to ask him not to go. "Only six blocks away," he said. "I'll take Anthony's car. It's out on the curb."

Anthony tossed him the keys. "The gas gauge is screwy. Don't pay any attention to it."

"Got it." He was out the front door, and gone.

"Is he all right?" Anthony asked. He sat at the kitchen table and pulled himself up to it as if ready to eat.

"Would you fix those forks?"

"He's not okay."

"I'll fix them," she said.

"He's not."

She remembered that John once wore a close-trimmed moustache like Anthony's. His face, his pale, unwrinkled complexion had been much the same. "We've had a strange day," she said.

"A fight?"

She put the forks in the right places. "I think we're both excited about everything—with Peggy and the baby and everything."

"Me too," he said.

She sat at the table across from him. She pulled in her chair and looked at Anthony's hands. When her children were born, their tiny, vulnerable hands had enthralled her. "I'm going to tell you something, Anthony. When you go to see Peggy and the baby—they're both beaten up. You don't know. Men don't know about birth. It's violent. Lamaze and all the Lamazers say it's beautiful, it's natural. It's 'a passage.' You see them say that on television. Okay. If that's what you believe, all right." In the mirror above the delivery table she had seen her blood on their shoulders, slick on their soft, unclosed skulls. At birth, Peggy's hands had clutched crusty scabs where she dug her sharp nails into her own palms while still in the womb. Ben's right clavicle had to be broken to bring his broad shoulders out, and it was set by the doctor in her view. She saw the doctor's thumbs and fingers whiten as he forced the bones. She had been given medication but could barely stand the icy gauze pad with which the nurse had compressed the long incision from vagina to perineum.

"Some women have easy labor. They do all the talking for the ones who don't." Her tears surprised and shamed her. "The baby has to shed you like you're dead skin. That's the 'passage' baby and mother go through." She was thankful when she felt his hands close over hers. "I love you, Anthony. But I never said things I needed to. You never—how old are you?—you never ask me about *me.*" She somehow could not see him and could not hear what he was saying, if he was saying anything at all to her through her tears.

All at once, he took his hands away and stood up.

At the front door, John was saying, "I don't have the bread. You can't believe it. I went into the store and drew a blank. I walked up and down the aisles, right past the bread, but I couldn't remember."

After he washed up and joined them at the table, he said, "You know how it works. You pull up into the driveway and you still don't know. You get to your own front door. And—boom!—you know! Bread!"

"Who needs it?" said Anthony. He didn't look at either of them.

She served the meal. She made a ceremony of opening the champagne and pouring it. John said grace, adding, for the joke, that he was glad to God for helping him find his way home. He had frightened himself in the grocery store. He wanted them to know. "I bet if I went back for it right now I'd forget all over again."

Anthony lifted his glass and slightly tilted it toward her. He said, "Things really have gone to hell, haven't they?"

He had been her first baby, a son. Thirty-four days before this day, before Ben's death, she had had two sons.

"So," he said. "A toast."

The End

If I had been on target with Paula Analyst's phase advance program, I would have gone to bed at 7 P.M. and woken up at 5 A.M. I woke up at 8 A.M. I found my pill box. Tupperware. I took a lithium tablet, one-fourth the dose I had been taking in the early fall. Two days earlier I had taken my last Prolixin capsule, ever. The damage the drug had done to me and the damage I had done to myself by stepping down off it were in precarious balance. I will take the lithium in low dosage all my life, I guess.

Francis was handwriting a long letter at Anthony's kitchen table.

"You need your typewriter at Everview," I said.

She didn't look up. "Good morning."

"He's gone?"

She finished the sentence she was writing. "He made me breakfast. He talked with me. He's a nervous kind, isn't he?"

"I think he means well, Francis."

She said she couldn't talk yet, she had to finish. All over her rumpled clothes and in her sleep-tangled silver hair was brown cardboard lint. Some of the lint clung to the corners of her eyes. She looked like a person just unpacked from a long stay inside one box. She looked like a gift.

When she put her pen down she asked, "Where will I go?"

"You'll have to go back," I said. "To Everview."

"Today?"

We both tried, but could not avoid each other's eyes. "I'll have an extra room for you at my new place," I said. "Help me move in, and I'll show it to you."

"Then I can wait until tonight to go back?"

"Francis."

"Tonight?"

"One thing," I said. "There is the matter of all the medicines you've destroyed. I've got a feeling Marva's going to try to run interference for you about that."

"God help me," she said.

When she stood to hug me, I said, "You're going to get that lint all over me."

"Yes, I am." I felt her holding me very close before I ever stepped into her arms.

PART THREE

Stick

"I esteem [a woman's hand] not because it gleams,
but because it grasps."

Sor Juana Ines de la Cruz

1 · *Ladders*

(DECEMBER 1988)

Before I delivered Francis to her room at Everview, we bought onion rings. Francis and I call onion rings "the O food." Naming and renaming was a simple important juvenile pleasure in our adult friendship. Frances was Francis. Paula Henry was Paula Analyst. Any occasion for celebration was a "holy day" and every holy day naturally called for onion rings. Onion rings are, in fact, one reason I have never been mystified by the physical similarity of friends, spouses, lovers, any cellmates locked in horrible or happy prolonged cohabitation. The same diet, the same furniture, the same bathroom and shower fixtures, the same surfaces under our feet and the sounds through the same bright-white plaster walls, the seasonal rhythms of natural light, all the shared mundanities lathe us as if we were the supplest tulipwood.

We were halfway through the third order of rings. We had already agreed, again, that The Golden Bull Restaurant on Solano was the only good place to buy the O food. We debated both the matter of salt and the matter of ketchup. We agreed that only yuppies put ranch dressing on onion rings.

People starved of ritual and myth might say this seventeen-year routine was pointless. Sometimes, we ourselves wondered.

But then Francis said, "I'm better now, Peg." Her cheeks were greasy and her smile shining.

"You are *so* fine," I said. "Have I ever told you that?"

"Nope," she said. "Really. Never once." Her oily face defied contradiction. "Will you take some of my things with you for the apartment? You know: insurance."

After we filled a Hefty bag with some of her Everview life, I asked Francis if she would read Tim Hutto's story, "The Cartographer." She took it from me and curled over it at once like a storybook character disappearing into a mirror. I left her alone in the room and visited Marva.

When I returned, Francis said, "I finished. I don't remember Hutto. Which one was he?"

I explained that he was one of The Invisible. "So," I asked, "what do you think of 'The Cartographer'?"

"Pretty good typing. Good writing."

"Real good. He's plagiarized 'Bartleby the Scrivener.' " She wouldn't believe me. I said, "Herman Melville wrote it."

"My." She had rolled the pages up in her hand. She unrolled them and leafed through the story. "The same thing happens over and over."

"Masterful."

"If you say so." Probably worried that she had hurt my feelings, she said, "You must feel good when one of them writes so nice."

"I would," I said, "I would feel great." In fact, the typing was excellent. Professional.

"But you're going to write your own?"

"Naturally." I told her about "In Your Hands," the story I had written to replace Hutto's story.

She frowned. "What I want to know is if you're going to tell Hutto he has plagiarized."

"Hmmm," I said. I hadn't thought of that.

Timothy Hutto
1212 Nashua
Las Almas, N.M. 88001

In Your Hands
(John O'Crerieh, 1971)

Up and down the aisles I talked to myself, trying to remember. *Pampers, thirty to a carton, a dollar sixty-eight,* my wife's voice inside me said. *Don't get the wrong kind.*

I wobbled the grocery cart past Dairy Goods and stood there under a big ceiling fan where I could think of things one at a time and not complicate them with everything else. *Infant Size. Pampers.* Truth is, I was afraid to go visit my daughter and new granddaughter in the hospital, so I was dragging my feet in the store.

I didn't have one good reason. So much had happened. I'd given up thinking you could explain any of it with one good reason.

She might want some Twinkies or cookies or something, I thought. I looked at the windmills and wafers she liked, but none of them looked right. *Thirty to a carton.* Thirty diapers? I had asked my wife about that, because it seemed like a lot of diapers. How many times did we change ours when they were babies? "Sixty or seventy times a week," she said. That was amazing to me. She asked, "Didn't you ever change a diaper, John?" We had had three children. Of course I changed some diapers. It just wasn't a regular part of my orders in our household. That isn't how things worked for Marcella and me.

I stood in front of the Pampers and I went over everything again. *Buck sixty-eight, all right. Thirty.* The fan overhead made a whumping noise. You think you move free through the air until you hear one of those fans working so hard to slice it up.

Before I came into the store, I had used the pay phone outside to talk to the National Cemetery System. A woman had to connect me to another woman who had to connect me to another woman who was Keeper of the Questions. Branch of service, term of service, disposition of the body? A long list. I'll say this, the woman was a real soldier in the way she asked her questions. If you have to make a call like this you'll see how kindness or meanness comes out in a single plain word. The woman said, "Sir." She waited for me to say, "Yes?" before she said, "We have been asked to tell people this." The goddamnest thing. "The national cemeteries are overfilled. We're having to close some of them down." She was real apologetic about it all. It's too much to believe. You crack up inside, I tell you. It's one of those things where you crack up, but it comes out sounding, even to you, like you're laughing. I told her I didn't believe her, that I wanted to talk to somebody else. She said, "I am sorry, sir."

I am sorry, sir. She could have been a tape recording, for all I knew. Trying to explain better, she read off some more bullshit.

"Okay," I said, which only made her get more technical. I looked out over the Albertson's parking lot while she did her spiel. In a corner of the lot, two fellows in sloppy aprons were roasting green chiles in a metal basket contraption revolving over jets of flame. The chiles burst open, spilling seeds out of the basket and exploding that odd chile sweetness into the air, a green sap and old car muffler smell.

The woman wanted me to know about the two-hundred-and-fifty-dollar statutory burial allowance my son Ben was entitled to. Could she take more information from me?

Back inside the store, my wife's voice circled after the VA lady's voice: *Don't get the wrong kind. We have been asked.* Sixty or seventy times a week my wife changed his diaper when Ben was a baby. And before that, Little Peg's diapers. And before that, Anthony's. That was how we divvied up men's work and women's work. Little Peg, who got so liberated and so well educated, hassled me about that. My job, the man's job, was to pinch-hit sometimes. I could do that. I changed some diapers. But I had a job description of my own. I helped them ride the bicycle without training wheels, and I kept them in line at church. Any time we were out in public, Marcella wanted me to be chief of children police. I spanked them. Whether it was her idea or mine at the time, I did that. It was also my job to—this was clear as day, I tell you—to stand at a public phone so my wife wouldn't have to hear, so she wouldn't have to listen to me ask for a hole in the ground to bury Ben. *I am sorry, sir.* I told the lady that they could take the two hundred and fifty bucks—you can imagine what I told her they could do with it. Then I cried some. I put my head against the wall beside the phone. All those questions hissed in me like the furnaces hissed in the brick factory where I worked. Maybe I did cry for Ben or for my family. Or from self-pity. From shame and anger. Not from any other one thing.

In the Candy, Nuts, Baby Supplies aisle, I tried to lean down for the diapers and blood rushed to my head. I could feel that fan bear down on me, hovering, lower and louder. It pushed me down on my knees. I couldn't right myself. I was drowning.

Some guy had to help me up. I don't think I said thanks to him even. He had to stand me up and hold me still until I found my legs.

I put the diapers in the cart. I went to the rear of the store to drink some water. I found cupcakes, the devil's food kind, for my daughter. At the checkout line, waiting to buy the diapers and cupcakes, I looked at the headlines. Hank Aaron had hit his 600th homer. Manson. In the framed "Item" next to that, a handful of sentences—right in your face—about Lieutenant Calley, his crew, Charlie Company. My Lai. It was the 114th session of the Vietnam peace talks. All the Supreme Court busing stuff. None of it got the space there on the front page that Tricia Nixon's wedding plans got.

On my way to the grocery store I had visited Anthony in order to check up on him. He always did the same for Marcella and me, and none of us made any masked ball out of it. When he dropped by he'd announce, "I'm checking on you." We did the same. We asked about his job or his car or some of the things you ask about with your children. Of course, we asked about how he felt, although we've never known him to be ill once in his whole adult life. Between us, Marcella and I had a dozen diagnosable troubles to report. My blood pressure was her favorite one to harp on. We had our comfortable routines in these conversations with Anthony, and we had ruts we wore deeper all the time.

He took me back to his dining room, where he was replacing a cracked windowpane that he said his landlord kept promising to replace. He pulled out a chair for me, handing me a tube of caulking. He didn't give me directions because he didn't need to. He nodded at the window, and I knew what to do. The window was an old roll-out; he had broken the bad pane out of the steel frame but hadn't yet swept up the glass. On the floor near him was a hammer with a rag wrapped over the head and claw. Picking glass from the groove in the frame, he collected the pieces in his left hand.

"You should wear gloves," I said.

"Yeah?" He had leathery, wrinkled palms. That was from being a hod carrier. Mine were that way too. All working stiffs have monkey paws. Marcella says all men look like some animal or another when you look close, but I think she's talking about blue-collar guys. To my way of seeing, most white-collar guys look awfully human. It isn't any great compliment.

We fit the window, and caulked it, and rubbed the caulking into neat, thick lines. Sweeping up, Anthony asked if I was still on my way to visit Little Peg. "I sure am," I said. "You want to tag along?"

He emptied the dustpan, and grinned. "Nervous?"

"Me?" I asked. I thought about my daughter, how she was. "Sure."

"You'll need this." He handed me the hammer.

We laughed together real easy. Always did. When he had put away the broom and dustpan and hammer and everything, I told him I'd better get going. There was a battery of things we asked, the usual things, but important. Was Mom okay? Would I say hi to her? Would he drop by next week sometime? Did he need anything?

At the door, he asked me straight, "What are you going to say to her?" It came out sounding like a challenge.

"Well," I said, "I'll tell her she's okay. She's got the stuff."

"Right," he said.

"She can move on now."

He nodded. "I'll see you," he said, still nodding, waving his half-opened hand near his face like he was making a sloppy salute.

I bet plenty of well-meaning people said things to Anthony and his buddies since they came back from Vietnam. You know the sorts of things: he did his duty, he was a patriot, he could hold his head high. They said the same to Marcella and me about Ben. You always wanted people to say something else.

In the hospital elevator I decided I should be firm with Little Peg. (My wife said not to call her that. *That insults her, don't you know?*) I felt the best thing was to find out just what the problem was, root it out, watch her. All of us were like wounded people since Ben died. It hadn't made all of us cave in, though. Why should she let herself break down, especially with her new baby born healthy and thriving and with her husband ending his tour in Vietnam and on his way back home soon? It was like a slap to us, an insult. She had—we all had—plenty to be thankful for.

Right off the elevator, I was facing the glassed-in nursery where all the newborns squirmed in their neat open trays. Some of them were blue and naked under lamps that pinked them up. Some of them had their butts arched and their shoulders hunched and were sleeping with their faces down on their fists. The nurses in there were expert. I mean, their calmness, sureness. A hospital, top to bottom, is a world where women rule. The mewing from the trays and the crying and bawling are in a dozen codes these nurses have to break down and answer back to a hundred times in a workday. I was out of my element, no question about it.

In the glass I checked my reflection over. I looked determined.

I was a foreman on the job, and I knew how to be forceful but fair. *Don't you call her Little Peg,* my wife's voice said. *She needs you now. You have to be different with her.* I noticed two incubators in the very back of the glass room. The tiny preemies, scary-quiet, looked tortured in all that brightness. Nobody lets them escape it. I bet there's a reason. Maybe if you don't stop them, those little spirits crawl into even the narrowest darkness.

At the nurse's station, an RN lady acted like she knew who I was, said that my daughter was nervous about seeing me, but excited. Walking me to her room, the lady whispered, "She's had lunch. The doctor prescribed sedatives for after her lunch. Your daughter won't take them."

"Is she acting crazy?" I asked.

"She has a good sense of humor."

That puzzled me. "So?"

"She has her own room," she said. "She sees our staff psychologist."

The conversation was plenty dizzy. "What about the baby?" I was trying to ask whether the baby couldn't heal a lot of my daughter's hurt. How in the world would the nurse ever make that out? I think she did. I think she chose to ignore me.

She flicked on the light switches as we entered the room, and she knocked on the back of the door. "Peggy?" she asked. "Your father is here. May we come in?" Before an answer came, she left.

Little Peg had Molly next to her on the bed in a tray, only nested up in blankets and things. I said, "Little— Honey. Hi." Little Peg was probably pretending to sleep. My new granddaughter looked like an acorn next to my giant daughter. That's the joke in her nickname: she's at least six foot one, and I can tell you, she's no featherweight. I didn't make the rules about our family's teasing, and I never felt I had to explain them. It goes back. If you couldn't take teasing you weren't one of the boys. And, girl or not, if you weren't one of the boys, well then, more teasing was called for, naturally. I still went through it. Whenever I saw my dad, who was in his seventies, he'd still try me out to see if I could take it. "Did you eat an old man?"

he'd say. "You got an old man's gut." It disarms you. You have to keep your guard up.

"Hey, Little Peg," I said, "hey, sweetheart, you're looking awful." I laughed, but all alone. If she was asleep, it was for the best. I might have time to get my nerve up. Molly looked bad too: her left eyebrow was bandaged and the skin on her face was kind of a scalded red. Marcella had told me the delivery didn't go right.

I put my grocery bag next to the chair near her bed. I could reach her bed lamp, so I turned it on before I sat down. Molly, who was curled on her side, wound herself tighter, tensing up her face in a way that had to do with her genes. At even a glance I could see some of my wife's traits. Looking for some of me in her, I leaned closer and could hear her sighing. This doesn't make any sense, but that reminded me of how my dad would hold his pocket watch in his left palm and rock the stem back and forth between his thumb and the very tip of the index finger of his right hand. He did it slowly and privately, and he watched what he was doing so that if you were with him you'd be watching too. He would close the face and hold it to his ear, then hold it to your ear. "Hear?" You had to pay attention to him. If you were rotten, his belt struck you like a snake.

We're strong people, my wife's people and mine. I couldn't remember any of our relatives ever who'd had a mental breakdown. I ran through some other words for it. Crack-up. Collapse.

When Little Peg's in-laws asked us why she and the baby had stayed in the hospital a week after Molly's birth, my wife told them, "Peggy has had a nervous episode." I was sitting at the kitchen table where I could hear Marcella on the phone. What? A nervous episode. Why? They wanted something, some one thing as an explanation.

My wife held the receiver away from her face. "The war," she said. That was her explanation.

An absolute truth is never absolutely acceptable, is it? I could guess what they asked next: But what is the problem really?

Marcella answered, "It could be the medicine they gave her after Molly's birth." They had what they needed.

After she hung up, she sat down next to me. "What was I supposed to do?" she asked.

Now, I wished Marcella was with me at the hospital. She made me come alone. "None of us has been any good," she'd told me; "she won't talk about it."

"You go ahead. Sleep," I said to my granddaughter and daughter.

I decided some sunlight wouldn't do any harm, so I opened the curtains to the left of her bed. Of our children, my daughter had gotten luckiest in the looks department. Like a maple: pretty every season of her life. When she was nine or ten and she shot up to be so big, my wife and I used to thank the Lord she had looks to compensate. If the world wasn't that way about big girls anymore, then we were just wrongheaded, weren't we?

It was the middle of the afternoon, and she should have been dressed. She had on a hospital gown, one of the ones with broad stripes across it that make all the patients look like zookeepers. Without budging in the bed or so much as cracking her eyes open, Little Peg said, "What did you bring?"

She sure threw me off guard. "What?"

She opened her eyes to look at me. "Hi." Large hazel eyes, like my wife's. "Bring anything?"

"You bet," I said, "you bet." I held up the bag to show her. I pulled out the diapers.

"The hospital provides diapers."

"Your mother said I should buy them." When she reached her hand through the bedrail, I stood up to hold it, which I did wrong at first. She wanted to hold my hand inside hers instead of the other way around.

She said, "They're not for here. The diapers are in case I come home."

"Oh." *You're going to come home,* I thought. I needed to be firm with her. That wasn't easy, I can tell you.

"Did you meet Molly?" she asked, and then almost in the

same breath, "Did you open my curtains?" She brought Molly out of the tray and into her arms.

I said, "She's a beautiful girl." I reached back and closed the curtains. "She's got a lot of her grandma in her."

"What does that mean?"

"What? I don't know." I felt like I was pitching wild with the bases loaded, every runner stealing base at the same time. I looked again at Molly's bandaged eyebrow, her face so boiling red. *She's got a lot of her grandma in her*. I was plenty embarrassed. "Her *eyes* are like your mom's," I said.

"She's asleep, Dad. And one eye is bandaged."

"Okay. You got me."

She cocked her finger and thumb, leveled them at me, fired. "It's my job," she said. She blew imaginary smoke away from her fingertip. If she'd wanted to remind me about Ben, put him there in the hospital room with us, that did the job. Before he left for Vietnam he had gotten some sort of fix on that *I Spy* show. He could do either of those two characters, Culp or Cosby. They were always putting their finger guns right up against each other's head and shooting, then saying, "It's my job."

I leaned down to ask Molly how she was. I had done that with my own babies too. "You doing okay there? Get enough sleep?" Marcella always did most of her communicating differently, touching their closed eyelids or folding their fingers or toes, and unfolding them, and singing nonsense songs right into the tops of their heads where their skulls were still slight as wax paper. All our children already had heads full of nonsense before they were a month old.

Molly woke up while I was talking to her. Little Peg said to her, "He's dumb, but he's sweet, isn't he?"

I ignored her and asked more questions, all dumb ones: "You're pretty, you know that? You know who I am? You want to be held by your grandpa?" Calling my bluff, Little Peg put Molly in my arms. I remembered to support her neck, but she kind of kneed my chest and arched her back so that I didn't know how to hold her, except to cradle her, which made her cry.

I offered her back. "Here." Little Peg shook her head no.

"Dad, the hospital psychologist says I need some time out somewhere."

Lifting Molly up so she could look me in the eye, I said, "You don't want to cry, do you? No? No." As if that made sense, Molly stopped crying. I asked, "You need what?"

"I need—I want to go to this halfway house. Everview."

Jesus. Everview. "What? Are you crazy? Isn't is a place for crazy people?"

"No." She lifted herself to a better sitting position on the bed. Handing me a little baby bottle, she said, "It's a halfway house. It's near you and Mom's neighborhood."

"I know where it is." As far as I was concerned it was a place for the half-crazy. Molly wouldn't take the bottle; she was getting frustrated with me. I leaned down again to hand her back to Little Peg, but instead of taking the baby, she took the bottle. She touched the nipple to Molly's lips, then stroked her chin. When the kid locked onto the bottle, I took over the whole operation again.

"Don't let her take so much."

I tilted the bottle at a different angle. Hell, I had done this before, you know.

"Little Peg," I said, "you're—she's *thirsty*—you don't belong there and you know it. Now this kind of talk is just stupid."

We both looked at the baby glugging away. A baby drinking like that stretches out so you feel like you're holding something already growing beyond what your arms can hold. I wondered when they'd take the bandages off her head. I thought this might be the right time to offer my daughter the cupcakes I'd brought. I really did think that. I've never been accused of being deep. I thought about all kinds of things: the big fan in the grocery store, the newspapers, Tricia Nixon and Martha Mitchell, the overfilled national cemeteries, Hank Aaron's 600th. It's unbelievable, isn't it? I wish I had thought of the one right thing to say to my daughter.

"It's been rocky," I said. "You're over that. You're—"

"Dad," she said. "Here. Give me Molly. I'm going to get the two of us dressed." It was a pretty clear invite for me to leave. Then she relented. "Do you want to meet us in the hospital chapel in a few minutes?"

That was a great idea, I said. She had offered me an honorable retreat from her room is what she had done.

The hospital chapel didn't have kneelers. No windows. The three-wall mural was modern art, if you know what I mean, and probably the story of creation, but I couldn't say that for sure. It was plenty nondenominational. My guess is, no denomination of any kind would ever feel comfortable having a service in it. Our family was what priests call Sunday Catholics. I'm really not sure what we were Mondays through Saturdays, but on Sundays we went to Mass, heard the Gospels, took Communion. Our church had just started doing guitar Masses. My oldest son, Anthony, was always wisecracking about that: "Who says Catholics don't swing?" And he called us "locksteppers," which we were, and which we still are. Why should I be ashamed? Humility, ritual, spiritual discipline, all those things are good. And being always faithful. I won't apologize for every goddamn Sunday of my life.

One of the last days I saw Ben before he went to basic, he and I were dishwashers for the church pancake breakfast. We hadn't kept up as well as we thought and after the breakfast ended, the stack in front of us was chin-high. Alone in the church kitchen, we both did the job right. He didn't leave crud on a plate, front or back. I didn't dry those plates and all the silverware; I *polished* them with a whole stack of towels.

Swear to God it's true: the towels were printed with the words Palms Motel. We joked some about that.

All totaled, we hadn't really said much between us; we were concentrating on the job. Scouring the sinks and counters off with Old Dutch, Ben told me to give my feet a break and sit down. I want to describe Ben now, because no one ever asks you—with all the questions they ask, no one ever asks you—what was he like, what did he look like? You get to where you want to be able to tell someone.

Ben was slight. His sister was big and tall; his brother had a frame like his bones were lodgepoles. But Ben had skinny legs, skinny arms. When he was seventeen I bet you could still close two fingers around his wrist. I never did that since the time he was a boy. I wish I had.

Even though he was short, his shoulders were no wider across than his hips. He didn't have that physical alertness some boys have who play sports. Those bowed shoulders and that straight neck, that head of thick brown hair he'd always just pitched up out of the way of his glasses—you'd look at him and see he had a special inner concentration. Anyone could feel good around him because, when he connected with you, that inside person was reaching out, paying complete attention to you. I think the reason I always could be more comfortable with Anthony than with Ben is because Anthony gave you plenty of room to stay at the surface of things. Ben wanted to haul you out to deep water as soon as he could. That's what he was like.

In the church kitchen, he didn't wait long after I sat down to saw a leg off my chair. "Dad, maybe now might be the time—before I go away and all." He didn't say what it might be time for. Ben was careful with words, and I think he was quietly choosing. You could see his weight shift onto his hands as he stopped scrubbing.

He looked at me with a kind of terror that I'd seen on his face when he was five or six and I woke him up from bad dreams. His trust in me back then was infinite. He'd tell me the dream. I'd hold him in my arms, where he'd relax and stretch and fall right to sleep, without it ever occurring to him that he had any risk of another bad dream ever. Now, when he didn't say anything, I could see how much of that trust was gone. I tell you, this is what is so unbelievable, that so much trust could be gone without his love for me lessening for a minute. I can't think of even one reason for it, but that doesn't make it less true.

He didn't say anything. He finished his work. We drove home. What was he going to say or ask?

"Dad?" Peg closed the chapel door behind her. She sat down next to me. She had at least six inches on me in height, and putting my arms around her, I felt tiny. I think she was surprised at first that I hugged her.

I needed to be hugged. She sat rigidly next to me, but I hung on to her all the same. "Peg," I said, "please don't go to this Everview place. I'm asking you. Please."

"Dad." She leaned herself over me, but her voice was as far away as if she was in another country or something inside had snapped shut. "Will you take me there?" she asked. "This Monday. Will you take Molly and me there?"

I still didn't loosen my hold on her. "I want to—this is the time—I want to say something."

Into the very top of my head, she whispered, "I love you too, Daddy."

That isn't what I was going to say. Something else.

I do love you, Peg. For God's sake, you know that, don't you? I want to say something else.

The End

In order to finish the last of my packing, I spent the next day at James's house. At 1 A.M. I was still sitting at James's kitchen table, writing remarks on the stories "In Your Hands" and "The Cartographer," and on the other newest stories the students and I had written during the first nine weeks of the ten-week session. I gave Mr. Hutto's story, "The Cartographer," an A plus plus. I would have done no less for Mr. Melville. Ah, Hutto! Ah, Humanity!

I gave my own story, "In Your Hands," the same grade. Even in the Nontraditional Program if you give an A to your own work or to a student's plagiarized work people will, strangely enough, call that "grade inflation." Those who have always deflated the importance of learning by inflating the importance of grades do not like to see people like me with a finger on the valve. I don't blame them.

I did my best.

When Molly surreptitiously came into the house through the front door, I said, "Hi. Glad you're home. I'm going to bed now."

She had not gone farther than three steps into the dark living room, and she stood very still. "Mom?"

"No," I said, "it's the Holy Ghostess."

"Hey," she said, "is Francis okay now?"

I didn't answer. The silence that froze under us tilted us toward each other without perceptibly moving us. Then she walked into the kitchen. I said, "She's alone now."

"And?"

"She's okay. Come sit down."

She stayed one step inside the kitchen, only one step within the light of my table lamp. "You waited up?" she asked.

"You had a good time?" I asked back. I think the very best expert ufologists would be mystified by the landing patterns of Peter's lips and teeth on the skin under my daughter's chin and around her right ear. Tiny, precise hickeys.

"Daddy's asleep?"

"Probably," I said, loudly enough to wake him up.

She sat down at the kitchen table. "Well," she said, "good night."

Her fixed staring at me made me feel I might as well have been the chair she had slumped on so heavily. I was already thinking, *She wants to ask about James.* Her head did not move. Sitting down across from her, I said, "All right. Tell me."

She wanted me to explain again that the next day I really was leaving James's house to move into my own place. I had to remind her that James agreed we would keep things open about visiting each other. She also wanted to be reassured again that

I knew what I was doing in stepping down from the Prolixin.

"So. You've explored all your alternatives?" she asked.

"You're being a smart aleck, Molly."

"He thinks it's okay?"

"This isn't James's choice," I said.

"But—"

"But." There were a lot of tiny hickeys, more than I had noticed at first. "What if you get an infection?" I asked.

"Mom. They'll heal."

"There. Everything does. It's that easy."

"All right," she said angrily.

"All right." I didn't get up from the table and neither did she. She put her closed fists one right next to the other on the tabletop and kept them there through the long, quiet thawing time between us.

"Are you okay?" I asked.

She said, "It's never boring anyway."

"What do you mean?"

"You know. You moving in and out." She touched her temples with her fingertips, then pushed up the dark hair there and held it up in a tidal wave to make me smile.

"I didn't use Spock to raise you, okay?"

"No?" Her hands plunged deeper into her thick auburn hair, like mine, crow-black around her face and ears.

"I mean, I didn't know what I was doing. We—"

"You didn't raise me," she said.

"Is that true?" I asked indignantly. *Is that true?* I wanted to answer myself, but couldn't

She mimicked me: "Is that true?" I could hear my own playful but angry three-syllable imitation of my mother: *Don't you know?*

"God," she said, as if making a little dam made of God that might hold back other words. Then she broke down her own dam. "Fuck," she said. "You didn't raise me. You loved me lots but—you know—"

"I hate that. I hate that—'fuck.' "

"You know! Fuck! You didn't raise me. You raised yourself."

"That's not true," I said. *Is that true?*

"Oh. Right, like I'm lying, right? You were the first child. You got fed first, then me. You got your hugs, then I got some."

Is that true? Somehow I could barely hear her. I heard my mother say, *Don't you know?*

Very quietly, Molly asked, "Am I right? You've done a fine job of raising yourself. You've run away from home a lot. But you're turned out okay, don't you think?"

I couldn't answer, except to lower my head. When she got up from the table and gripped my shoulders in her arms, I hurt as deeply as if she were wringing out my stupid heart.

"It's over." She couldn't hold back the last hurtfulness. "You can finally go out in the world now. Go out and make your own way."

I wished she would cry. Still, I never loved my daughter more than when she hurt me that much. "It's true, Molly. It's all true," I said. "Where did you learn to be so mean? And honest?"

"Probably Sunday school," she said. She moved her hands to my neck, pretending to throttle me.

It's true that when Molly was a child I was her best bad example. We had always been jaywalkers, always line cutters-in. We could not behave ourselves in public. One time, when she was about thirteen, we were at FootSoar trying on shoes, and the young man fitting her looked up her dress.

She asked him straightaway, "Did you look up my dress?"

I demanded, "What did you see?"

The young man answered her, "No!" and me, "Not much. Honest!" They were expensive shoes, and as we left with them, I explained to Molly that I had bounced a check to buy them. We hurried out of the mall, giggling criminally.

I need my daughter. You hear of people attesting to how they need their children, but they don't mean that as I do.

Later, as I was packing I remembered the summer day in 1971 when James bought the Nova.

We had car-hunted at most of the dealerships in the valley, and James had set his heart, finally, on that Nova. I had liked the Granada, but we both implicitly understood he would make the decision.

On the hot afternoon we went to close the deal, he insisted on wearing his uniform. Even with the odd national sentiments about Vietnam veterans, he felt it was a safe bet that car salesmen would be suckers for a boy in uniform. Either he was right or the salesman was especially slick about making the "veteran discount" pitch sound sincere. Through all the paperwork and inspection of the car and lease review, he asked James about his service in Vietnam.

Handing us the keys, he said, "There you go. Zero to forty in nine seconds. It's going to feel good. And you've got it coming, Mr. Aigley."

"Thank you," James said. He shook the keys like dice in his palm, and he put his arm around my waist. James had always liked getting what was coming to him.

I snapped my briefcase open.

"I know some of you are angry with me about what I have done to your stories."

Burns said, "Fuckin' right."

"Pay attention," I said to Norm. "Some of you have waited all semester—haven't you?—for me to pass out these teacher evaluation forms."

Mitchey brushed her hair back with a curved wrist; threading himself through her eyes, Norm curved his own wrist and glided it through his flattop. I said, "I know many of you will not appreciate that I have already filled out the forms for you, offering myself the highest undeserved praise possible, while respecting your individual first-person points of view."

The folder of evaluations before me said *Confidential*. "Questions?"

Mitchey dipped her right pinkie in a small fingerpot of bright grape-green lip balm. After she daubed her lovely young lips, she passed the balm down the table to Norm. I passed out the completed forms. As they read my thoughtful, well-written comments, I saw smiles. I saw flinches, and I saw flinching smiles. I especially liked Mitchey's and Norm's.

Burns said, "You did a better job than we thought."

"I did, didn't I?" I collected the forms, sealed them in the confidential envelope, and thanked the class.

"By the way. I will not post grades this semester. Those of you sitting here, the ones who have survived this experience, will all receive A pluses, A's, or A minuses. My department head will not like the curve, but the pluses and minuses might appease him."

Burns asked, "Do you sleep with him?"

Do I sleep with him? Of course not. But I had to answer because the question had quieted everyone. "Yes," I said, "in my worst nightmares."

"What'd he get?"

"A plus."

"Fuckin' right," said Burns.

"Okay," I said, "you may assume the high grade is meant as an inducement for you to remain quiet about our course design. Incidentally, I want to remind you that I can submit a change of grade form anytime in the first three years after the semester ends." I looked at how their wrists and hands rested on the single long table at which they all sat. Mitchey's and Norm's intimate hands. Peter's alert concrete hands, and Andria's: delicate, unwrinkled. Burns's hands. Oh, Burns, I said to myself, you chew your nails *and* knuckles, don't you? I should have paid more attention. The Invisible all had their hands on their books and notepads, like fishers, watching their bobbers, waiting for strikes. Burns, I should have paid more attention to you and even less to them.

"Okay. What I hope you have learned is simple: Watch Out.

"Imagine you're on a busy street. A womanhole is open. Repairwomen are down inside, below a sign that says *Women Work-*

ing. Watch out. Put this in your notes. Your last chance. I required you to write my story. After you did that, I took back my own story from you. You couldn't stop me, it's my life, right? Some of you didn't want to stop me. It made me happy. You know that, I guess. It helped me out."

Peter raised his hand. End of the semester, and he was still raising his hand. He said, "I want to say, I—" He lowered his arm. "Just—you're welcome, Mrs. O."

"Thank you, Peter." I looked again at my lecture notes. "But listen, I have never once promised you people greater happiness or personal growth as a result of storymaking. Don't try to tell me I misled you. Here's what you get. You get complication, confusion, and conflict, crisis and more crisis, uncontrolled development, useful and useless revelation, no climax, no catharsis, and, in a lifetime of writing, finally more questions in the place of more clarity. What did you expect?"

Andria, I knew, expected an A plus. You got it, I silently said to her. Peter still had sleep gunk in his eyes at 6 P.M. I knew what he wanted: Molly.

I took off my blue-black pumps. I held them up as Mr. Rogers would do on the television, and put them in my attaché case. I snapped it closed. "Can you say 'Freytag's High Dive'? Do you remember that? Can you promise me that you will? You make your own ladder as you go up: each rung a weak sentence or strong one. At the top: a place to jump from. Do you see?"

All The Invisible nodded yes.

"Key-rist," said Burns.

Norm blew Mitchey a verdant kiss.

"I have the final story for us today. A very tiny family portrait. This one has the same title as the story Andria Charley wrote instead of 'One Set, Proofs' that I said she wrote. This is not your story, Andria. But it is your title."

She did not thank me.

Andria Charley
2322 Houston Ave.
Las Almas, N.M. 88001

Actual Size
(Max Tibbets, 1987)

How I learned was I shot a lot of clients named Joe. Hundreds of Joes. What do you think about that? If I had those pictures, that's what I'd show you. I don't have one.

Scoot your chair up. What're you—a high school graduate now? Want to learn this business? Look at this set. The Aigley family.

Face it, sometimes you can't get one good proof of people you shoot. Shoot all day, you won't get one. So. You have to let the proofs tell the truth, and that means you don't make a sale.

I'll explain about Joe. I haven't forgotten.

The Aigleys. It's got nothing to do with whether they're pretty. You think this family is ugly? Well? Huhn-uh. This has all got to do with subtraction. That's what I want to teach you about: what minus what minus what. How much truth can you subtract before people stop looking like themselves?

Let's spread them out. Go ahead. See what I mean?

The mother was the real problem. A big problem. They wouldn't let me do pairings or I could have done a nice father/daughter portrait.

Don't laugh. I swear I wouldn't show them to you ever except to teach you. Show a little self-discipline. Pay some attention.

One thing you want to know right away is what poses you can make work. This woman here was over six feet tall. Built like a bouncer, maybe a hundred seventy-five pounds. She had a—you can't see it here—a person fitted inside her. An outside person plus an inside person. A coldness over life you can see when you squint at people who are half an inch high in your lens. But you look at the three of them, and this has to happen fast: your decision. Father standing, Daughter and Mother sitting.

You're going to have to angle Daughter in front of Mother and put Father on a lift. If your eye is ready, your guts tell you not to choose Mother and Father together in one shot.

You try to pose. This is the first time you get behind your lens. Here's part of what I mean about subtraction. You're trying to subtract size because size, actual size, is part of what might make them people instead of pictures. Her shoulders are less giant inside the lens. Her chest is still big, so you say to the daughter, "Lean a little more in front of your mother."

Father doesn't match. He's like a starched sheet behind that peachy brightness and roundness. You don't want that. That might not even be a professional way of seeing him. So?

You ask Father to put his hands on their shoulders and bend forward some.

"Like this?" he asks.

"No," says the mother, the giant. She's the real problem. She's the one who makes this family hard to get a bead on. Daughter is normal size. I mean, an eighties-model sixteen-year-old.

Hey, I don't blame you for staring at her. But to me a sixteen-year-old girl always only looks like the starting kit for a woman.

Father is trim, crisp shirt, short hair smartly combed.

Now you get out from behind your lens. They're actual size again. You even hear them better. Mother's saying to Daughter, "Be whatever way you want. It's not up to him." Meaning the father, Mr. James Aigley. It's written on the back of the picture.

The daughter says, "Can't we all just pretend?"

"Some of us can," says Mr. Aigley.

"Mom," asks the daughter, "how about it?"

Okay, I hear you. That same grim jaw in the whole family. See? Perfected in Molly. I get the feeling you're not a jaw man, son. Here's something I can tell you that I wish I had known forty years ago. Before you fall in love, take pictures.

Look hard. Think like a photographer. Subtract. Poor posture, a slack mouth. Age. Four chins minus three chins equals what? Pay attention. Almost every fact of a person can be subtracted.

The father had two pens, I subtracted one. Makes a difference.

This is stuff you do in front of the lens. You make him a one-pen man. You straighten them up. You get the knees pointing one direction, the shoulders the other way, so that—let me ask you. Why do that?

Torque? You call it torque? I like it. Right. You get torque that way.

The mother says, "This wasn't a good idea," or something like that.

Mr. Aigley steps off the lift, says, "It was your idea."

The mother was in a cotton dress. Her legs and feet were out of frame or you'd be able to see her white lacy-edged bobby socks, low down on her ankles. Look. I think you can tell. She fit in her clothes like she fit in her body. Her heaviness wasn't soft.

No, I can't remember. What is her name? You get—it'll hang me until I remember—but you get blocked. I told you before about how I was a medical photographer? Second World War. Like I said, I shot Joes. See, I'd get blocked on their names so I'd have to call them all "Joe."

A nurse would take off the dressings and help me turn Joe like a pipe cleaner so I could get good shots for the docs. You never heard about this, did you?

Someday all those shots are going to be spilled out of all those doctors' files. Then what, huh? Who sends those proofs out? A wound has a face—you can't subtract the truth from it. That's all I did from 1942 to 1944: I told the truth. Maybe five, six hundred truths.

Okay, enough. Here's these Aigleys that you can't shoot a good proof of. Mother says, "Get this over with." You put Mr. Aigley back on his lift. You pose them all again because you haven't given up on them. Professionalism. You regroup. Try to keep in mind how light erases the surface of people. Filtered light erases bad skin texture; angled light subtracts fleshiness. I wanted to soften their hair, make them look more comfortable, get their heads—do something with their heads to make them look lighter. I crouched behind the lens and aimed.

They looked like something exploded behind them. I could flick off all the light. They'd look the same way.

The daughter was a softer version of her mother. Two glaring faces. See? And Mr. Aigley had a bluffing smile. I could recognize that.

I wonder what happened to them. Those boys, I mean. I could've shot (I was supposed to shoot) only the wounds. Just them. All right, one second. I'm saying something, please, I'm getting to what I have to say.

This is what. Subtract some of yourself. The part of you that wants to know the truth. Or—no. Subtract the part that wants to tell the truth.

Even if I was shooting an injured foot, I'd get the boy's face in the picture. A nurse might have to hold his arm up or cradle his hips a certain way. She might be crying or cringing, or glaring at me. I made her part of the picture. The Joes, the nurses, they were like this giant woman, this mother here. No matter how much of her I subtracted, she would not be different.

You get behind the lens. Subtract time by holding your breath. Think, *Now minus then minus then minus then*. You're not thinking, *Now plus next plus next plus next*. It's not a movie, I mean. You aren't making a frame in a reel of frames leading to the end of things. See. Look again. It *is* the end of things.

The mother said something to me when I finished. Because, you know, she could see how I felt. And she cared. She said, "Hell with it." So we could both laugh.

You see what you need to see in a face. That's what I mean.

I saw the mothers. The sisters, daughters, wives of all those boys.

The End

* * *

Everyone quietly read. In only a semester, even though I am stepped off the Prolixin, I'll have forgotten most of their names. Not them, but certainly their names. That's how I am. Oh, I'll remember Norm, who has repeated my writing class three times. When he sees me he'll even help me recall his name, he'll say, "Mrs. O! It's me, Norm." Although he will have been one of thousands of my students and I will have been one of forty or fifty of his teachers, we will feel—no, I'm storytelling— Am I? We will feel attachment.

The first finished reading, Lewis looked up from the story. His face hid something.

I nodded yes, that I knew.

Very quietly, to me only, he said, "More shit."

"No. The truth." I wish Lewis and I could trade dog tags. I don't want to forget his name. I don't want him to forget my name. But I don't have dog tags.

When everyone finished, we had a brief discussion of "Actual Size."

Norm asked, "It's a short short story, right?"

Susan Orstal offered that she thought it had a bad title. The Invisible all nodded in agreement with her.

Out of the blue, Mitchey said, "Something's screwy with my period." She said it out loud. Norm wiped his mouth clean.

"I *like* the title," said Erminia Maestas.

Lewis seemed to be looking everyone over in my own method of sizing them up. I considered calling on him.

I said, "You should be proud of this one, Andria."

Andria said, "I didn't write it."

"Nevertheless," I said. Someone knocked on the classroom door.

In the hallway, my supervisor's secretary, Helene, whispered, "Dr. Millidge wants to see you before you turn in grades." I thanked her. She said, "You don't have shoes on."

"I love them," I told her.

"I know, Peg." For all my thirteen years in the Nontraditional Program she had been that kind to me.

When I went back into the classroom, their books and papers were in neat stacks on the conference table and their chairs were scooted back from it. Peter stayed pinioned to the table edge. "Peter," I asked, "are you going somewhere?"

"No," he said, his fists closing.

"I have another story," I announced. "It's entitled 'Visiting.' We can't discuss it because we have no time. We probably couldn't anyway since it doesn't stand up right on its own. Take it home. Live some more. Marry the wrong person. Have children. Then read it, okay? Remember what E. M. Forster said: 'The master uses whiteness, wordlessness more than the novice.' " That was a lie, but I was confident that E. M. Forster would have said it. On a bad day.

I could not get anyone's attention until I opened my attaché case again. I methodically tried to make eye contact with everyone. "You understand," I announced, "that you can repeat this class for credit?"

Lewis and Burns started chuckling. Erminia couldn't help herself. Norm was nervous at first, but that didn't last. Their laughter sprung out in little bursts that grew into drumfire, then became chain reaction explosions, then bells striking and deeply fracturing, and striking again. I found myself laughing with all of them past the time that some and, finally, all of them stopped.

I took out my shoes. I put them on again, snapped shut the attaché case, and said, "I'll miss you."

I got hugged by some of them, or got my hand enwrapped in their warm, whole hands and shaken. Like the two halves of a shell, Mitchey and Norm reached around me into each other. "Everything'll be okay," Mitchey said to Norm.

"Sure," I said. "Well?" They let me go.

Peter repeatedly churned my hand up to my chin and down to my waist. He didn't say anything. He looked at my face without arriving at my eyes. And I looked at my daughter's mouth imprinted everywhere over his neck.

Lewis made me reach down to his height so he could take hold of my head and shoulders and pull them into his chest. He whispered, "And only we two to tell the tale." He did not let go until he was sure I understood: an embrace after battle, a man-to-man embrace.

After he left, it seemed I was almost instantaneously alone in my classroom. Most of them had left their copies of "Visiting" on the table.

Peg Nearing
795 Sombra
Las Almas, N.M. 88001

VISITING
(Peg, 1974)

"Yipes!" said my daughter Molly. She was three years old and not able to understand the idea of custody, that her father was "fit" to live with, and I was "unfit." As she rocked her head up and down and back and forth, it jingled.

I was jingling my head the same way. "Yipes!" I said, leaning forward in the seat of the K Mart Freedomcopter where our ride was coming to an end. It was a camouflaged comic-copter, not a 1970 evening-news-copter, and it was a regular part of our Tuesday visits together. Sundays, Mondays, and Tuesdays were our agreed-upon visiting days. Because she lived with her father, I never saw her in the evenings.

The new identical stocking caps I had bought for us were watercolor light blue with golden glitter in them and with jingle-bell puffs at the top. But the 3-D life-size bumblebees perched above the hinges on our new sunglasses were what we liked best. When we moved our heads just a certain way, their wings raced, their bodies dipped into our eyes and drew nectar from them.

Molly stayed in the Freedomcopter as I got down. "Girl's Friend," she said, "wants to know 'Do you have a million of nickels?' "

"Girl's Friend?"

"You know."

Girl's Friend. I suppose I did know her.

I already had the change out for another ride. I put it in the slots and got back inside. I knew some of the things Girl and Girl's Friend and Monster *did*, but, until that moment, Molly had never told me what her imaginary friends *said*.

"Do you have a million?" asked Girl's Friend.

Behind her sunglasses, Molly's eyes squinted at me.

I did not hurry. I had been curious for two years whether I would meet Molly's imaginary friends before she grew older or before our family dissolved. The Freedomcopter rose up and whirred, turning us left, then right, then touch-landing and lifting away. I looked at the stationary blades overhead.

Girl's Friend, who was always breaking rules, making up new ones, persisted. "Do you have a million?"

"Me?"

The stillness of the blades in the late morning desert glare seemed like the illusion of stillness created by extraordinary speed. For a second, I couldn't catch my breath. I bowed my head to be safe. When I lifted it, a voice floated from my throat. "Me? I have millions of millions," said Pigbird-in-me. I had not heard from Pigbird since I was Molly's age or younger. *Where did you come from?* I thought. I had believed it was gone, that part of childhood when you are convinced the coin the magician brings from behind your ear was there all along and when you accept, at the same time, that sleight of hand put it there.

And why was I surprised that Pigbird sounded like me? I had never been the least surprised that Molly's imaginary friends were Molly. "Me?" Pigbird asked. "I've got zillions."

I looked at Molly, who looked at me looking at Girl's Friend talking with Pigbird. We must have all had the same thought at once, because together we grabbed for the control stick and rattled it. It had a red thumb button that we pressed. Pigbird and Girl's Friend shouted, "Stop! Boom!"

When the ride ended, Molly calmly asked, "Can we fly again?"

"Molly!"

"Can we?" she asked.

I fed change to the machine. "Here goes." When the whipsaw sound began, I swore I could feel a downdraft.

On our first sweep to the left, Girl's Friend said, "Let's spit!" Girl's Friend did whatever she wanted without ever getting corrected. I already knew that.

"What?"

"You know," said Molly. "Spit," said Girl's Friend.

It shocked me when Pigbird said, "I can spit farthest!"

"I can spit more far than you," said Girl's Friend. She had Molly's controlled grin and her same single-jingle nod. The bumblebees held perfectly still on her sunglasses.

Pthew!

"That ain't much of a spit," Pigbird said. Pthew! Hers was no big improvement.

"Wow." Molly wiped her chin.

I was amazed too. I saw boys spit when I was a child. My mother did not approve of it for my brothers or me, but especially not for me. I had never allowed myself.

"I won!" said Girl's Friend. The copter took us straight up.

Pigbird said, "I won because I did and all the judges say I did." I had my hand over Molly's on the control stick. Just Molly's hands and mine.

Girl's Friend either said, "Fuck the judges," or asked—I hope so—"What judges?"

"Everywhere," said Pigbird. We rattled the control stick, then let it go. The Freedomcopter landed with a screech.

"Wow," said Girl's Friend. Or Molly.

"Where did we land?" I think I asked that.

In her father's house, we made half-slice peanut butter and jelly sandwiches. Molly used a chair to get potato chips from one of the cabinets, but we ate our sandwiches first. In James's house that was how we acted.

When we'd made our chocolate milk, we rinsed the spoons and dirty knives, and put them in the dishrack before drinking. "Cheers," we said, as though we were Hansel and Gretel getting away with something. We set the glasses on coasters. I should have taught her how to slosh and spill. At the least, I should have taught her how to leave the dirty dishes in the sink for the next person.

"Don't hurry," I lied when she went to the bathroom. In the living room, I picked up our 1974 family portrait. *Every year,* I said to myself. A handsome, kind man and his daughter. Behind them: her.

I put the picture back in its right place, on the low brass lamp table. We were estranged. That always sounds to me like the Spanish word for "strange." He and I were estranged, separated, eventually reconciled, estranged again. I guess I was mostly responsible for the estranged part. He was mostly responsible for the reconciled part. That is the fate of a married couple when one of them cannot break a pattern and one cannot, for the life of her, form one.

On the bookshelves he had all my books, and I knew he still made an effort to read my favorites, to understand. If Molly didn't hurry, he would be home soon.

Molly and I drove to the university duck pond for our regular Tuesday afternoon visit. In the car, she asked a familiar barrage of questions about when ducks had babies, how many, whether the babies could talk, hear, did they have bad dreams, did people really *eat* ducks?

To deflect her, I said, "Baby ducks are called ducklings." I didn't want to answer all her questions, because I knew they led to more questions. Were they killed, who killed them, couldn't people eat something else? Molly was always tireless in asking the very same questions again and again until her memory formed a version she could stubbornly defend. Sometimes I would loathe myself as I heard her echoing even my own vocabulary in an explanation to someone. She would look sad and solemn as she said, "Only certain people eat certain ducks. They kill them quick." There would be particular emphasis on the words "certain" and "quick."

To finesse her away from all that, I asked, "What are baby geese called?"

"Goslings," she said through her teeth. She was not easily finessed.

We parked the car and walked to the duck pond. We sat on the low stone bench near the curdled, swampy bank of the water. Our bread was too gross for the ducks, and the two who deigned to leave the pond in order to check the menu took the pieces in their bills only long enough to toss them away. Their heads tolled slowly up and back at us as if their bright necks were bellpulls.

I guess a dreamier mother than I would have helped her child name the ducks. Papa Duck Duvalier came to mind. Tricky Duck Nixon and Le Duck Tho. But, after all, they didn't like us, so why should we make the effort?

"The ducks're cold," said Molly. Her head burrowed under my arm, and I thought I heard my heart make a muffled jingle-noise.

"They're university ducks," I said. "Spoiled."

"They have in stinks?" she asked.

"They have *no* instincts, Molly." In our visits to the pond I had been at least motherly enough to explain about nesting and mating and migration. She put her hands in her coat pockets, sinking herself into me. A breeze sugared the water with dust from the cotton and chile fields on the edge of the valley. The air around us smelled like pescado seco, the smoked fish in the Juarez markets.

Our stillness had almost become sleep when she whispered, "Mom?"

I whispered back, "Molly?"

"You could go way away," said Girl.

"Girl, is that you?" I asked. Her forehead had more wrinkles than a three-year-old's should have. "Girl?" When she hunched her shoulders, they relaxed only very slowly.

"We can go way high." Girl lifted her head and tilted it up, looking past me for the sun. "Way high. See everything."

"Shout," I said. "Screeeeem if we want to," said Pigbird.

Girl dive-bombed. "Shhhooooohoom!"

Pigbird screamed. All the ducks bumped up off their butts and screamed back, which made Pigbird dive-bomb too. "Shhhooooohoom!"

We leaned forward, lost our perch on the bench, and barely righted ourselves. Teetering, I heard Girl's Friend say, "You're exploded!" with the snide enthusiasm she always had when she said things that weren't nice to say.

Pigbird said, "You're—"

"You're exploded!" said Girl's Friend. "And you're flushed down!"

Flushed. Pigbird had to think fast. She said, "I've got magic words." *So there.* "I can come back if I want."

"Yipes!" said Molly.

Damn right, Pigbird thought.

We had a teetering standoff, the ducks quietly concentrating on us from behind the weeds. I heard my heart skipping, and my magic words coming to me like a skip-rope snapping pavement. Then, from nowhere, Monster appeared. She growled at Pigbird, frightening her—and me and even Molly, I think. "Grarrrgrrrrr!"

Christ!

"I EAT UP MAGIC!" said Monster. The bees on her sunglasses trembled in a rage, and her head jangled back and forth, her teeth bared. "You won't come back! EVER!"

"I will." Won't I? "I will."

Monster jumped away from me. Tears streamed down her face, around her hissing mouth. I had been told that Monster could smash anything that wanted to hurt you. Molly said that even when Girl or Girl's Friend was gone, Monster stayed. "Grrrrrrr."

I'm not sure what I would have tried to do if I had been completely there, or what I might have said to Monster. Pigbird knew. Pigbird stood up: a very big Pigbird, with great wings reaching out in front of her, like palace gates. She said, "Molly?"

"Yes?"

"I'm not going away, Molly."

"No?"

Pigbird recited a jump-rope spell. "Leetseeleetsee on me in me from me come me out me—free!"

Nothing happened. I tried to help Pigbird by saying it backward. "Free me out me come me from me in me on see eetslee eetslee!"

We laughed, and that did the trick. We let ourselves fall off the bench. All of us.

At a booth in Jerry's 24 Hour Restaurant we looked out the window for the lights to change in sequence along El Paseo. I explained I would pick her up at her father's house again next week. The chili the waitress brought made our heads warm, but it would have ruined the fun to take off our stocking caps or sunglasses. When we blew on the steaming food, our heads jingled, and we had to look at each other through wavering ghosts.

The End

2 · *Freedom*

TO THOSE WHO FOUGHT FOR IT

I had moved from Everview to James's house, to my own apartment and then back to James's house many times in our years of marriage.

The night before I moved out permanently, James was so silent in his sleep that I suspected he was awake. "James?" I asked. "James, are you awake?" I had not forgotten how he had betrayed Francis. "If you're awake," I said, "I just wanted to thank you again for helping me look for Francis."

Once I even touched his waist. But he stayed still. All night long I wondered what I would change my name to. I would not be Little Peg O'Crerieh Aigley. I would not be Little anything for anyone ever again.

N seemed like a good place to start. From *N* I could work backward or forward through the alphabet. Peg Nearing occurred to me. Peg Next. Peg Nexus. Peg Noxious. Numerous. An aristocratic name: a trail of silk: Peg Nowmore Newand Impudent.

I slept too much. My sleep phase advance program had not advanced. I rarely dreamed. Then, an unrealized dream, like my dream about the Eclipse Plant, would surface in full daylight.

I imagined a plant that germinated, unfolded, branched, and blossomed, entirely underground. Close to the surface, but beneath it.

Whenever I decided to stay up and watch the late, late movie, we had a fight about me violating my sleep schedule. James, as always, gave in. I think he stayed up with me in order to annoy me. I sat apart from him. I told him about the Eclipse Plant.

"Like a potato?" he asked.

"No. Some of a potato grows above the surface."

He finished a handful of popcorn, turned the television down, asking, "All right if I turn it down?" After every bite, he wiped his hands with a paper towel. He said, "I think a flower like that—that kind of thing probably really happens. Underwater. Deep down there where the fish look so strange. What do they call that?"

I still loved James for how he would work that way to figure out something for me. But sooner or later, I melted his kindness with my smartassedness, and he shut up. That was his way of adjusting.

He quietly crunched his popcorn. At the beginning of the movie he said, "I can't think of the name." He sat himself next to me on the sofa, his back straight, his legs primly together, both feet next to each other on the floor. He wiped the oil from his lips. "This looks like one of the old ones."

"Yeah," I said, "you can sure tell." Behind giant words scrolling upward on the television screen, an elderly woman bent over a table to scrawl an intimate letter. Accompanied by faint harpsichord music, her oddly unintimate film voice read the letter as she wrote.

> ". . . and how I shall miss the golden dusk light as lovely on your hair as upon the sycamore leaves . . ."

James said, "A tearjerker. Are you ready for this?"

"Can't wait." I was always ready to swallow another dose of

sadness. "Depression is addictive," I said, "you know that." He didn't. Not really.

"James, everybody needs some lice in their lives." I had on my black and red silk toreador pajamas that always threatened to make me unreservedly happy. (Francis had sent them to me. She had enclosed a beret and cape.)

"It's so late. I wish you would let me tape it, Little Peg."

"Not that again. I'm—"

"You're breaking your sleep routine. You're sabotaging yourself."

Wind-in-sycamore sounds came from the television. Golden light around the bird-like shadow of pen and hand over paper. Everything darkening. The windiness becoming whirling propellers. The shadows of bombs over targets. Her dearest husband pushing his flight cap back. Unfolding her letter.

"I'm going to sleep," I said.

James said, "Thanks. I'll be right there."

I took all my clothes off. I took the thing off my breasts. I wasn't finished. I thought of that word, "panties," that one word defining children's and women's underwear, and that mattered to me. I took them off too.

An AWOL housesoldier in peacetime is an aggravation, not A Symbol. In peacetime when a woman betrays her allegiances no one will insist her life has cost other lives. So, when James was standing in the bathroom in his underwear and I announced that I would move out of his house again, he was calm. I guess he had expected it but all along had not been able to make up his mind whether he wanted me to move or wanted me to stay. He asked why.

I said, "I'm leaving because you're screwy, James. I'm screwy and I know screwy when I see it." He plugged in his Remington. Christmas gift, 1978. (He could disassemble and service and reassemble it in less than twenty-five minutes.) He was shaving, moving his closed mouth left and right and up and down in order to mow his stubble.

"*I'm* screwy," he said. He did not open his mouth after he splashed his face with water and toweled dry.

"James," I said, "you—lie down with me, and let me tell you."

We should have had clothes on. I probably shouldn't have suggested we talk with my clothes off or with his clothes off, but he did lie down with me before I could decide a clothing-optional goodbye was wrong.

He got up to put his underwear back on. I pulled on my long yellow tee shirt. "James, you're alone. Nothing changes that. Do you see?"

We were on our sides, facing each other the way we had been facing each other in the boat on the Elephant Butte reservoir so many years earlier. The pink, scrubbed skin of his knees touched my knees, and the accident of it made me continue. "You believe—I bet you've always believed you're accountable for me. But you don't think you need me. You don't think Molly needs me." He moved on to his back, crossing his arms over his narrow chest. "So," I said. "Do you think that's freedom—to be needed but not to need?"

I asked, "Are we going to talk about this?" His stillness answered my question. I said, "We should."

The bed felt small, and he seemed very near. When he turned his head away, I could see how short his hair was and how high it had been cut on his clean neck, how balanced and straight the barber had made the line for him.

By the dawn's early light I huddled, tired and bored, with about twenty other women—all women—at the Ellis Island of the eighties: my grocery superstore. I leaned against the grill of the Nova and had what felt like my first thought ever in English. *This is a nation on the move.* Within our boundaries we are always finding new frontiers to conquer, dismantle, build upon, desiccate, abandon, and rediscover.

In the republic for which we stand you don't think about how many people want boxes until you're at the Albertson's superstore on the Wednesday morning produce stocking day. You quietly, respectfully stand around with the other box hunters, who have all apparently been told the same whispered secret by a stock clerk: "Get here early on Wednesday."

We wanted the liquor boxes, canned food boxes, produce boxes that smelled bitter from oranges and ones that were sticky and damp from juicy peaches, overripe plums and pears. Anyway, we waited for The Produce Man. I couldn't help sizing us up: a Young Recent Unemployed, a Mother Box Hunting For Daughter Moving In With The Bum, a Volunteered To Be Den Mother, a Helping Son Finally Leave The Slut, a Soon To Be Sentenced To Nursing Home, four Graduates Going Home, three New Promotions, two Friends Having An Adventure, one Little Peg Moving Out Once More. We hovered like Produce Man groupies, nervously offering starting line smiles to each other.

From youngest to oldest, I think we all knew about boxes; how they have to open and close nicely, how they should be new or look new; how they must hold up, travel well, bend though not buckle, be light but have firm bottoms; be deep, carry plenty, come in sizes you can lock your arms around, lift easily, easily pick up, put down, empty out, and pack full again.

Finally, the Produce Man came out with his crew of muscled Produce Boys, heaping boxes against the wall where PICK UP was painted in five-foot letters. By way of an abbreviated greeting, the Produce Man pushed his chest out, nodded his head, and said, "Ladies."

We nodded our heads. Maybe we could have said, "Produce Man!" back to him but our hen-like twitching was friendly enough, I guess.

Except for Helping Son Finally Leave The Slut and Volunteered To Be Den Mother, we were polite in dividing the boxes. Helping Son swiped an onion box and a peach crate I wanted —she took *all* the peach crates—but I still carried away nine boxes, which I flattened out and stacked into the Nova. On the drive, I smelled the good, acrid odor of limes and oranges and the sweet awfulness of cantaloupes. My open senses invited in a better mood.

I speculated about how rich I would become if I manufactured fruit-scented spray starch. In the driveway, I settled on Red Delicious as first in the Peg Nearing product line. Folding open my boxes, carrying them inside, assigning certain ones to certain rooms, I began to feel in a good mood. I did not careen or swing toward my good mood. Like the bus lady, I had my hands on the wheel, my foot at a constant place on the accelerator. *Slower*, I said to myself, because normalcy is a strange ride too.

I began with the kitchen, then packed up the den, where most of our books and plants were; I took things from the closets, and from our bedroom. My questions shifted respectively: What will he need? What will he want? What will he miss? I kept in mind that he would have Molly with him.

Before two in the afternoon, I had my nine boxes full and two giant plastic garbage bags bulging with my clothes. It wasn't much. In the years of vacillating between James's house and Everview and my various apartments, I accidentally or consciously lost favorite jeans and tee shirts and dresses and paperbacks and notepads and even big objects like turkey roasting pans and standing lamps. What followed me were useless tennis shoes I had not thrown away and drafts of three novels all marked "Almost Final." And lecture notes written on prescription pads borrowed from Paula Analyst. In the same bushel basket with the violated stories of my students, I kept Molly's spitty bibs and first drawings, her first poem.

Jars.
Jars.
Jars.

The completest illustrated poem I've ever read. Three words inside carefully sketched jars. I had shown it to James, who marveled over it with me.

He asked if anyone else on earth was as lucky as we were. I do remember that. Later, he said something harmless enough. He said, "Let's work on helping her stay in the lines when she colors." Why have I remembered that? Where have I stored that kind of memory?

In a small Albertson's grocery bag I had all my letters from Ben. He had written eleven times from Vietnam. Once, Paula Analyst asked me to reread the letters and, if I wanted, to bring certain ones to a session to read to her. I have never read any of them since the very first time I received them. I don't owe anyone an explanation of that. But, look, I think if all the lovers, friends, and families of all the Vietnam dead gathered ourselves in Washington to tear down the goddamn black marble wall, and went back to our homes where our bloody hands might heal, we'd feel better than we feel staring at our reflections in that permanent national expression of our private loss.

I have pondered on the anger I felt when James told me how before he left Vietnam he destroyed my letters to him. He couldn't explain, he said, and when I got angrier, he said he didn't owe me that. His platoon had a motto: "Freedom to those who fought for it is a flavor the protected never taste." Loosely translated it meant, Fuck you if you weren't there with us.

I had my letters from James, which I burned in late '71. Together we watched them burn in our barbeque grill. We put the grill on so that the ashes wouldn't fly. We didn't hold each other or cry or reach some dramatic moment of rosy, patriotic reconciliation. That would make a better story, but we didn't do that.

He said, "Makes the whole thing over. For today."

Now, I put some of the boxes in the trunk of the Nova and stacked them in the passenger seats until I was surrounded. Except for the front driver's window, the boxes blocked my visibility. I could have leaned out my window, but I liked backing up blind, executing a fine reverse curve as if I were a skater doing compulsories, and moving forward right next to the curb.

I turned the car off in order to have a final look at James's fine, solid bunker. No matter how you huffed and puffed, it would not come down around him. I recalled the builder's ad: "The Maple: Stately Southwestern Styling!"

I have never been thankful enough. As I remember my father and mother's home it was a nest that neither inspired flight nor ever invited rest. Isn't that a good nest to be raised in? Shouldn't I be thankful?

Inside his garage my father had mounted a big spotlight and he had put in two windows. He told Ben and me once that he put the windows in because he had always wanted to know how to fit and frame a window and the back wall of a garage was as good a classroom for that as any. One of the windows ended up being a little tilted, and since the two were eyes right next to each other, that face of the house seemed to have arched one brow in stupid amusement at nothing in particular. A month after that project he had professionals install a picture window for our living room. He liked light. He wanted the curtains always wide open, and he wanted so much wattage in the ceiling fixtures and the fixtures so big they might have been industrial. The shade of a tree was fine in the backyard but unwelcome falling onto or inside his house. Outside, he painted the adobe surface a lighter pink each year.

Into all this my mother brought color and pattern and form. She cared about that, and could be made happy ("transported" was her word for it) by a new florid bedspread or a single line of stamped cornflower-blue tiles above her kitchen counter Formica. I was with her once when she picked out a radio because the ivory-striped green burlap covering the speaker matched her ice-vine dining room curtains. I heard her explain her choice to my father, and I still remember his good-natured laughter.

She armed herself with Lysol and Comet and Pledge against odors in her home. The good things she cooked fought with the fresh artificial smells. From her garden she brought late-winter daffodils and dutch iris and early-summer ranunculus and golden branches from our Mexican broombrush, and white roses called Church Roses, but they all were taken to her and my father's bedroom, which was off limits to us even on cleaning days.

No visitors were ever allowed to hang their own coats in her closets. No one was permitted into her refrigerator or cabinets. They were her secret riot of disorder. People were always impressed; if they stumbled as they complimented her she would help by saying how thankful she was for such a "cheery and bright" home. She was genuinely thankful.

Whether or not he was planning on it, I intended to keep James's Nova. *Thank you, James. And what are you going to do about it?* I thought, looking at the front door with its decorative carved tiger doorknock.

I remembered the pretend James I had made when James himself was in Vietnam. My pretend James would have admitted that he loved that Nova. "I'm attached to it. I'll miss it," he would say. The pretend James wouldn't just adjust. He wouldn't just benignly say, "All right. What else?"

In my dream version, James would make our goodbyes memorable for their bitterness and confusion. He would really believe I had the strength to leave without returning, and then I would believe that all the more myself, and he would hate me for that, wouldn't he? He'd put his head halfway in the car window, his handsome pale mouth and chin heated red, and he'd say, "You'll be back. You'll come back!" with hatefulness admitting to helplessness, hopefulness.

Oh, James. You came back to me after your tour of duty. Liet Si. A hero. Sometimes I hated you for coming back at all after I had prepared myself to lose you. Or I wished you had not come back unwounded, unneeding. I resented your life—here is the truth—when Ben died, I resented your life. You saw that. How could you have forgiven me for that? This is madness, isn't it? I don't belong out of Everview. How can either of us really believe I will stay out for long?

And as for you, how can either of us expect you to venture from your sweet brick cottage? You and Molly. Papa Bear and Baby Bear. The porridge is just right, the bed just your size again, the war a series of redundant docudramas flickering in your gingerbread television. Two hours long, not counting commercials. You'll only lack a Little Peg now.

I know it should be enough that you love me and are loyal to me. You have defended and protected me and served me honorably. "Freedom to those who fought for it is a flavor the protected never taste." That should be respected. Who is this bitch wanting more from you? What right do I have to ask for healing?

I loved you. There.

I'm surprised to know it too.

I love you.

3 · *Air*

So, I drove to my new place. The neighborhood was an oxbow, an odd, small island the city had formed as it changed courses years earlier. From West Espina, one of Las Almas's main drags, I turned right onto Lindero Street, past Los Reinos Avenue into five square blocks invisible behind the new sprawling Alpha Beta Plaza. My street was named Sombra. I had asked Rosa at the Albertson's checkout to explain the word. She said, "Means some shade from the sun." An old woman in the line next to mine told Rosa, "No. *Esta es Limbo*. Where the unbaptized go." My Spanish/English dictionary said a sombra is a reflection in water. Anyway, Sombra was unlighted, and in the shallow front and back yards of its homes were trees humbled by bad soil.

At Number 795 an R & R Real Estate sign lay facedown in my front yard. Rickee had explained to me that the first and last *R*s were her: the Rickee who versified, and the Rickee who diversified. Both Rickees had cooperated and, between 1976 and 1987, her business made it possible for her to buy six rentals. All were about like mine, more like large holding cells than homes. But all six were more like home than Everview.

Rent was $100 a month, not including utilities. I thought that was charity, and I had told her I didn't accept charity. Her response was that the house was a bad deal, a dump, and if I painted and repaired it my rent would be even less by whatever I invested. The logic appealed to me. I asked if I could postpone my first three months of rent payments until March. What the hell. After all, accepting charity and soliciting it are two different things, right?

Rickee, ever agreeable, said I had until May 1. What is more, on my front door she had posted a poem.

HOUSEWARMING

Here is a pin rocking
in the eyes of a hinge.

Here is a hinge upon which hangs
the weight of a door wanting to swing
out and in.

Here is the handle made to fit
the swinging door risking its weight
on the eyes of a hinge
depending upon
a rocking pin.

Here is the doorframe
shrinking from
and swelling around
the heavy door creaking upon
a hinge's eyes stabbed by a pin
rocking out and rocking in.

The handle turns to open a tongue
fitting a lock made to stop
the weight of the door from swinging
free, rocking a pin inside a hinge
inviting out or welcoming in

the person whose hand made the wall,
placed the hinge, and provided the pin
without which there might never have been
a door at all.

Rickee

I liked it. I started to fold it up, but had to read it again to know whether it was a warming or a warning. Behind me, the loud, long honk from the bus and the shushing sound of its doors and the bus lady's hollered "Peg!" and Molly and Francis clambering down the bus steps, all came at once. The bus lady made the engine roar as if to show me machines could rejoice too.

"Mom," Molly said, hugging me, "Mom—hey—God, what a place! Spooky!"

Francis closed her arms around us and asked, "So this is it? Samba."

"Sombra," I said.

She closed her eyes, hugged me more tightly. "Same thing."

The bus lady shut off the engine and stepped down. I took presents from her arms. Her handshake was firm. Her right hand folded around mine and her left hand embraced my shoulder near my neck, as Lewis had done. At the front door, I looked at what she had brought. A bag of table levelers. Homemade oven mittens, snow-white. A tiny flower press, the size of my palm. She saw my wonderment and said, "I bought it in Hatch."

"Oh," I said.

She tore the tissue wrapping from two very anatomically correct male and female "Thinker" bookends.

"Hatch too?" I asked. We giggled.

My key worked, and the front door opened. Molly carried the gifts inside for me. "Smells like new paint," she said. "That's good, huh?"

Francis and the bus lady went to the bus to bring a few of Francis's things. We had agreed that she would bring an extra toothbrush, and combs and clothes enough to sometimes leave Everview and stay with me for the weekend. Then Francis also hauled in Larry's tool kit and his cleaning implements, the brushes and mops and buckets. It took the four of us to bring in the Dirt Mister.

"Let's open some windows," said the bus lady.

"Good idea," said Francis. None of the windows would budge open.

I flicked on a light switch. No light.

"Well," said the bus lady. She tried the light switch. We stood quiet and close to each other. I told her I hoped she'd visit sometimes.

She took my hand and my shoulder again. "I'm going to," she said. "If I tell you I'm going to, you know I will."

Francis and I both answered yes at the same time. The bus lady wiped one hand with another as if they were wet or dirty. "I was only dropping by," she said. "The place looks good, doesn't it?"

I answered, "It looks good to me."

"I'm going to bring a Christmas tree."

"Great!" I said.

"It's just a giant green wire brush thing in a box." She held my hand on the way back to the bus. From the driver's seat, she said, "Peg, I don't have any advice, you know."

"No?"

"No."

I thanked her. She said I was welcome or she said to watch out, I couldn't tell which through the roar of the bus engine.

I had to wipe away tears, I admit. "That is the biggest damn bus," I said to Francis.

"Ain't it," she said, which was not any more nor any less than what I needed for her to say to me.

My new home had one bedroom and closet, a bathroom, a kitchenette, and a large living room with sliding doors leading onto a kind of patio where the floor and wall frames for an uncompleted room claimed most of the backyard. Rickee had stored things everywhere in the house but had been kind enough to push the three televisions and five or six dryers against the walls. She had large original oil paintings stashed in corners. Francis leaned one toward her, frowned, then turned it so Molly and I could see. Probably Rickee's own work, it was a remarkable abstract of—"The awfulness," said Francis—of, well. I guess it was some kind of artistic activity.

"Nasty," said Molly. The way she pronounced the *N* I thought she might be echoing some rock and roll code. But I tried it out as a name: Peg Nasty. Nah. Peg Nah. No. "Nasty" did nicely describe the painting.

As Francis turned it to face the wall, I said, "Don't."

"It's going to stare at us," she said.

"We'll have to stare right back."

The bedroom had a dozen screen doors and forty or fifty aluminum window screens leaning against the walls. How many people's homes were inside our home? More paintings crowded the small closet. Francis leaned into it and shuffled through some of the canvases, most of them about two feet wide and five feet long. Molly looked too. "I bet Rickee did 'em."

Francis said, "They're all the same thing."

"Freaky."

The thing in the paintings had two bloody stump-like maybe-arms plunging into (or tearing themselves from) a sink-or-oven-dryer-or-dishwasher full of cracked-human-heads-or-broken-chinaware with larger-than-life-size eyes and open mouths. The thing was unfriendly. But it wanted to be friends. I fixed my eyes on it because I felt that was the only way to hold it from attacking me.

Before we did anything else on the house, we hung three of the things triptych-style in the bedroom, three of them in the living room, three of them in the bathroom. Some of them had more mouths than others; some of the mouths had teeth; some of the teeth were human; some not.

"They grow on you," said Francis. "Don't they?"

"Wacky," said Molly. She grinned knowingly at me when she

said it, and I remembered the *Wacky Things* storybook I had read her so often when she was little. Over Grimm and Silverstein and Sendak, all of them, we liked *Wacky Things* best. Its refrain, "How many wacky things now?" was a question that genuinely challenged us. For many years after the question became figurative and then finally ironic, we kept asking it.

"Okay," I said, "where do we start?"

Molly leaned against the wall where most of the window screens were stacked. "Dad's supposed to bring some stuff. He's worried you won't have a bed or things like that, so he said he'll bring you his—or yours and his. You know."

"Yeah," I said, "I know. His."

Francis had picked up a window screen and was taking it outside. She asked, "Is that bed the real small one?"

"That's the one." I had explained to Francis in Everview how much I liked having a big institutional bed, because the one James and I had shared was too small for me. Even as a teenager at home, my twin bed had been tiny. In beds like that you jackknife yourself, you angle yourself a thousand different ways, or you dangle your ankles and feet off the end, but eventually you have to learn to make yourself smaller. You throw the net that gathers in your dreams closer and closer to the bed. You bring up more strange, gasping bottom-dwellers. After you wake up from that kind of bed, it takes a day to fully unfurl yourself.

Molly and I took window screens outside to make a stack in the uncompleted room outside. Then the three of us carried out door screens and some of the fat rolls of old carpeting that had their butts shoved against the bedroom walls and their uncoiling open heads bent forward. Later, we moved four of the carpet rolls back inside to my bedroom so we could bind them into a raft and lay foam rubber on top of it for a good, long bed.

We took all our boxes outside in order to clean the floors. We barely got the Dirt Mister roaring when James and my brother Anthony came. That faint, halfhearted knock was Anthony's, I knew. Molly got the door, hugged them, brought them inside with such ease that I suspected her of engineering their visit. I asked them to come back to the kitchen, where I introduced Francis, who said, "Glad to see you again," and without pause, "The bed you've got for her is too small. You already know that?"

"Ummm. No," said James.

"You do now."

Anthony offered his hand. "Good to see you."

"I know you," Francis said. She said it in a friendly way, but I could see from his expression that he nevertheless found it strange.

"We brought you something else," Anthony said. Francis stood between him and me, so he had to say it through her.

Anthony didn't ask if I wanted the something he brought. He turned around with James in tow, James saying, "Wait'll you see," and they went to Anthony's little pickup to unload my childhood swingset. I followed, and stopped them from unloading it all.

Anthony said, "We could build it for you. Why don't you let us?"

"Anthony. This is how you want to make peace?"

By saying it, I thought I had given him his fair chance to back away. He said, "I want to make peace."

When I held my arms out, he embraced me nervously. I gripped his shoulders. "This is how men make peace, Anthony; you build something. You build some stupid thing, and that makes peace, right?"

That was his second chance, in just so many minutes, to give up on me. Finally, he said, "Peg, I don't know any better. What do you want?"

He moved away, but let me keep one hand locked on his shoulder. "I want it left in parts," I said. "For now."

"You want me to take it away, Peg?"

"Nope." I thought he intended for me to notice that he was not calling me Little Peg, he was calling me Peg. I noticed. "We're on different terms, aren't we?" I asked.

"What do you mean?"

"You can bring the swingset back some other time. I think I would like to have it. I mean, I know I would. Come on," I said. In the bedroom where my boxes were, James was backing away from one of Rickee's paintings as Molly said, "Nasty, huh?" Francis nudged James and Molly out of the room when we came in. I heard her say, "You want one to take with you?"

I found what I wanted. "You remember this?" I asked Anthony. Handing him the folded map of rivers, I said I wouldn't wish the thing on anybody but that I wanted him to have it. "What do you think?" I asked.

He didn't unfold it. "I remember it," he said.

As he and James were leaving, James asked me if I was going to need anything else. Because I couldn't think of anything, we didn't have more to say. "You've got my Nova," he said.

"I'm not giving it back."

"What?"

"I'm not going to." I dared him: "Am I supposed to explain?"

He kicked at the dead grass along my sidewalk. "How?" he asked. I could see he wanted that grass to be edged. That bothered him. "Where are you going to begin to explain, Little Peg? How?"

"Yeah," I said, "there's a lot of shit still under the bridge. And neither of us is halfway across."

Molly interrupted by asking whether it was all right with me if she went with James and Anthony to dinner. Later in the evening, she and Peter would drop by again on their way to the movies, she said. She hooked James's arm in her hand and began to lead him away, with Anthony following.

I said, "See you around, James."

"Okay."

All I wanted was for him to look at me. If he had only turned around, I don't think I would have called him back. "One more thing," I said.

I waved for Molly and Anthony to leave us alone. "He'll be right there."

I kissed him on the cheek. "James. James?" I touched his chest, flattening my palms on it. His heart beat so fast under my right hand that I could not tell him now. I could not tell him I knew about his broken promise to look for Francis.

"We both have a lot to forgive," I said. I pushed him away.

Francis was more polite in saying goodbye than she had been in greeting Anthony and James. But after they drove away, she said, "They make me sad."

She asked if she could show me something. It would be time for "The Brazilian Hour" soon but she said we had enough time. When she brought her letter out of one of her boxes, she also brought the radio. We sat together on the floor of our bedroom, tuned in FM 92.2, set the volume low. We leaned over her notebook.

Dear Molly,

I have asked myself to stop writing these letters after this one. You can see why. I am better now.

What I mean to tell you is that I am unpoisoning myself and seeing better because of it. A certain dosage of the end of things is what I mean to say I have taken. I might want to take less. Step down to the beginning.

I will see you now without letters, without handing you letters. I liked writing them. I guess you see that I like pretending, medicine or not. You see?

I have been quiet. But one last thing. It doesn't explain everything, I won't say it can. You had an uncle beside your uncle Anthony. I have told you. You had an uncle who meant so much to all of us. When you were about to be born he died. How do you understand that, ever?

I was the person your mother told all this to. I am Francis. You know that, right? You need to know that, because I have more to say before you will see that I have not signed this with your mother's name.

She told me once that if she had to give up sunlight she would not give Ben up in its place. He would have held you, heard the sounds you made, smelled the goodness of you. That's what she wanted. Something I have told your mother is that I have been her: I have also lost my life in another place. Three times. Who mourned? Who asked me—my husband, my family that advised I have psychiatric treatment—how I had been wounded?

Three stillborn children. Each time, I held myself still for seven months. I waited. Three in nine years. I did not name my first daughter. To make a promise with myself, a threat against God, I gave the other two names. They were lost in me, so far away that they might have been lost in a foreign land. You see, I want you to see how dear their lives were inside me though such a distance from me.

Without me ever asking, your mother was mother to me. Here is what I want to ask, stupid kind of, but here goes. No more letters. Be my daughter too.

I will love you.
Francis

I asked her not to give the letter to Molly. "Tell her," I said. "Tell her all of it."

We listened to a radio report about President Reagan's newest nose tumor. Said to be harmless. Bethesda Hospital. The First Lady's visit. What Nancy says. What experts say.

Francis said, "Okay, I'll tell her. You're right. That'll be better."

"It's a good letter and all, Francis."

Skin cancers. Kinds. Activities in the White House despite the President's nose.

"Will you let me hold you, Peg?"

And now. "The Brazilian Hour." Our sponsors. "This is listener-supported public radio."

"He's starting," Francis said.

Sergio must have thought he could begin without us. He was already introducing the first music of "The Brazilian Hour." "In Brazil we szay in the music zhou hear only—how zhou szay? —only what is zo muszh as zhur heart know. Whad zhur heart know? We do a test. Zhou hear how muszh. Liszen thisya one."

It would be challenging, living in peace after being at war so long. In war, your heart expands from the fear always pulsing just underneath; your eyes, your fingertips and breast and lips, are pressed outward by that ballooning heart. For so many years my senses were never at my command. Now, after war, I will never again draw such faint breaths, never be so full of breath.

"Let's be real quiet," said Francis. "We have all this quiet to ourselves."